RUN RUN CRICKET RUN

RUN RUN CRICKET RUN

America's Secret Wars in Laos

BY TOM THOMPSON

CASEMATE

Philadelphia & Oxford

Published in the United States of America and Great Britain in 2021 by
CASEMATE PUBLISHERS
1950 Lawrence Road, Havertown, PA 19083, USA
and
The Old Music Hall, 106–108 Cowley Road, Oxford OX4 1JE, UK

Paperback Edition: ISBN 978-1-63624-036-7
Digital Edition: ISBN 978-1-63624-037-4

A CIP record for this book is available from the British Library

Printed and bound in the United States by Integrated Books International

Typeset in India by Lapiz Digital Services, Chennai.

For a complete list of Casemate titles, please contact:

CASEMATE PUBLISHERS (US)
Telephone (610) 853-9131
Fax (610) 853-9146
Email: casemate@casematepublishers.com
www.casematepublishers.com

CASEMATE PUBLISHERS (UK)
Telephone (01865) 241249
Email: casemate-uk@casematepublishers.co.uk
www.casematepublishers.co.uk

This is a book of fiction. Mentions of historical events, real persons or places are used
fictitiously.

The views expressed in this book are solely those of the author and do not reflect or
imply official policy or position of the United States Air Force, Department of Defense,
or the U.S. Government.

Dedication

At the outset, I would like to acknowledge the contribution of the late Mr. Walt Disney to the 23rd Tactical Air Support Squadron, the Forward Air Controllers (FACs) who directed the air strikes on the Ho Chi Minh Trail in Laos during the Viet Nam War. Mr. Disney was contacted by the pilots of the Squadron and was asked if he would design a Squadron emblem using his most famous character, Jiminy Cricket, since the Squadron's official call sign was 'Cricket'. Mr. Disney graciously designed and sold the patch to the Squadron for one dollar. The parachute he added to the Jiminy Cricket image was appropriate because of the hazard of the Squadron's mission: flying low and slow to find North Vietnamese trucks and anti-aircraft guns and then directing fighter-bombers against them. As the Southeast Asian con-

flict intensified, the size and scope of the 23rd Tactical Air Support Squadron grew much larger and more sophisticated. The call sign of the squadron was changed from 'Cricket' to 'Nail' for brevity. Nevertheless, the use of Mr. Disney's contributed image remained on the squadron logo and was cherished by the pilots and navigators who wore it.

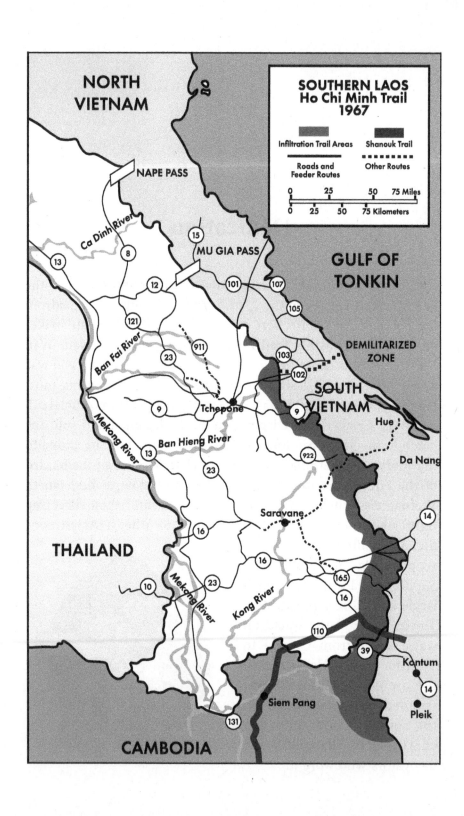

One war we should have never fought
One war we should have never lost
and
The End of the Viet Nam War

Ho Chi Minh Trail
The Ho Chi Minh Trail was not a monolithic road in
most cases, but a series of parallel dirt roads threading its way
through jungle, mountain passes, and occasionally abandoned
rice paddies. Road cuts by American air strikes were often
bypassed by road crews who were permanently assigned to
specific sectors. Their living quarters were later found to include
the typical road construction and repair equipment as well as
underground hospitals and even R&R facilities.

Run, run, Cricket run,
Ho Chi's coming with a loaded gun.
He's mighty angry, you've caught his eye,
He's throwing flak up in the sky.
Run, run, Cricket run,
One thing is no lie,
If you wanna get back to your wife in the States,
You better damn well fly high.
You've been blowing up all of his guns,
And killing all of his trucks.
You keep doing things like those,
And Ho Chi, he's fed up!
So, run, run Cricket run!
As fast as you know how.
If you wanna be a Cricket any more,
You better be a chicken now!

1

A Young Pilot's First Mission

Early on the morning of December 24, 1969, as the Laotian sky began its transformation from black to deep blue, a young North Vietnamese Corporal arose from his slumber in the Laotian jungle a few hundred yards from the Laotian/North Vietnamese boundary line. The Corporal's family name was Ca, and he was the eldest son in the family. He had left his wife and young son in Vinh, North Viet Nam a year earlier. He was working under camouflage netting, oiling, and reloading his 37mm anti-aircraft gun with his assistant, Corporal Le, a recent replacement for a crew member who died of malaria a few weeks before. It was a cool early morning, 58 degrees, so they and their two ammunition bearers wore jackets as they went through the morning checklist. The day started with a breakfast of South Vietnamese rice, something their families back north would have very much appreciated, given the failure of the rice crop there the past year. South Viet Nam farmers, by contrast, were feeding surplus rice to their animals.

Ca's gun crew had seen ear-splitting action the night before, shooting hundreds of streams of brilliant red anti-aircraft shells into the inky-black Laotian sky at attacking American airplanes. At night they could hear but could not see the American planes, so they fired in pre-arranged patterns, hoping to get lucky. Ca had five

American aircraft kills on his resume and adding another would result in more honor to both him and his family. His father had defeated the French in 1954 and returned home with no medals and no right arm. Ca was determined to make his aging father proud, and he picked up the banner. He was only 19 but had already been fighting for two years. The family name 'Ca' meant 'brave warrior' and he was honor-bound to uphold the tradition. The brave warrior was promoted to gun commander when the previous commander was killed by American planes a month earlier. Just as Corporal Ca finished his preparations, an American O-2 Forward Air Control aircraft appeared 5,000 feet over him. The noise of twin engines caught Ca's attention. The early morning sun illuminated the underside of the gray aircraft with an orange glow. The aircraft was slowly twisting and turning, obviously looking for a target.

Piloting the plane was a young American Lt., Roy Harris, only three years older than Corporal Ca. The enemies did share one thing in common other than youth: Like Ca, Lt. Harris too was excited. He found a barely camouflaged North Vietnamese truck just a few hundred meters south of the North Vietnamese/Laotian border. This was in the first hour of Harris' very first solo combat mission over the Ho Chi Minh Trail! The mix of excitement and nervousness produced a heightened sense of awareness of everything around Harris: the lush green of the jungle a mile below, the swirl of the cool air rushing through the opening on the right side of his O-2 aircraft where the window was removed for ventilation, the steady hum of his twin in-line engines. Sweat was already running down his neck and back like rivulets in a shower, but it was from nervousness, not the early morning temperature.

Like all Forward Air Controllers, or FACs, Harris was, in essence, a battlefield commander. His job was to locate North Vietnamese trucks, guns, and enemy troops and destroy them. To succeed, he could summon the impressive power of American fighter-bombers against those targets. He and he alone determined what to destroy and how to do it. No one was looking over his shoulder. This power was rare for a 22-year-old Lieutenant and he relished it. What glory might await him! As captain of his high school football team, he was used to accolades, but this was on a far greater scale. He was preparing to direct the most sophisticated attack aircraft in the world flown by the most highly trained and skilled pilots America could offer. Most were older and outranked him. But he had the power to choreograph their attack like a Broadway play, telling the actors what bombs to drop, the directions to come from and break to after dropping their bombs, and the precise spot for the bombs to hit. He did that by marking the target by firing one or more of the 48 white phosphorous marking rockets called 'Willy Petes' slung under his wings. He could also direct an attack on any nearby gunners foolish enough to challenge him. The shock wave from the bomb explosions would be heard and felt clearly, even a mile high; a cone of dirt would leap 50 feet into the air before slowly falling back to earth. The truck would be twisted scrap metal in a hole on the ground. Lt. Harris wouldn't be buying any drinks tonight at Nail Hole bar!

He pressed the mic button on the yoke and called the airborne command post controlling Ho Chi Minh Trail air attacks during the day, a C-130 code-named 'Hillsborough.' Hillsborough had replaced the night-time airborne command post, Moonbeam, an hour earlier and this would be their first request for ordnance.

"Hillsborough, Nail 86."

"Nail 86, Hillsborough. Good morning sir. What can I do for you?" The voice on the other end was from another Air Force First Lieutenant sitting at a radio console in the back of a C-130. He and a team of other combat controllers parceled out available attack aircraft to FACs based on availability and the degree of urgency.

"Hillsborough, I have a truck just south of Mu Gia Pass. Anything available?"

"Roger that, 86. I'll divert two F-105s to your location. They're carrying 18 Mark 82s."

"Roger that. Thanks." Harris tried to sound matter-of fact, but a little quaver in his voice probably gave him away. Destroying an actual truck always took precedence over targets such as road cuts or suspected truck parks. Diverting the F-105s was allowed based on "eyes on a target," not sensor readings or previous intelligence reports. Eighteen 500-pound bombs were more than needed to destroy one truck, but once an airstrike began, anti-aircraft guns would disclose their locations as well, becoming secondary targets. Killing a gun was an added bonus to Nails, worth an extra pat on the back and a round of drinks in the bar at night. Spending at least four hours a mission over the trail, Nails were the most frequent target of the North Vietnamese.

While Harris was wishing, Corporal Ca was issuing. He was shouting out orders to his assistant to uncrate additional 37mm anti-aircraft shells in the event his first salvo missed.

The stage was set. It was a chess game with both opponents representing the higher powers they served. It wasn't unusual in ancient times for champions to fight each other as proxies for the armies they represented. Psychologically, this wasn't much different. And sadly, regardless of the outcome, it would be replicated every day until the Viet Nam war was resolved. America's war-making capability over the jungles of Laos was perfected to a high degree. The availability and quick reaction time of the system was truly remarkable. Trucks were what the war was all about in southern Laos. Nails flew where the 'spigots' opened, the mountain passes where hundreds of trucks poured out of the mountains of North Viet Nam into Laos headed to South Viet Nam. Detoured to the flat land of Laos by necessity, and for no other reason, the North Vietnamese trucks carried everything necessary to wage protracted war against the wealthiest nation in the world: ammunition, guns, food, medical supplies, and a generous supply of parts to keep everything operating in the face of constant American bombardment.

The American strategy for winning the Viet Nam war, unknown to the American public, was not face-to-face combat in South Viet Nam. That was a last resort. It was preventing enemy ammunition, supplies, and troops from getting there in the first place. Theoretically, if American fighter-bombers could interdict all the North Vietnamese trucks, there wouldn't be any face-to-face combat: the war in South Viet Nam would be over. No trucks meant no ammunition, no food, no medical supplies, and no way for North Viet Nam to support the Viet Cong in South Viet Nam. And most importantly, no, or at least fewer, American casualties. Every American killed in South Viet Nam was killed by a bullet that came down the Ho Chi Minh Trail. And every American death added to the daily questions being asked by the folks back home: What in the hell are we doing there? And all too often: Why is my son (or daughter) coming home in a casket?

To the sources of this war-making supply chain, China and Russia, the Viet Nam War was a gift. They had little economic interest in agrarian, tropical countries with populations who could neither read nor write. The Communists were delighted to distract their arch-rival Americans from other issues which might have caused them more problems. There was no compelling economic or strategic value of Viet Nam to either Russia or China, but the enormous cost in time and money to the United States represented a huge drain on assets which couldn't be used against communist causes elsewhere in the world. And America fell right into the trap. Secretary of Defense Robert McNamara, ever the number cruncher, read summaries of the Nail airstrikes on a daily basis. Before he left office, Secretary of Defense McNamara had come up with what he considered a brilliant plan for tilting the advantage to the pilots. He knew Russian supplies coming down the trail were the only means of keeping the Communist threat in South Viet Nam alive. His strategy, indeed his reputation, depended on winning the war by starving the Viet Cong of ammunition and war-making equipment, allowing U.S. Forces to maintain control, and giving the South Vietnamese time to grow into a self-sustaining power. In so doing, Viet Nam would be a barricade preventing the scourge of communism which infected other parts of the world, especially Europe. And here, at least for the moment, Secretary McNamara was depending on a lieutenant he had never met and would never know, Lt. Harris, who was the tip of the spear of his strategy.

Ca stepped on the firing pedal of his gun and the first salvo of seven 37mm anti-aircraft shells screamed out of the six-foot barrel, one shell after the other, less than a second apart. The string of shells barely missed Lt. Harris' O-2, although they were behind him and he never saw or heard them. Engine noise and his combat helmet prevented hearing anything except very loud explosions near the window.

Harris circled once again above his intended victim. To score a truck kill on his very first solo mission would give him bragging rights at the Nail Hole, his Squadron's bar/lounge, TV room, BBQ pit, and home away from home. In his first few days, he observed with envy the veteran FACs entering from their missions, sweaty, thirsty, and ready to party. The other FACs crowded around them, ready to share stories, and were rarely disappointed. No one even noticed the 'New Bean,' a term applied to newly arrived Nails until replaced by the next New Bean. New Beans didn't have anything to report. Tonight, though, they would be crowding around him! They would hear his story! At the end of his one-year tour, after many more successful airstrikes and stories, he would go home. There would be a hometown parade, bigger than the one the football team enjoyed his senior year's winning season. His girlfriend would be impressed, and his parents would try hard not to look too proud but would not succeed.

Ca reloaded again, but intentionally withheld his fire. The pilot above him, he finally realized, was unaware he was a target; even more, the pilot was doing something Ca did not see very often: he was flying in a predictable pattern, a perfect circle above the dysfunctional truck Ca's crew had positioned as bait. Obviously, this pilot was not a veteran. Veteran pilots only flew in unpredictable patterns; they called it 'jinking.' Ca didn't know what they called it, and he didn't care. To him, this inexperienced pilot was a gift. He grinned, took a deep breath, and waited for just the right moment.

One more time, Lt. Harris left the safety of the trees to circle over the trail proper. Once again Ca stepped on the triggering mechanism of his anti-aircraft gun. This time, before the F-105s arrived to make Lt. Harris a hero, the string of anti-aircraft shells from Ca's 37mm anti-aircraft gun abruptly removed the right wing from his O-2. Harris froze for a moment in a state of unbelief. O-2 pilots flew from the left seat of the airplane, but unfortunately, there was no ejection seat and, inexcusably, the only door was on the right-hand side. Pilots, wearing a backpack parachute, had to undo the seat belt, squeeze over the throttle quadrant to get to the right seat, pull a lever to jettison the door, jump out, and then open the parachute by pulling the rip cord manually. On the ground, with no aircraft movement, exiting (or even entering) the aircraft could take more than a minute in the cramped cockpit. The aircraft was spinning violently in random directions and Lt. Harris, encumbered by his backpack parachute, didn't have a minute. Seconds later, his gut-wrenching terror ended with screams no one heard, and dreams of glory forever stilled. His aircraft was reduced to a scrap metal coffin. There would be no immediate search and rescue attempt because there was no radio signal from his parachute to indicate a bailout. No one would expect him to have managed to bail out of an O-2 anyway. Over 170 O-2s would be lost during the war, with only one successful bailout. The F-105s, arriving a few minutes later, were unable to establish radio contact, and went to another target. The wreckage of the O-2, documented by aerial photos taken by an RF-4 reconnaissance jet an hour later, showed no sign of a deflated parachute or an intact body in the tangled wreckage. Bailing out of the aluminum coffin of an O-2 missing one wing and spinning widely out of control was impossible, given the few seconds before a near-vertical impact. The Ho Chi Minh Trail claimed another American pilot. His body more than likely was removed and buried by the North Vietnamese hoping to dissuade any attempt at recovery, which was unlikely in any event. Harris' O-2 would be one of 194 O-2s lost in Viet Nam. OV-10 losses would total 73. The OV-10 had an ejection seat.

Harris' roommate, who barely knew him in the few days he had been there, would pack up his belongings and ship them home. Secretary McNamara's morning report would have another digit, but it would have no name. Ever the self-assured optimist, he would remain blind to what most Viet Nam vets already knew: the War was unwinnable. Most of the Nails drinking and playing cards in the Nail Hole that evening would not remember Harris. A chaplain would visit his family to console them. Harris' name would be chiseled on the Wall in Washington D.C., but there would be no body in a cemetery for his family to pray over. On Memorial Day each year, the VFW, Viet Nam Veterans, or American Legion would read his name along with the other hometown boys who were lost in wars. At the end of the ceremony, a bugler would play taps. His family would grieve. His girlfriend would too, for a while. As the years passed and the family diminished in size, there would come a year when no more tears were shed.

Corporal Ca would be decorated once again for defending his country against a foreign invader.

2

Baker 22 Bravo

Four hours after Lt. Harris met his rendezvous with death, a chartered American Airlines Boeing 707 taxied to a stop at Cam Ranh Bay, South Viet Nam. The 125 passengers—military officers, civilian contractors, and Civil Service employees—stood up and crowded into the aisle after hours of flight. Their weariness was mixed with greater or lesser degrees of apprehension, depending on their ultimate destination. For some, it meant a desk at one of the dozens of U.S. bases in Southeast Asia. Few people understood the enormous clerical and logistics demands of the supply lines necessary to fight a full-fledged war on the opposite side of the Pacific Ocean. For others, it meant a one-year tour of life-threatening existence beginning in just days. Two of the latter, Captain Ted Thatcher and Captain Jerry Underwood, yanked their carry-on bags from the overhead compartment and followed the slow-moving crowd to the exit ramp. Thatcher, at six feet tall, was slightly taller than Underwood, and sported dark brown hair; Underwood's hair was black, but they could easily have been taken for brothers. Both were handsome, but neither was cocky; they both shared a reserved demeanor in contrast to the nervous chatter of the younger lieutenants disembarking.

The blast-furnace heat of the Southeast Asian tropics reached them before they even got to the door. Their khakis, already wrinkled, quickly became stained by perspiration. One of the busses, marked BOQ for Bachelor Officer Quarters, awaited them at the airplane's underbody luggage compartment. The tropical sun beat down mercilessly as they found their B-4 bags and transferred them onto the air conditioned bus. Thirty minutes later, having checked in at the BOQ, they walked into the Cam Ranh Bay Officers' Club Stag Bar, mercifully cool and surprisingly well appointed. It could have been in New York with one exception: the club was tastefully decorated with a profane sign stretching the length of the bar. It consisted of two words; each three feet high. The second word was COMMUNISM ... It was Christmas Eve, and the Club was tastefully decorated with a palm tree covered in a few strands of tinsel.

The bar was a melting pot of American officers of all ranks and branches, although there were a few from Australia and New Zealand as well. The conversation was lively. Thatcher and Underwood found two adjacent seats at the bar and ordered beer. After a toast to something or other, they sampled the cold brew and found it excellent, as any beer would be after the stifling heat outside. On the barstool next to Underwood an Air Force First Lieutenant wearing wrinkled khakis was nursing something amber, probably Scotch. His light brown hair was disheveled, and he was a few inches shorter than the recent arrivals. There was an empty glass next to the one he was nursing. A prominent gash on the right side of his nose looked nasty and fresh. The officer introduced himself as Wade Bennett and asked where the two captains were headed.

"Nakhon Phanom, Thailand. We're O-2 pilots, Forward Air Controllers, FACs," Underwood responded. While neither Underwood nor Thatcher could be described as gregarious, Underwood had a slight edge, usually initiating conversations.

"Shit hot! You're gonna be Nails. Those guys helped save my life! I'm buying, put your money away!" Lieutenant Bennet's enthusiasm was impressive. Something told the two recent arrivals there was a story somewhere. They exchanged glances, wondering if the story might tell them what the next year was going to be like.

The young lieutenant wasted no time, apparently eager to tell his story. His drink sloshed a little over the bar as he turned to get a better angle from which to talk.

"I was a back-seater in an F-4, call sign Baker 22. As the back-seater, my personal call sign was Baker 22 Bravo. We were being directed by one of your squadron mates, a Nail O-2, on a target on the Ho Chi Minh Trail early last week. We were loaded with Mark 82s, 500-pound bombs. Our target was a suspected truck park near a section of karst on a river bank. The karst was about 200 or 300 feet long and about 500 feet higher than the flood plain around it. If you haven't seen karst yet, it's a gray-brownish piece of rugged limestone riddled with caves and ledges. It's scattered all over the trail, especially in the flat flood plains, and rises almost vertically from the flat ground to as high as 1,000 feet. Think of the buttes in our western States. As we found out, this piece of karst was a literal stone battleship. In fact, we called it the Battleship Karst. What we didn't know then, and I guess no one else knew, was the karst we were bombing was pockmarked with caves hiding anti-aircraft guns, lots of them. My front-seater and I were number two in a two-ship formation. That meant the gunners could improve their aim after our leader made his drop." He paused, almost out of breath, and took another swig from his glass, spilling a little more in his haste to relate his experience.

"After we rolled in, we felt and heard a loud thud and our aircraft started shaking violently, like it was coming apart. We only had one option: we punched out. Our chutes opened normally, but we were only 100 feet off the ground because we ejected near the low point on our drop. We didn't make what you might call a textbook landing. My front-seater, Hank, injured his leg on landing and limped into some brush on the bank of the river at the northern end of the formation. I landed about 300 feet away from him near the southern end."

Another pause, another drink, another deep breath.

"We both landed on the flood plain of the river bed. It was 20 feet or so under the river bank itself. The river bed was dry, except for 30 feet of slow moving water in the center of the channel. This is the dry season here; the rainy season starts in a few months. Guns were hidden everywhere: in caves at the base all the way to the top of the karst and in the nearby trees at ground level. The camouflage was incredible. The guns in the caves were usually rolled out at night, but in this case they were pulling out all the stops and doing it in broad daylight."

The Lieutenant took another drink, wiped his forehead with his arm, collected his thoughts, and regained his composure. His listeners maintained a respectful silence, wondering what they had gotten themselves into.

"The Nail directing our airstrike wasted no time putting our flight leader, Baker 21, on several of the guns he'd spotted. He had enough fuel to stay another ten minutes. After he ran out of rockets, he made false passes on the guns until he reached bingo fuel and had to RTB. The Nail had already ordered Jolly Green rescue choppers and A-1 Skyraiders, who use the call sign 'Sandy' when they're flying rescue missions. Until they got there, he continued to shoot rockets and make dry passes to keep the bad guys' heads down and away from me. He had found the location of a lot of the guns by the time the Sandys and Jolly Greens finally arrived. Hank and I were the top priority on the trail."

He paused to catch his breath and take another deep swig. The alcohol didn't seem to have much effect. His words were never slurred and despite his machine-gun delivery, he never stumbled. It was as if he would explode if he didn't get all the emotion out.

"When the A-1s Skyraiders from NKP arrived 30 minutes later, they saturated the area with Mark 82s and CBU 29 cluster bombs. When they thought they had it under control, the first of four Jolly Green attempts at pickup for Hank was made. Hank ran out of his hiding place dragging one leg. The anti-aircraft fire was unbelievable, and the first Jolly Green retreated with battle damage. On the second rescue attempt Hank was moving even slower and the second Jolly Green had to hover a long time and suffered even more flak damage. One of the door gunners was killed."

A twinge of emotion, a pained expression, and a voice cracking slightly were the first signs of what the listeners perceived as a possible loss of control; they remained silent. Another pause, another swig, another brush across the sweat-covered forehead. Then the lieutenant continued, but more somberly. "At some point in all of this, Hank radioed me there were enemy troops close to him. There were four pickup attempts the first day. The gunfire didn't seem to diminish though there were many direct hits on the caves. The A-1s and F-4s were dropping enough ordnance to open the gates to Hell, pieces of the rock showering the ground at the base of the karst after every hit. After the first Jolly left, we both hid as best we could and waited for morning.

"On the second day, the Jollys tried about six more times to get Hank again, but again, they all retreated with battle damage."

Lieutenant Bennet paused for what seemed like a long time, and then spoke despondently. "The gomers finally found Hank and shot him late on the second night. I heard him scream and then I heard the shots. I'd never been so depressed. I can't tell you how I felt. And still feel." He looked down at his glass, exhausted, despondent or both.

The Nails waited respectfully for a few moments without speaking, not sure of what to say. Finally, Captain Underwood, his face showing obvious concern, broke the silence with a touch of admiration mixed with incredulity. "You made it. How in the hell did you do it? It sounds hopeless."

Lieutenant Bennett took another pull from his glass before he answered. He took even a longer time to respond than before. Whether he was collecting his thoughts or controlling his emotions, the listeners couldn't tell. They exchanged more furtive glances with each other but still maintained a respectful silence. Finally, Bennett regained his composure and continued.

"I made up my mind not to give up. The third day I continued hiding in the brush beside the river, waiting for a rescue. I used my compass to direct the airstrikes since I had a better view of the guns than anyone. There were eight more rescue attempts before sunset. I moved after the sun went down because the gomers were getting closer to my clump of bamboo. I grabbed a bush and draped it around me, swimming along the bank, sliding in and out from under bank of the river."

He paused and polished off his drink. Thatcher motioned to the barkeeper for three more. After another short pause, Bennett continued. "Your Nail buddies never left me. They were there 24 hours a day. They couldn't put in airstrikes at night, but they let me know they were there," his voice quavering.

His refill was delivered. He pounced on it and it wasn't out of thirst. Underwood glanced at Thatcher, a genuine look of compassion on his face. Trying to imagine themselves in such a hopeless situation wasn't pleasant. The lieutenant had been on the ground for three days with people all around him trying to kill him. He had been subjected to the physical trauma of living in the muddy water of a tropical, snake-infested river, and was starving.

Thatcher put his hand on the lieutenant's shoulder and asked, quietly, "how did they finally get you out? A hovering rescue chopper would have been dead meat. The Jollys had already lost one door gunner and all the Jollys apparently got shot up pretty badly."

His question snapped the lieutenant out of his temporary depression. "That's the miracle! Have you ever noticed how one man can make a difference? Well, one man made a hell of a difference in my situation. Captain Stan Marcucci, the pilot of one of the Jolly Greens holding high in a safe area near me, knew the Sandy pilots directing the rescue didn't want to put another Jolly into a suicide situation. So, on his own, with no permission from anyone, he flew downriver to a safer area and dropped down to the water level. Remember, I was 20 feet below the bank because of the low water. Then he flew upstream to me. The gunners went crazy, but they couldn't lower their barrels enough to hit him. The chopper crew pulled me into the Jolly Green, Marcucci reversed course, and here I am. Who wants to buy me another drink?" The lieutenant, relieved at having emerged from the ordeal or catharsis, the listeners didn't know which, finished the chance meeting with his last drink of the day. Bidding each other farewell, they left the cool, urbane setting of the Cam Ranh Bay Officers' Club, stepped into the sweltering heat of Viet Nam, and went their separate ways.

A chance meeting one afternoon in an air-conditioned bar in a very warm foreign country; three Air Force officers, all pilots; one headed home; two others wondering what stories they would tell at this same bar at the end of their one-year tour. At a briefing on the incident after arriving at Bien Hoa Airbase the next day, Captains Thatcher and Underwood learned Lt. Bennett not only kept his wits about him, but even collected water samples for testing after he consumed the emergency fresh water supply. His continued calm transmission of information on the location of guns, the suggestions on tactical approaches, and the warnings on impending defensive moves by the NVA, would become legendary in the lore of combat in Viet Nam. Every rescue helicopter in Thailand was damaged, a total of ten.

3

Bien Hoa Air Base:
Welcome to the War

The next morning Thatcher and Underwood emerged from the air-conditioned BOQ into the hot humid air of South Viet Nam and mercifully boarded an air-conditioned bus. They were driven to Bien Hoa, a major United States air base an hour's drive inland from Cam Ranh Bay. To their surprise, the road was a four-lane, newly constructed asphalt highway. There was no vegetation for hundreds of yards on either side, thanks to Agent Orange. The bus was full of officers of all services and ranks, each wondering what the next year would be like. After the drive, they arrived at Bien Hoa. Like Cam Ranh Bay, it was heavily fortified with a massive concrete and cable fence topped by concertina wire in endless coils as far as the eye could see. Observation towers were spread uniformly along the fence, with armed soldiers manning machine guns. The travelers clambered off the bus and stretched their legs before entering a large, concrete block building.

Once inside, there were no formalities: they were seated in a small sparsely furnished conference room on metal folding chairs where they received a confidential briefing on the war. The briefing officer, an Army first lieutenant, wearing camouflaged fatigues and horn-rimmed glasses, dimmed the lights and put up a map of Southeast Asia. His presentation, including questions, took about two hours. The room was well air conditioned, whether to ensure the audience stayed awake or simply to combat the tropical heat didn't matter much to the listeners, who were grateful.

The young lieutenant removed his glasses, wiped his forehead with his other hand, and then replaced them. He was fully aware most of the officers in the room outranked him. Six months ago, he thought to himself, he was back home in his frat house drinking beer. He recovered from his reverie and began to explain very succinctly how the French government in Viet Nam was dismantled in 1954 after being defeated by Ho Chi Minh at Dien Bien Phu and how South Viet Nam became 'temporarily' divided into northern and southern sectors. He carefully avoided any explanation of why reunification elections scheduled for 1956 were never held or why the U.S. decided suddenly to commit combat troops into South Viet Nam in 1964. He never mentioned the Gulf of Tonkin incident in which the United States government claimed two attacks on the destroyer U.S.S. *Maddox*, one of which was true.

During a pause in the briefing, someone asked, "what exactly is our objective in Viet Nam? Why are we in this room?" Although only one officer posed the question, everyone in the room was watching intently, waiting for the answer, wondering why they were being asked to risk their lives. The growing dissatisfaction back home in America hung over the room like a dark cloud.

The lieutenant, although young, had heard this question dozens of times in the past year, and always delivered his message with the standard Department of Defense response:

"We are here to support the governments of South Viet Nam and Laos and to defeat the communist insurgents." He was hoping to move on to more mundane questions such as R&R procedures, pay issues in a combat theater, or when the heat would subside. But he knew it wasn't going to happen. It never did.

"Are we expanding control of South Viet Nam or Laos, geographically speaking? Let me put it another way, are we winning or not?" The questioner asked directly but politely, although there were quite a few snickers in the room. Anyone reading a newspaper knew the answer. The briefing officer knew the importance of giving the officers all the information he could, knowing they would be in harm's way within a matter of days. Even those assigned to desk duty in Saigon would be subject to more and more frequent suicide bombings.

He took a deep breath and responded, "we have begun to reduce our presence here. For example, we abandoned the Marine bases at Dong Ha and Khe Sahn, just below the DMZ. They were both positioned to interdict enemy supplies and troops moving down the Ho Chi Minh Trail and across the DMZ into the south. They were our two northern-most bases, both with air cargo capability. Their abandonment means more opportunity for the NVA to move farther south without serious opposition."

"How about truck traffic on the Ho Chi Minh Trail?" an officer asked. "This is essentially a war being fought at the end of a supply chain." He had obviously studied the war. Any army attacking a territory needed a lot of supplies: arms, ammunition, food, medical supplies, and clothing.

The briefing officer didn't pause this time before he answered, "you are correct major. The old adage about an army traveling on its stomach has always been one of the bedrock principles of warfare. By the way, who gets the credit for that saying?"

Thatcher volunteered the answer from the back row, "Napoleon, who, by the way, was French." Underwood noticed Thatcher appeared to know quite a lot about Viet Nam in previous conversations. And now Napoleon? Underwood reminded himself to pursue this a little more the next time in a more liquid setting.

"Correct. To respond to your question, truck traffic has more than doubled since we quit bombing the North. The NVA are just now opening a third route from North Viet Nam into Laos, called Ban Karai Pass. They now have ten more miles of safety in North Viet Nam, since we no longer bomb there, and it puts the trucks closer to South Viet Nam. The NVA has increased truck capacity by at least 100 percent since last year, to about 300 per day."

"What are we doing to prevent that?" another officer asked. It was obvious these officers weren't there to wave pom-poms. Their skepticism was not unexpected by the briefing officer. Their lives would be on the line soon and this behavior was becoming the norm for new arrivals.

"You Thailand-bound FACs in the room are the answer to the question. We are intensifying our Laotian interdiction campaign. FAC-directed missions over the Ho Chi Minh Trail are our best offensive weapon because Nail FACs and RF-4 reconnaissance aircraft are the only ones literally looking at a bona fide target. B-52 strikes are a good offensive weapon but are often several hours—or even days—behind the Intel. They are really good on road cuts and underground storage which is prolific on the trail. We'll discuss Intel in a moment, but there is no substitute for eyeballs on the target. Whatever slips through your grasp one day will be killing soldiers and Marines in Viet Nam a few days after it passes your stations in Laos. The targets of opportunity increase in proportion with the increase in truck traffic. There are hidden truck parks, hospitals, and infrastructure such as gasoline lines and, believe it or not, R&R centers. You FACs staying in Viet Nam will be dividing your time between infantry and fire base support missions."

"As everyone knows, the American public is about to revolt over this war. I assume we have some sort of exit strategy. Could you share that with us?" The speaker this time was a major wearing navigator wings. As with everyone else in the room, he wasn't smiling.

The briefer paused and took another deep breath, "let's just say the North Vietnamese aggression hasn't diminished; it's accelerating.

If we draw a curve, metaphorically speaking, the term 'exponential' comes to mind. Our estimate is we will be increasing air strikes, particularly on the Ho Chi Minh Trail. If we can stop the trucks, or slow them significantly, it might open opportunities for negotiation. But that's not official policy, just my guess."

"Have the South Vietnamese military forces shown any more capability to assume the bulk of this war?" A Major in the back of the room chiming in.

"I don't feel I'm in any position to respond."

More sarcastic glances among the officers. They were being told their lives would be in danger in a war not going well. If the South Vietnamese weren't giving 100%, why should they? The rest of the briefing went into more detailed plans to slow or impede the flow of supplies down the Ho Chi Minh Trail, which extended along several passes from North Viet Nam into Laos and from there into South Viet Nam and, even more recently, Cambodia. The most important tactic was 24/7 airstrikes by Air Force and Navy/Marine fighter-bombers directed by FACs. They ensured 'eyes on the target' along with details of the explosions: secondary explosions indicated ammunition and were the most important indicator of progress, or lack thereof.

Another tactic included seeding the trail's tributaries with mines as well as seismic and acoustic sensors designed to record truck traffic in real time. Trail Watch teams, consisting of Green Berets out of uniform coupled with a few indigenous mercenaries, had been developed to an art form, although a very hazardous one. The teams were inserted by Jolly Greens a few miles from the intended observation point but rarely walked out on schedule. They were very productive in locating truck parks and mining roads but were increasingly being discovered and rescued under hazardous conditions for both the team members and Jolly Green crews rescuing them.

There was also unspoken awareness by those in attendance that the supply chain relied upon by the North Vietnamese, while not the only key to their success, was so important the U.S. government was devoting an increasing share of its resources to disrupting it. Deny the enemy ammunition, food, and other supplies, and the communist advance might diminish, stall, or regress. There was also an unspoken awareness in the room 48,000 dead Americans gave the U.S. government little political room to maneuver. It was win soon or get out. U.S. public opinion had been drained of its patience and the antiwar sentiment was reflected every day on the pages of the *New York Times*. Just a month prior, over half a million people marched in Washington protesting the war. Many were veterans. Although the press was aware of Laos, they were denied access to it because there were no safe areas from which to observe or report.

In the final analysis, the statistics by the briefing officer showed no correlation between bombs dropped and truck traffic. In fact, he admitted, there was a negative correlation. This was disturbing because real damage was confirmed after many B-52 and FAC-directed air strikes. Apparently, the U.S. wasn't bombing fast enough to overcome the acceleration in the logistics of the North. For those in the briefing room, the news was not good. For those remaining in South Viet Nam, it meant more mortar and rocket attacks and hence more American casualties. For those headed to Thailand, it meant the war on the Ho Chi Minh Trail in Laos was intensifying, and with it, more risk. The lesson was not lost on Thatcher, Underwood, or anyone else in the room. None of them were aware preparations for secret negotiations between the U.S. and North Viet Nam were already underway.

When the briefing concluded, the participants were directed to their respective liaisons for travel arrangements to their bases throughout Viet Nam and Thailand. Thatcher and Underwood were the only Thailand-bound pilots and were scheduled to leave immediately. They walked out of the air-conditioned building and into a furnace of tropical heat and wasted no time boarding the bus waiting to take them to their chariot, a C-123 to NKP Thailand.

4

Nakhon Phanom, Thailand, Christmas, 1969

Bad Sam was having a bad day, which for him was normal. Sam once read about the evils of drinking, so he gave up reading. Not only was he hung over, but two New Beans were coming in on the afternoon Bangkok bird. New Beans meant more orientation flights instead of a real combat mission. It meant the predictable questions about winning the war or the cost of local whores. Sam didn't give a damn about saving democracy and he'd sort of lost interest in local whores; a 40-year-old alcoholic captain tended to rely more on Black Label than brown skin. Although it was mid-afternoon, it was morning to Sam, along with many of the other Nails. Covering the Ho Chi Minh Trail 24 hours a day meant flying schedules took precedence over circadian rhythms. He swung his legs over the edge of the bed, knocked the alarm clock to the floor, and reached for the bottle on the nightstand. He knew it was empty—it always was—but he held it up to his lips anyway. You could never tell, thought Sam. There might be a god. The bottle was empty, so it followed the alarm clock, and a cigarette took its place. His lungs ached from too many cigarettes, and his head was throbbing. He wondered how long he could keep this up, but he realized he didn't really care. He wasn't suicidal, but this war was all he had. He had married twice, and both wives had divorced him. The thought of selling cars or life insurance made him nauseous. When the war was over, which it would be as soon as someone figured out the emperor wasn't wearing any clothes, his career would be over.

Who was stupider? Kennedy? LBJ? Nixon? McNamara? It was a close contest. None of the Nails in the 23rd Tactical Air Support Squadron thought the war could be won, regardless of the definition of victory. Victory, in their minds, was surviving for a year. Since the Nails were the northern-most FACs in the Viet Nam War, they were the first to witness changes in truck traffic. They had what amounted to the clearest crystal ball concerning the key to the Viet Nam War: daily changes in the supply chain of arms, ammunition, and troops. It was their daily reports being read by the President on a daily basis, and what they saw gave them no hope whatsoever.

Sam often gave a great deal of thought to the subject of the war while sitting on a barstool in the Nail Hole. The Nail Hole was a home away from home for the FACs. It featured a brick BBQ pit, a lounge area with overstuffed sofas, and a billiard table. Several well-worn card tables completed the ensemble. An Akai reel-to-reel tape deck and two large Jensen speakers provided a superb collection of folk music and Johnny Cash. Johnny Cash, an Air Force veteran himself, would never know how much his music meant to warriors 12,000 miles from home. His song, "What is Truth?" about the Viet Nam War, was an instant hit with all the troops in Southeast Asia, including NKP.

Sam put out his cigarette and headed for the shower wearing a towel and flip flops. A chilling sight, he thought, to an enemy surreptitiously photographing the Nail compound. He entered the latrine/shower area, looked in the mirror, and sucked in his stomach but the towel didn't even fall off. That depressed him. He stepped up to the urinal and leaned way in to make sure he didn't dribble on the floor. That depressed him even more. When he was young, he could knock the boards off the side of a barn; now he couldn't even miss his shoe.

* * *

Captains Thatcher and Underwood awoke when their C-123 touched down on the runway at NKP. In a half-sleep, Thatcher heard the whine of gear and flaps being lowered, but after six years in the Air Force he had mastered the art of sleeping anywhere, anytime, and he didn't bother getting up until the aircraft was parked and the tail ramp lowered. The C-123, originally designed as a WWII glider, was later fitted with two radial engines. To complete the absurdity, in Viet Nam it was often fitted with two additional outboard jet engines, used primarily for additional takeoff thrust. Like most of the equipment in the war, it ironically mimicked the strategy of the conflict. It was something pieced together at the last minute, a patchwork of responses to unforeseen needs driving action in direct proportion, not to some overarching strategic purpose, but to some brushfire problem no one anticipated. For Thatcher, Underwood, and the two enlisted passengers on board, however, the C-123 was as good as a feather bed.

The comfortable pile of parachutes on the floor complemented the somnambulistic drone of the twin radial engines. The plane's crew, like most crews in Southeast Asia, was so proficient the pilots flew with minimum physical effort, mostly fingertips and trim wheel control. Flying over 300 hundred hours a month yielded a level of expertise producing ultra-smooth flights and landings so soft the wheels seemed to start rolling before they even kissed the runway. As the rear cargo door was lowered, the stifling heat of Thailand crept through the interior of the fuselage, capable of overwhelming the unsuspecting with a combination of shock and hyper-perspiration.

The two captains had already experienced high heat and humidity, both in the Philippines at jungle survival school and at Cam Ranh Bay and Bien Hoa, but the tropics never became tolerable. They pulled themselves onto the web seating which ran down both sides of the cabin. Before the engines whined to a stop, they had B-4 bags in hand and were headed toward the tailgate ramp.

Thatcher put on his regulation sunglasses, tucked his wrinkled shirttail into his wrinkled khaki trousers, and stepped onto the rusted pierced steel planking stretching for miles down the shimmering NKP flight line, followed by Underwood. He scanned the tarmac for a long time, occasionally wiping the sweat from his face and observing first the rows of old Korean War vintage, single-engine A-1s occupying the acres to his left. Half were painted black and their huge, four-bladed props told the experienced eye there was a lot of horsepower hidden somewhere. These were obviously night fighters and used for truck attacks on the trail.

The other A-1s were camouflaged. They were used both for daytime strike missions on the trail and for rescue missions such as the rescue of Baker 22 Bravo. What the eye could not see on these birds was the armor plating and superb survivability in heavy anti-aircraft environments.

To the left of the A-1s were the gliders-turned-airplanes-turned-jet assisted cargo carrier C-123s. Unlike the one he rode from Bangkok, some were painted black for night flare missions over the southern part of the trail in Viet Nam proper, where the flak was less intense than in Laos. Others were camouflaged and used to spray Agent Orange on the Ho Chi Minh Trail, not just as a weed killer *per se*, but used to reduce vegetation and enable better visibility from above. Unfortunately, it was also sprayed on areas used by U.S. troops with catastrophic results. C-47 Dakotas occupied space as well, many of them having flown in China in WWII. In Viet Nam they were used as gunships, but in the uber-hostile skies over Laos, their missions were electronic surveillance accomplished well to the west of the trail itself. In less than a minute, they had visually toured a large sample of America's first line of defense in the Viet Nam War. All that were missing were the jet fighter/bombers used over Laos which were based on aircraft carriers, Danang AFB in South Viet Nam, or Thakli, Udorn, and Ubon Royal Thai Air Force Bases in Thailand.

But the airplane Thatcher spent the most time reconnoitering was a Thai Airline C-46 on the tarmac. Captain Underwood dragged his B-4 bag and other paraphernalia over to the exit ramp where Thatcher was standing.

"What the hell are you looking at?" His wrinkled khakis had been dried out by the rush of air through the cabin while at 8,000 feet, but the heat and humidity of Thailand wrapped around him like a car going through a car wash and the perspiration had begun anew.

"You know what that is?" Thatcher asked, nodding toward the C-46.

"Not really. Sure is a big mother though. It looks like it could carry the Goony Bird next to it with room to spare."

"That, my alcoholic friend, is a C-46, affectionately known as Dumbo. It's a giant aluminum tube with two P-40 engines strapped to the wings. There are very few left. It was the first cargo plane that could fly high enough to get over the Hump, the Himalayan Mountain Range, in WWII. It was designed solely to get fuel and supplies from India to the American troops and Flying Tigers in China. It led to the discovery of the jet stream."

After a long pause, Underwood asked "How in the hell did it do that?" Underwood was curious, as any pilot would be at the sight of such a rare and large aircraft, one with obviously a lot of age on it. Thatcher didn't answer immediately, still transfixed by the aircraft. Underwood was having a hard time reading his companion. He continued sweating profusely standing on the concrete ramp under the hot Thailand sun, wishing he was back at the Cam Ranh Bay Officers' Club.

Finally, Thatcher spoke, although quietly. "It climbed up to 25,000 feet and flew there for up to ten hours. Fighters could get that high, but they couldn't stay there long enough to chart the drift. It took C-46s over ten hours to get from Dinjan, India to the Flying Tiger Base at Kunming, China. It wasn't uncommon to get over the Hump and have no reception from any navigational radio beacon because the aircraft had been blown 100 miles or more off course. At first, none of the crews could figure out why their navigation was so poor. Then it dawned on them. There was one hell of a crosswind. Often, over 100 miles an hour. And so, *voilà*, the discovery of the jet stream."

Underwood's pilot brain finally kicked in. "So, what did they do if they ran out of fuel?"

"They sent an SOS, taped the transmission key down, and jumped out."

"Damn! Then what?"

"Some were able to walk out. Others were never heard from again."

"They teach you that at the Air Force Academy?" asked Underwood, continuing to wipe his arm across his forehead.

"Nope."

"Where did you learn it?"

Thatcher didn't answer immediately. After a very long pause, "My Dad died in that airplane. June 23, 1944. I was 34 days old."

Thatcher was in deep thought, so Underwood decided not to intrude for a moment. Finally, he asked, almost reverently, "Did they ever find his airplane?"

"Yeah. At the approach end of the runway at Dinjan in India."

"He didn't get lost over the Hump?" Underwood was getting more than curious.

"Nope. They got back to India after a 12-hour flight, bingo fuel, and zero visibility in a monsoon downpour. They tried three fields, 30 miles apart, and all three were socked in. They set up a crude instrument approach back then that relied on using a stopwatch to time their descent from a radio beacon. Under the best circumstances, planes might end up in a rice paddy, but on average they lost one plane a week. His was one of those planes."

"Damn! What are you doing here then? You're a sole surviving son. You're exempt from anything but a declared war." Underwood was characteristically a 'cool customer', but Thatcher's story brought out more emotion than usual. And it was genuine.

"Pulled some strings." Thatcher hefted his B-4 bag and headed down the ramp. Underwood assumed it was the end of the discussion.

The two pilots walked toward Base Ops, passing by the FAC aircraft: OV-10s and O-2s. The O-2s, with an engine both in front and back of the fuselage, came in two flavors: black for night missions and grey for day missions. There were no front windows on the right-hand side of the O-2 cockpits, left open for several reasons. The open window on the gray models, flown during the day, facilitated supply drops to troops in South Viet Nam but not over the Ho Chi Minh Trail. There were no friendlies to drop to. The air flow did, however, provide a better air conditioning system than the anemic ventilation fan installed at the factory. On the black versions, the open windows allowed navigators in the right-hand seat to use handheld starlight scopes at night in the search for enemy trucks on the Ho Chi Minh Trail. The O-2s had one distinct disadvantage in the intense anti-aircraft fire environment over Ho Chi Minh Trail: they did not have ejection seats. The flak could easily remove a wing or simply demolish the plane. The grey OV-10s with their bubble canopies were next in line and appeared even in number with the O-2s. They were twice as large, had the disadvantage of very loud turboprop engines, but the advantage of faster speed and ejection seats, both front and rear. The ejection seats worked flawlessly in all cases that did not involve a direct hit on the cockpit.

Before the two pilots reached base operations with the ubiquitous welcome banner found on every airbase everywhere, a jeep announced its arrival on the flight line by taking a corner on two wheels and racing straight toward them. It skidded to a stop inches from their feet. What must have been the oldest captain in the Air Force—and possibly the ugliest—slowly removed his sunglasses. His eyes reminded Underwood of his first civilian flight instructor, a 50-year-old alcoholic whose eyes looked like two festered rooster's nuts in a bowl of cottage cheese. The flight suit of the pilot in front of them was stained with sweat and he hadn't yet shaved, although it was past noon; his face was pockmarked, his hair unruly. The white nametag sewn on his flight suit read, 'Bailey'.

"Who the hell are you?" growled Bad Sam.

"I'm Jerry Underwood, and we're here to win the war."

"Who's the other asshole?"

"His name is Thatcher, but he doesn't talk much. Where's the nearest bar? We're a little hung over."

"If you're going to be a Nail, you better learn to drink better than that or else just hop back on the crate that brought you here," growled the old captain. "I'm Sam Bailey. The General asked me to personally escort you to the Nail Hole and buy you a beer. We're welcoming a Nail back from the dead today. Get in."

Underwood jumped in the back with his B-4 bag. Thatcher hefted his bag into the back of the topless jeep and then tried to seat himself on the passenger side up front. Not fast enough, however. As soon one leg was fully in, the over-the-hill captain popped the clutch and the younger captain was thrown back into the seat, hanging on to the door post with his left hand, his right foot dangling in the slip stream. With some effort, he managed to recover and seat himself.

"Didn't know there was a general on base." Thatcher, forcing an air of calmness, was still trying to get comfortable on the front seat.

"Well, hell. There was one here when I arrived in 1945." Sam obviously had a self-deprecating sense of humor. It worked. The two new pilots smiled; before fully seating themselves in the dusty seats, the jeep was in second gear, and the red dust of NKP Thailand was billowing up behind them like smoke from a worn-out blast furnace.

"Do you always drink before noon around here?" Underwood was shouting to overcome the noise of the wind zipping by the topless jeep.

"Only when we can find an excuse," the grizzled old captain growled. "Today we've got a doozy. Successful rescue of a Nail. You'll see." As all men are wont to do, they were mentally assessing each other in terms of physical appearance, size, and attitude. For his part, Bad Sam was grateful to see some pilots with experience. They were obviously not excited, like the recent wave of young lieutenants, at being one step away from combat and perceived glory. Fortunately, neither of them had asked if the U.S. was winning the war.

"So," yelled Thatcher, "are we winning the war?"

The ancient captain turned slowly and looked at the younger captain next to him. Thatcher was looking straight ahead with a half-smile on his face. Bad Sam grinned what those who knew him called his famous Bad Sam grin, a mixture of mischievousness and sarcasm. Thatcher liked him immediately. Most people did. Those who didn't were usually in positions of authority. As the oldest captain in the Air Force, many people wondered what—or who—allowed him to stay in. Usually, it was move up or get out. They would have to keep wondering. Sam wouldn't talk about it. There was a rumor Bad Sam took a general on a cross country flight and found the general the next morning in his room passed out, propped up in bed, and wearing a red wig, obviously not his.

Painted female toenails were also rumored to be sticking out from under the covers by the general's head.

How that affected Sam's future promotions was never clearly understood. Did he share the story with other officers and embarrass the general? Did the general's wife find out? Sam never told, but rumors like that were the fabric which made the Air Force such a great branch of the service. The Navy had their Filipino waiters, linen tablecloths, and 'Officers' Country', areas of the ship where enlisted sailors were not allowed. Air Force officers and enlisted men were often eating beanie-weenies together in the shade of an airplane wing. There was no 'Officers' Country'. As a result, there was rarely the arrogance of the Naval officers, and thank God, there was no perpetual requirement to abuse oneself as in the Army or Marines. No one in the Air Force even talked about Marines. They were all considered insane.

Nakhon Phanom was dry and dusty for the nine months called the dry season. Red clay dust painted the few sparse trees and banana plants with a sickly rust color. The lush, green, tropical side of Thailand was far to the south. NKP looked like Utah with rusty trees. The jungle-shrouded mountains of Laos, visible to the east, were green however, and looked like an oasis to anyone choking on the dust of northern Thailand.

No one talked on the way to the Nail Hole. The ride was too harrowing, the wind too noisy, and Bad Sam was enjoying himself, double clutching and taking the corners almost on two wheels. Underwood, hung over, fell asleep, laying down in the back of the Jeep with a B-4 bag as a pillow. The buildings they sped between were all similar: teak siding, metal roofs with a generous overhang to relieve the monsoon rains, and an occasional zinnia or rosebush probably sent by some warrior's mother. Mothers were one of the constants in life, Thatcher mused, all of them hoping a bit of home might somehow protect a son from the horrors of war. His

32

mother would soon be sending chocolate chip cookies and asking in every letter if he was all right and if there was anything he wanted to tell her. The jeep skidded to a stop in front of a large, dark brown teakwood structure, one of many that lined the streets on the way from the flight line. This one was distinguished by a sign on the side of the building proclaiming it was the 'Nail Hole'. Banana plants decorated the sides of the building. Four smaller but longer buildings flanked each corner of the Nail Hole. On the doors on the four larger buildings were two silhouetted airplanes with room numbers stenciled on each silhouette, apparently living quarters. About 20 cheering, whistling men dressed in a random mixture of green flight suits, Bermuda shorts with no shirts and camouflage fatigues were tightly clustered in a circle near the side of the Nail Hole.

Bad Sam stepped not too agilely from the jeep and sauntered over to the men. Thatcher and Underwood followed, B-4 bags in hand. As they approached the crowd, they could see a sweat and mud-stained flight suit covering an obviously happy airman who held a bottle of champagne in one hand and a Thai woman with the other arm. Red dirt smeared the airman's face, but Laotian clay couldn't hide the expression of relief. He was smiling like a man who had found a men's room after ten cups of coffee.

"Jensen. Got shot down today." Bad Sam laughed, as Thatcher stopped next to him. "Didn't know if we could get him out before dark or not."

"How?" asked Thatcher.

Bad Sam chuckled. "Shot himself down. Trying to strafe a truck with his AR-15 on full automatic from the right side window of his O-2. We've been trying to get him to stop that crap ever since he came here. Jensen's about half a bubble off plumb. His barrel jumped up as he fired and started his right wing on fire. Lucky it didn't explode. But it was burning so he jumped out. He keeps putting himself in for the Medal of Honor. And if that isn't enough, another O-2 hasn't returned and there wasn't even a beeper."

"Come on, I'll show you your room so you can dump your B-4s. Then we'll have that beer I promised." As Thatcher walked away, he noticed the anti-hero known as Jensen swinging the Thai girl upside down to the escalating cheers of the crowd.

"Who's the girl?" Jerry Underwood asked.

"She's Sonni, the hostess from the Officers' Club."

* * *

Across the base, Lt. Col. Everen, the Squadron Commander, was having a bad day. A first lieutenant named Jensen with severe judgement deficiencies had shot himself down. Another O-2 was missing, and given the elapsed time, was presumed down. The pilot of that plane was a first lieutenant as well. Everen wondered when the brass would see a pattern emerging.

It wasn't just O-2s and lieutenants: last month it was an experienced but overly aggressive captain in an OV-10 hitting a tree. Although that bird made it back to base, the crew chief took pity on the pilot who he knew would automatically be disciplined for flying too low. The crew chief pulled out his pistol, shot a hole in the wing, and wrote it up as combat-related. But it didn't work. The accident investigator spilled the beans in the report to headquarters. Fragments of a tree limb stuck in the wing didn't leave him much choice. Lt. Col. Everen, unfortunately, was judged on the performance of the subordinates under his command. And now, how could he hide the loss of this second O-2 due to pilot stupidity? He couldn't.

A knock on the door interrupted his grim thoughts. It was his clerk, Airman Baxter. "Sir, Captains Thatcher and Underwood were on board the afternoon run. Captain Bailey picked them up."

"Thank you, Baxter. I want to speak to Lieutenant Jensen this afternoon. He's probably celebrating at the Nail Hole about now."

"Yes Sir. I'll arrange it."

* * *

Thatcher and Underwood deposited their bags in the room to which Bad Sam brought them.

"Thatcher, this is your home for the next year. Underwood, tomorrow morning you'll be flown over to our detachment at Ubon." Bad Sam crossed the room and turned on the window air conditioner. Two gray metal lockers and two metal-framed beds were the only items in the room. Plywood paneling tastefully decorated with *Playmate* centerfolds and green linoleum tile on the floor, recently waxed, completed the décor. Thatcher had seen worse, much worse, and thought of the grunts in South Viet Nam sleeping in rain-filled foxholes. One of them had been his half-brother, a Marine at Dong Ha, an easy half hour flight southeast of NKP. Dong Ha, along with the infamous Khe Sahn were the two northern-most bases in South Viet Nam, just south of the DMZ, now abandoned, unable to function with a constant barrage of rocket fire. The two bases were, for all practical purposes, the canary in the mine. The war was over for his brother. His right arm was mangled, permanently, two years before.

"You can scrounge for some other furniture later." Bad Sam was headed for the door. "Ready for that beer?"

Bad Sam, Thatcher, and Underwood walked over to the Nail Hole where the party had moved from the lush but hot lawn to the welcome relief of the air-conditioned bar and lounge area. As they entered, Sam and Underwood took off their flight caps, but Thatcher was a little late. Someone rang a big brass bell and the 30 or so revelers all grinned at him simultaneously. Sam pointed to the 'Rules of the Nail Hole' on the wall. Rule number one was, "He who enters covered here buys the house a round of cheer." This referred to anyone wearing a cap or hat in the bar. There were other

35

rules, such as, "He who rings the bell in jest buys a round for all the rest." Thatcher slapped a $20 bill on the bar. At ten cents a drink, it would cover all the Nails there plus any others who might wander in. Since the rules in stag bars were uniform across the Air Force Bases, Thatcher's indiscretion was a planned introduction to the other Nails. It worked; those present came up at random intervals and introduced themselves.

The Nail Hole wasn't just a party hooch, it was a home away from home, a place to share laughter and sorrow, often on the same day. It was known for its cuisine: boiled eggs and popcorn any time of day, and thick steaks every night. The fellowship there would become a page in the memory scrapbook the Nails would carry with them the rest of their life. It was a room full of warriors, and the warriors were full of war stories only hours old, fully as dramatic as any tales from any war ever fought. Unlike the infantry that went on search and destroy missions followed by days of recuperation, the Nails fought every day (or night). On the wall opposite the door hung a mangled, twisted O-2 propeller, obviously damaged by flak, a vivid reminder the Nails weren't in a frat house back in the States. A mahogany bar dominated the left wall, bottles of almost anything alcoholic and well-worn card tables covered in green felt occupied the center of the back half. The *pièce de résistance* was an oil on canvas copy of one of *Playboy*'s well-known centerfolds, a red-haired beauty known to the Nails as 'Big Red'.

The Nails came up one by one and introduced themselves. Two were navigators. One was "Big Jim," a six-foot-two wild-eyed navigator who appeared to be slightly psychotic; he was not only big but was playing bumper cars using sofa cushions as a shield with two other navigators, all of whom were feeling no pain. He was shirtless and had enough hair on his chest to weave an Indian blanket. The contestants seemed to take great delight in knocking each other on their ass. Another was Steve Johns, a pudgy, short first lieutenant, also a navigator, but one who looked a little too young for the rank and definitely not material for the bumper car game. His family owned a huge flower nursery in California. He was planning to complete his five-year commitment and return to civilian life to grow carnations. In less than ten minutes, Thatcher would learn enough to start his own greenhouse business. Sam led Thatcher to the bar where they both ordered Johnny Walker Black Label. Beer sounded good in the searing heat of the Thai airstrip, but the hard stuff seemed a much better idea in the cool, dim light of the Nail Hole. Next to them were two ancient majors with white cloth navigator wings on green flight suits. Both appeared to be on the north side of 40 years old. Sam introduced them as the Martini Twins, a sobriquet neither seemed to mind. They were the only martini drinkers in the crowd, and both seemed to be well past a few. The navigators sported bleary eyes, paisley skin, and thinning gray hair. They looked and acted as if they were unsure of where they were, a testimony to the magic of gin. They were in the middle of an animated discussion and insisted both pilots join them.

"I can get it up anytime I want," garbled one, his arm wrapping itself around Bad Sam, drawing him closer. His slurred speech perfectly complemented his spastic movements. His friend looked at him unsteadily, teetering on the edge of a barstool. After a few seconds delay for the message to reach his communication center, he managed an equally slurred response, "I think I'll have another drink."

The first martini twin continued the fantasy. "Any time I want I can make it stand up like this." He held, up his finger. Unfortunately, his finger had been broken or malformed in some way so instead of being straight, it was quite bent. The effects of too many martinis caused him to sway violently; Thatcher caught him to prevent him from crashing to the floor of the Nail Hole, perhaps injuring his outstretched, but malformed phallic symbol even more.

After his rescue, he took another swig from the martini glass on the bar and struggled to reach his wallet located in the right breast pocket of his flight suit. "I have a name right here," he mumbled. "This is a girl at the Orchid Club in Bangkok. You ask her. She'll tell you. I can get it up anytime I want."

Unsuccessful in negotiating the zipper on his flight suit, he ultimately forgot what he was looking for and resumed the attack on his martini. His bleary-eyed friend fell asleep on his bar stool in the meantime, balancing himself with remarkable precision, no doubt the product of years of practice. Bad Sam and Thatcher moved slowly away after ensuring the twins were at least in some form of bodily equilibrium.

Lt. Jensen stumbled in, flight suit still wet from perspiration and stained with the red dirt of the Ho Chi Minh Trail. He was slim, his head full of black hair smeared with the same dirt as his flight suit, and appeared to be a little exhausted, not surprisingly. Sam motioned for him, and he managed to thread his way over.

"This is one of the New Beans, Ted Thatcher. Ted, this is Houdini. Got himself out of one hell of a pickle today."

Thatcher offered his hand, and Jensen shook it. "How in the hell did you bail out of an O-2? I've never heard of anyone bailing out of one before."

"Beats the crap out of me. I can't remember. Just crawling over the throttle quadrant to get to the right seat in in the middle seemed to take forever. The plane was in a spin, and I actually don't remember how I even got to the right seat to open the door. Why the Air Force would put a pilot in the left seat of a combat aircraft with no door on the left side is … well you other O-2 pilots know what I mean. Anyway, once I finally got to the right seat, I couldn't get the door release to work. I figured I only had a few more seconds and was about to give up. I tried to squeeze out of the window on the right side, but my backpack parachute was too big. When I was halfway out, the door finally fell off. I remember falling and trying to get the damn door off me. The next thing I knew, I was sitting in a tree. We lost another O-2 earlier this week with no chute spotted. He was a New Bean, like you guys, so pay attention to what Sam tells you."

Airman Blake, the squadron orderly entered the dim light of the Nail Hole, found Lt. Jensen, and whispered something in his ear. Jensen excused himself and left with the Squadron orderly.

"Well, shit's about to hit the fan," mumbled Sam. He didn't need to explain shooting one's own self down was frowned upon. The Lieutenant was not seen again.

What Lt. Jensen did not mention, as the Nails learned later, he had started a fire with the tracer rounds from his AR-15, and the O-2 was ablaze. He was lucky to have gotten out.

Another captain entered the Nail Hole wearing a flight suit, also sweat-stained and wrinkled. He was slightly taller than Thatcher, with sandy hair and what appeared to be a permanent grin with a mouthful of teeth. Before the arriving captain noticed him, Thatcher lurched forward and bumped into him intentionally.

"Sorry, I didn't see you."

The arriving pilot turned and exploded into a grin.

"Ted Thatcher! What the hell are you doing here?"

"I was told there was some serious weakness in the pilot ranks here. Now I can see why! If Bill Stancil is here, the rumors about losing the war must be true."

"Ted and I have been through a lot together!" Stancil wrapped his arm around Thatcher.

"Yes, we have, and most of it was your fault!" Thatcher didn't miss a beat. "I'm beginning to smell a conspiracy. Is all of Moody Air Force Base here? You all need to know this psychopath was in Section B and I was in Section A in pilot training. They adopted camouflage ascots to wear with their flight suits; my section picked red. Since they were invisible because of the camouflage, we kept bumping into them. They never did figure out why."

"Well, you can see him now, so why don't you just go ahead and kiss him?" Sam shouted, to hoots of laughter, the loudest from the newly reacquainted friends.

The crowd got the joke and laughed a little louder than might have been customary under normal circumstances. But the booze, the party atmosphere, and the unspoken bond enveloping those who shared a common danger added a heightened sense of emotion to the situation. The danger the Nails faced in Laos on a daily basis permeated every experience from taking a shower in the morning to falling asleep at night. Theirs was a war with no interludes, no periods of inactivity, and no possibility of coming back with unused marking rockets or, at night, red ground flares. Targets of opportunity were too numerous; most missions had pre-arranged (fragged) targets as well. Nail aircraft would be the target of hundreds of anti-aircraft shells announcing their presence with red balls snaking up in a line, especially visible at night, or black puffs of smoke during the day. Comradery was, in a very real sense, therapy.

"How long have you been here Bill?" Thatcher resumed the conversation with his old friend.

"Got here six months ago and got picked to fly special missions with our Green Beret friends. Their code name is Heavy Hook. They're all over the trail, out of uniform, of course, and are the source of much of our intel. They see things under the trees we can't from 5,000 feet. But they almost always get in trouble, sooner or later. That's where I come in. When they get discovered, I provide the air cover. Matter of fact, I want you to come over to their compound with me tomorrow and let me introduce you. There may be a time when you're called on to help."

"Great. What time? I might have an early flight tomorrow, so I'll be free after that. Maybe we can do lunch." Thatcher smiled at his own weak attempt at a joke.

"You never could tell a joke, could you? Sounds good, though. We can meet here at noon. The boiled eggs here at the Nail Hole are pretty good this month."

"My mouth is already watering. Those Green Berets won't hurt me, will they?"

Stancil laughed. "They will if your beer can doesn't hit the trash barrel on the other side of the bar. And whatever you do, don't look them straight in the eye. They're pretty tightly wired."

Thatcher remembered how Stancil was always smiling at Moody Air Force Base in Georgia where they underwent a year in pilot training. He was the eternal optimist. And here, in the midst of an unwinnable war, at the northern most FAC base and subject to the largest anti-aircraft guns in Southeast Asia, he acted as if he was at a frat party in college. Combat, at least at NKP, seemed to influence the behavior of men in different ways. Some, like Stancil, seemed to accept the danger and embraced the opportunity to rise above what Thoreau described as typical human behavior: 'The mass of men lead lives of quiet desperation.' The Nails, as with any combat squadron in Viet Nam, or any other war for that matter, had representatives from both camps: those who accepted the risks and took pride in their results and those who looked for ways to avoid risk and lived in the Hell that was a mixture of fear and dread.

The crowd in the Nail Hole grew slowly throughout the evening. The air was filled with smoke, Johnny Cash, Waylon Jennings, and war stories told by aviators wearing camouflage fatigues or olive-green flight suits. The stories were not about feats of old out of a book, but about real actions only a few hours before. Stories of huge explosions buffeting FAC aircraft a mile high, tales of ammunition trucks exploding in orgasms of fire, descriptions of black smoke curling up even higher than the fighter-bombers that caused it, vivid descriptions of red balls from multiple anti-aircraft guns spitting out their venom in pre-arranged patterns, evil spirits shrieking up toward the American aircraft, their explosive warheads trying to find their destiny in the flesh of mechanical birds, both the fighters dropping the bombs and the FAC aircraft directing them using marking rocket and flares. On any given night, there were more stories than time to hear them. Because of the press embedded in infantry units in South Viet Nam, the American public was getting a nightly summation of the war; what they didn't get was information on Laos, where 90% of the bombs in the Viet Nam War were dropped, which is why it was the most heavily bombed country in the world, ever.

Thatcher's khakis gave him away as someone different, a smudge of beige in a sea of camouflage green; most of the Nails referred to him as the 'New Bean'. In the Air Force, every time one switched bases he was a New Bean, so there was only a slight stigma attached to the term. At NKP, as at all Air Force bases in Southeast Asia, the tour of duty lasted one year, so the difference between a New Bean and a grizzled veteran was only a few months.

"Well, how do like your new home?" asked Sam, drifting over to Thatcher as Bill Stancil left. He was one up on Thatcher on drinks, but Thatcher noted it didn't seem to have any effect on him. He apparently had a lot of practice.

Thatcher paused, took a sip of scotch, and didn't speak for a minute or so. Finally, he asked, "we're not doing very well, are we?"

Bad Sam hesitated a moment and then grinned a half grin. He knew the question would come, and he was surprised it hadn't come on the Jeep ride earlier.

"Not really. Let me paint a picture. This is the so-called Secret War. We fly over the Ho Chi Minh Trail across the border in Laos and try to stop the bad guys from getting supplies into Viet Nam. If we succeed, the war in the South might be won. But when Nixon quit bombing the North, under political pressure back home, the North Vietnamese moved thousands of their guns down here. They line up trucks 200 or 300 deep across the border in North Viet Nam, thumbing their noses at us, and hope for a cloudy night. If it comes, they run like hell, and we try to find 'em. During the day, we try to find where they've hidden those that didn't get blown up the night before. The worst part of day missions is flak we can't see, unless we happen to be looking up, and you better get used to doing that often. Then we can see the black or white puffs of the shells as they airburst. So, we never fly a steady course. We call it jinking. Day missions mean jinking like hell. Night missions are easier and fun. We fly straight and level since they can't see us: our night birds are painted black. We can see the muzzle flashes of the guns, and the tracers start burning a few seconds later. Missing them is easy—we just wait until the tracers burn in. We're at 5,000 feet and we have a few seconds to alter course and it only takes a few degrees of bank. Once the tracers are moving on the windscreen, it means they're not on a collision course. Don't make the mistake of young pilots and rip the wings off. Let's get another drink."

"Look," Sam whispered after refilling, "over here, you take off and no one gives a damn where you go or what you do. Everyone knows there's no way to win this piss-ant war. Everyone except the politicians. The French taught us that, or at least we should have learned it. Ho Chi Minh doesn't love the Chinese or the Russians. He just wants the Vietnamese to run their own country. Imagine that! This war's been going on since the end of World War II. They won't stop fighting until they get it. And no, we're not doing very well, so whatever you do, don't die here." Another long swig.

Bad Sam put his arm around Thatcher's shoulder and pulled him close, whispering. "Listen Ted, we turn off our radar transponder when we cross the Mekong River. No one can track us, so no one knows where we are. So, you can circle over the safe areas for four hours or get down in the weeds and kick some ass. It's all up to you. But flying will never be the same again. You will look back on this, if you live through it, as the most memorable experience of your life. There are no friendlies out there. Everyone will be trying to kill you. Everything under you is fair game except for a few Green Beret ground watch teams hiding on the border of the trail which you'll know about before taking off. It's you against the North Vietnamese. Because of the Geneva Conventions, they're not supposed to be in Laos, and we're not supposed to be in Laos, so officially no one is even in Laos.

"The press concentrates on South Viet Nam since they can't come up here. But 90-percent of all the bombs dropped in the war are dropped so here, and you are the one who decides where they go. During the day, you will have what we call 'fragged' targets based on infrared photography from RF-4s or from sensors planted on the trail. You'll get briefed on them before takeoff. The fighter-bombers can't see the targets under the trees or at night, so it's up to you to direct them. Imagine having tens of thousands of bombs under your personal control. You're sort of like God, the God of the Old Testament."

Thatcher wondered if Sam ever read the Bible but decided this was not the time for a lesson on theology. Thatcher would have quoted his favorite passage from Isaiah: '*I form the light and create darkness, I bring prosperity and create disaster; I, the Lord, do all these things.*' Thatcher always prayed a little in threatening situations. There might not be many atheists in foxholes, but there were probably even fewer over the Ho Chi Minh Trail.

Sam paused for another swig and caught his breath. Then, he really got into the drama of the current situation. He sounded almost as if he were preaching some sermon on how to get saved. "The biggest problem," Sam began ... but was interrupted by a crescendo of cheers as a few visiting A-1 pilots from one of the other compounds on base showed up with guitars and started with their version of folk songs, substituting bawdy, occasionally disgusting, lyrics. A-1 pilots had a close bond with the Nails since the Nails were the ones who directed them night after night on truck-killing missions. Even more importantly, they were the ones in charge of the rescue missions of airmen, including Nails, shot down over the trail. The night passed quickly. Few left to eat at the Officers' Club, satisfied with the diet of boiled eggs, popcorn, and steaks from the grill. Everyone was drinking except the Nails who were flying the night missions. As they drifted out at their pre-arranged times, others drifted in, damp hair matted from combat helmets and flight suits or camouflaged fatigues stained a dark green by sweat.

The war stories would start anew, as each crew of pilot and navigator would relate their mission's success. Hands traced swooping paths through the air, depicting maneuvers only a few hours old. Because it was a clear night, the hunting had been good, with several dozen trucks destroyed and an occasional anti-aircraft gun silenced. And the night was young. Mounted on the wall, overlooking the crowd like an amulet, was an outboard section of an O-2 wing, a weird trophy with a gaping hole torn in it, a constant reminder of the business of the Nails. It had hung there for over a decade.

"The biggest problem," Thatcher reminded Sam, bringing him back to their last conversation.

"Oh yeah. The biggest problem is we are pullin' out of Viet Nam, quitting. We can't win because we can't fight. We've given them Cambodia as a haven and uni … unilalet … Oh hell. You know what I mean. We've stopped bombing the North without any concessions at all from Ho. So, the biggest problem is you may get killed in a fight we aren't even trying to win. How's that for a screwed-up war?"

"And this is supposed to be the highlight of my life?" Thatcher was smiling at the inebriated old captain, now beginning to teeter on his barstool.

"It can be. These assholes on the trail are bad. If you want to hear some sickening stuff, talk to the Laotians over there."

Against the far wall sat four Laotian officers in flight suits. As Buddhists, they weren't drinking. "They've all lost family members to the NVA and Pathet Lao. Women, children, it doesn't matter. And let me tell you right now, if you ever get shot down, don't let the NVA capture you. We don't know of any POWs from Laos. They're far too big a burden for the NVA to worry about. Just fight it out and hope for a quick end. From what we know of the treatment of the pilots shot down over North Viet Nam, through their own TV propaganda, they're animals. See! That's the point. It's black and white here. All the rest of your life, it's going to be shades of gray. If you blow up a truckload of ammo here, you can save 100 Marines in Viet Nam. Maybe a rice farmer and his family. When you go home, you can sell life insurance. Even if you stay in the service, at 50 years of age, you're out on your ass and no one cares what you did. You're never going to find life the same again. Enjoy it."

Sam paused and downed, by Thatcher's count, his fourth scotch on the rocks. Not bad for the first hour, thought Thatcher. Other than mispronouncing a word or two, it was hard to tell Bad Sam had even been drinking.

"There's another aspect to this," Sam continued.

Before he could finish, another captain walked in and stopped to let his eyes adjust to the dim light. His black hair was matted, damp from wearing a flying helmet and his flight suit still wet with perspiration. He saw Sam first and headed over, but halfway there he stopped and broke out in a huge grin. "Son of a bitch! Ted Thatcher!"

"Mad Dog!" Ted walked over to the sweaty captain and they tried to squeeze the lifeblood out of each other. "How's it hanging Roger?" Thatcher was laughing.

"Short, shriveled, and leaning to the left!"

Brown was six feet tall, broad shoulders, sandy brown hair, and sported an infectious grin which, those who knew him well, knew was present even when he was sleeping.

46

"What are you doing here Ted? I thought you already did your tour in hell."

Ignoring the comment, Thatcher ordered a beer from the bar for his old friend without even asking him what he wanted.

Turning to Bad Sam, Mad Dog, aka Captain Roger Brown, let Sam in on the relationship. "Academy roommates, Sam. Thatcher was my best man, and we haven't seen each other since my wedding on the day we graduated. There I was, my new bride on my arm as we walked through the arch of sabers and I feel something goosing me. You always did have a thing for my ass, Ted. I always slept with one eye open."

"In your dreams, flyboy. Say, how's Bobbi anyhow? Has she told you about us yet?"

"She's great. Staying with her mom. And yes, she told me you were a fairy." Laughter filled the Nail Hole once again as several nearby Nails heard the banter.

"Roger got the nickname Mad Dog by hiding a Chihuahua in his Academy dorm closet," Thatcher told Sam. "Trained 'em to get in and out of a basket so Roger could lower him six floors to do his business. Got away with it for two years."

"Then what happened?" asked Sam, the scotch lowering his humor standards to the point where Swiss cheese would have been funny.

"Well, one night a suspicious duty officer named Major Feirtag put on one tennis shoe and one regular shoe and ran down the hall. It sounded like he was walking since only one shoe made noise and he finally caught Roger before he could hide the dog in his closet."

"Damn! No wonder we're losing the war."

"Hell, Sam, Ted just got here. Slow down. Let's not give away all my secrets."

Thatcher paused, then asked, "How is Bobbi?"

Roger paused for few moments, the smile faded from his face, and then he said, "She told me last month in Hawaii she wanted a divorce."

After a visible moment of disbelief, Thatcher responded. "Damn, Roger. I'm sorry. I can't believe it." The smile faded from Thatcher's face, replaced with a look of concern.

"Can you believe she flew all the way to Bangkok from Maryland to tell me? Why didn't she just write a letter like a normal person?" Roger took a deep drink from the glass he held in his hand.

"First," Thatcher responded, "she respects you. She could have just sent a telegram saying, 'Roger, I've changed my mind'; but second, she isn't—and never was—normal and you knew that when you married her. She always reminded me of a hummingbird, intriguing, but never predictable. Remember the good times and sooner or later someone will come along who will make you forget her. Let's just drink to better times to come." That was the best Thatcher could do. He was compassionate but could have never been a marriage counselor.

Sam raised his glass. "Hell, I'll drink to that!" Sam was obviously willing to drink to anything.

"Roger, Sam told me we're winning the war. Has he had too much to drink?" Thatcher was trying to change the topic of conversation.

Sam laughed at the humorous perversion of his previous comments about Viet Nam. Roger laughed too and continued the analysis.

"Well, get used to the 'F' word, because that's how we all describe this war. And no, Sam hasn't had too much to drink. There's not that much scotch in Thailand. When you see him standing up asleep, just push him over to the sofa, and turn the lights out when you leave. But Sam wouldn't be the last person in this room to joke about winning. How in the hell can we tell these barefoot people who eat rice and pray to Buddha how to run their country? This war is like navigating a ship by the lights of other passing ships. Our strategy changes by the day, not even the month. We do blow up a lot of stuff. But what we blow up today is back tomorrow. If Canada invaded the U.S. and captured all our wheat growing states, would we bow down to them? Substitute rice for wheat, North Viet Nam for Canada, and South Viet Nam for the U.S., and that's what we have here. It's obvious to everyone we're losing, day by day. Kennedy, Johnson, and Nixon didn't learn anything from the French. These people have been fighting since before World War II to gain independence and they will never quit. It won't be long until the SAMs are here, and when that happens, you'll find me over the mountains, out of missile range. B-52 missions have doubled since I got here six months ago. You can hear the B-52 warnings on guard channel. They're broadcast as heavy artillery warnings. And if you hear a warning close to your location, Ted, you'd better get the hell out of there. Intel gives us a good briefing before take-off, but they're human and they can get as hung over as we can. Can you imagine being in the middle of 100 Mark 82s? This war will be over soon, so don't do anything stupid."

"Yeah, but where will we be then?" asked Sam. "Flying training missions? Dropping dummy bombs?"

"Well, was it worth 50,000 American lives?" asked Brown, getting a little annoyed.

"How about another drink?" suggested Thatcher, trying to head off what appeared to be a potential disagreement.

A voice behind him interrupted, "Get your chin in, smack!"

Thatcher turned and there facing him was a tall, thin captain in a sweat-stained flight suit, his light brown hair thinning, damp and disarrayed. He was bearing a toothy grin from ear to ear.

"How in the hell are you Ted?"

"Damnation! Tex Robertson! Another Zoomie! You're not going to make me do push-ups, are you?"

"It wouldn't do any good. When I told you to do them at the Zoo you just smirked."

Thatcher turned to Sam, who was looking perplexed. "Well, I guess you figured out Tex and I were in the same squadron at the

Academy. He was two years ahead of me and Roger. He's the man who made me what I am today."

Tex Robertson chuckled. "Look, don't blame me for that! I'm surprised you even graduated. All you did was ski every weekend and chase girls. Of course, you never caught one as I remember."

"You're right. I never did become an expert skier. And Tex, even though you always were a bullshitter, it's sure great to see you again. Have you destroyed that Corvette you bought?"

"No, Ted. I haven't, did you get that Volkswagen bus you always dreamed about?"

The nearby Nails laughed harder than Thatcher. Then, Tex got a little more serious. "Ted, you've won an all-expense paid vacation to the hottest area in Southeast Asia. Welcome to the Secret War."

"Thanks Tex. I've been getting quite an earful. As hard as it is to accept, it appears that some incredibly bright minds in Washington have been developing some seriously flawed concepts. I'd like to hear your side. I was about to get another drink." The two ambled back to the bar.

About that time, some A-1 drivers visiting from the Zorro Squadron with guitars started the Nail theme song. They were from one of the squadrons flying WWII/Korea Corsairs re-designated 'A-1's or 'Spads' on night missions directed by Nails. The Nail Hole reverberated with 30 or so voices, tinged ever-so-slightly with alcoholic lubrication, all somewhere between the key of G and A.

Run, run, Cricket run,
Ho Chi's coming with a loaded gun.
He's mighty angry, you've caught his eye,
He's throwing flak up in the sky.
Run, run, Cricket run,
One thing is no lie,
If you wanna get back to your wife in the States,

You better damn well fly high.
You've been blowing up all of his guns,
And killing all of his trucks.
You keep doing things like those,
And Ho Chi, he's fed up!
So, run, run Cricket run!
As fast as you know how.
If you wanna be a Cricket any more,
You better be a chicken now!

Another captain, apparently a new bean like Thatcher, was standing next to them at the bar. He asked the other Nails who or what the Crickets were.

Tex answered, "they were the first FACs here at NKP back in the sixties when the war first got started. They flew O-1 Bird Dogs and used the call sign Cricket. Walt Disney personally designed a squadron patch for them showing Jiminy Cricket holding on to an umbrella, using it as a parachute. We still use the patch on our party suits. You don't have one yet, but you will. A party suit is a black flight suit we wear at ceremonial functions like our monthly award dinners. The patch is on the right breast pocket. You'll get one after your first mission. Don't ever lose it. They'll be worth a lot of money one day."

The A-1 drivers started on another raunchy song and the party continued.

"Damn, Tex. I still can't believe you're here." Thatcher slapped his old friend on the back once more.

"You're not going to believe this Ted, but Ace Faircloth from our squadron is here in A-1s. Your classmate from the Fourteenth Squadron, Mark Tinga is also a Nail. He might get here later. And another FAC from our squadron is over in Laos flying as a Raven FAC, Paul Bartram."

"Bartram? Are you kidding me? He's the guy who trained me, my first element leader. He's seen me naked." Tex offered an explanation to the FACs around him who overheard the comment and were laughing and whistling.

"What Ted means is that when new cadets arrive at the Zoo they're taken into a large warehouse where they take off all their clothes and put them in a box. That's shipped back home to Momma and the new cadet starts with nothing, not even a watch. Their new element leader, a senior, or First Class cadet, takes 11 or 12 of these naked men, hands them some fatigues and combat boots, and begins transforming them into Air Force Academy cadets and future officers. Paul Bartram was Ted's element leader. Ted made it, but as you can see, he's not exactly the cream of the crop." His attempt at humor succeeded and received a respectable amount of laughter. Insult humor had been developed into an art form at NKP.

The party would continue until sunrise. Those with early day flights meandered out to get some sleep as the first of the two-man night crews, consisting of pilot and navigator/strike control officer, began entering at random intervals, hair askew from wearing combat helmets and flight suits or fatigues damp from perspiration. Each arriving crew immediately became the attraction of the moment as other Nails crowded around, looking for the latest war stories. They were rarely disappointed. Unlike the hit and miss experiences of conventional hunters back in the States, there were always targets. For the lucky hunters, stories of tanks or fuel trucks lighting up the sky like a giant blowtorch commanded superior bragging rights. The trail was, in a sense, a river with a perpetual flow of things headed for South Viet Nam: trucks, tanks, artillery pieces, and infantry columns. This logistical river was the artery keeping the war in Viet Nam alive.

The Nail Hole never really shut down. As the last of the night crews retreated to their rooms for sleep, the early morning pilots would gradually replace them, still groggy from an alarm clock that never showed mercy. The popcorn and booze would morph into coffee and boiled eggs, and the president and Congress would continue funding the insanity. God Bless America.

5

Welcome to the Trail

Bad Sam kicked on Thatcher's door at 0700 and announced their impending 0800 takeoff. He hadn't told Thatcher they were flying this morning, so Thatcher was understandably groggy. But, after a quick shower and shave followed by a breakfast of boiled eggs and coffee at the Nail Hole, he was back to normal and the two pilots caught the step van called the TUOC Trolley to the Tactical Unit Operations Center, the headquarters for all combat operations. With a slight hangover and six hours of sleep, Thatcher knew it was going to be a long day.

After disembarking at the center, Sam and Ted received weather and intelligence briefings. The briefings, except for specific targeting information for airstrikes, would always be the same: expect heavy anti-aircraft fire (AAA) and tropical heat. They were often given times and coordinates for B-52 strikes which would be broadcast over guard channel on the aircraft's radios as heavy artillery warnings a few minutes before the bombs were dropped. It was a warning to FACs not to be anywhere near to that location. The 'fragged', or assigned, targets for the day given to the Nails were accompanied by the strike aircraft information: Navy, Marine, or Air Force, aircraft type, ordnance load, and ETAs. This day their assigned target was right at the border with North Viet Nam: an anti-aircraft battery of five guns with radar guidance. The battery had already claimed one Marine A-4 and several F-105s had been targeted but not hit in bombing runs on trucks in the vicinity. Just the previous day, an O-2 with a young 'New Bean' lieutenant was lost and the gun complex was a suspect.

The pilots walked next door to the equipment room and checked out folding-stock AR-15s, .38 caliber revolvers with shoulder holsters, survival vests with radios, first aid kits, water flasks which they put in the leg pockets of their flying suit (Sam) or camouflaged fatigues (Thatcher), and parachutes which they slung over one shoulder. Sam stopped at an ammunition bin and dropped several clips of tracer ammo for the AR-15 into his helmet which was suspended by a chin strap. Thatcher followed his lead. It was still dawn and quiet. Like a morgue. Neither spoke. Both pilots had a slight nervousness. It would always be there. And it would always disappear after take-off. For most crew members anyway.

After a short ride to the flight line in a step van, they disembarked at the grey O-2 they would fly that morning. Despite the dim light of dawn, it was already getting warm, the tropics being the tropics. Airman First Class Bunker Powell, the crew chief, met the pilots at the plane, saluting smartly, and running to open the only door, which was on the right. "How's it goin,' Bunk?" asked Bad Sam.

"Great, captain. Got to play at the NCO club with my new band. Got to drink free all night long."

"Well, Bunk, it's barely morning. I'm sure you got gassed up last night. Did you remember to gas *us* up?"

"Have I ever let you down, captain?"

"No, Bunk, you haven't. And I want you to meet my new friend. This is Captain Thatcher. A new bean. He's Nail 79."

"Glad to meet you captain."

"Glad to meet you, Bunk."

"Is the bird safe Airman Bunker?" asked Bad Sam, knowing it was.

"Absolutely sir."

"Thanks Bunk. We'll take good care of her." Thatcher and Bad Sam deposited their AR-15s into the cockpit through the only door, which was on the right-hand side of the plane and did a quick walk around, checking the movability of the control surfaces, looking for any unpatched bullet or shrapnel holes, pulling the safety pins from the landing gear, and checking the oil level.

"Time to go, Ted." They strapped their parachutes on over their survival vests and climbed in. Thatcher went first since as pilot-in-control he would be flying the mission from the left seat under the supervision of the instructor, Bad Sam. Thatcher squeezed over the throttle quadrant to the left seat and began strapping in. Bad Sam followed, strapping into the right seat, and in minutes they got takeoff clearance from the tower while taxiing to the runway. As they turned on to the runway, Thatcher went through the standard engine checks and then smoothly advanced the power. In a few moments, the O-2 was clawing for the cooler air above. In less than ten minutes, climbing east, they could see the town of Nakhon Phanom, Thailand on the west bank of the Mekong River with Thakhet, Laos, on the opposing bank. Laos was still safe for the first ten or so miles, but gradually the North Vietnamese became more entrenched and the threat of anti-aircraft fire more pronounced.

"That's the Mekong River. Is it where you left it?" Sam was looking at Thatcher to see his reaction.

Thatcher paused, smiled, and then adjusted his helmet volume down to compensate for the hangover, and nodded. "How did you know?"

Sam grinned. "Well, first of all, you didn't even ask me which way to head. But second, I checked you out before you got here. Why in the hell would anyone come back for a second tour?"

Thatcher grinned back. "Maybe I was bored. And when I was here two years ago, we called the Mekong River 'The Fence.'"

"Do you remember how to check in with the airborne command post?"

Thatcher double clicked his intercom switch to acknowledge Sam's query and then transmitted on the UHF radio, "Hillsborough, Nail 79 is crossing the fence outbound for Sector Two."

"Roger Nail 79. Boomer flight headed your way. Two Marine A-6s with 28 Mark 82s each. Should be there in 20 minutes."

"Shit hot!" Sam was excited because that was a total of fifty-six 500-pound bombs. The explosion from that many bombs would buffet their plane even a mile high. It would leave a hole in the ground 300 meters wide.

"Turn to zero six zero degrees," he instructed Thatcher. "We can have a good time with that bomb load." The pre-takeoff jitters were gone for both pilots and the excitement of directing what was the largest bomb load of any aircraft in Laos, with the exception of a B-52, infused the cockpit.

The dry, yellow rice fields and green, dust-covered trees of western Laos resembled an impressionist painting, but they soon merged into a lush green, jungle-carpeted mountain range running north-south in front of them. As they passed over the range 20 minutes later, they entered the western boundary of the Ho Chi Minh Trail and leveled off 5,000 feet above the ground. The network of dirt roads on the flat flood plain beneath them meandered around karst formations which were thousands of years old. Bomb craters, between 30 years old and 30 minutes old, punctuated the land beneath them. The latter were marked by wisps of smoke curling upward. The karst formations reminded Thatcher of the sandstone sculptures of the American West. The formations, sprinkled randomly within and on both sides of the valley, had been given descriptive names by the aircrews, names such as the Battleship Karst, or the Banana Karst, reflecting their shapes. The gaunt gray/brown karst was often decorated with pools of aquamarine water trapped around the spires of the cathedral-like tops. Compared to landing on the valley floor below, they were great places to aim for a pilot swinging from a parachute and wishing to hide from the enemy. The downside? Landing in the rugged karst could be fatal due to the sharp, unforgiving spikes.

The trail itself was once a large rice producing area, even before the French. This day, it was a dry flood plain anywhere from a mile to two miles wide, and sprinkled with more green pools, but these were not natural: these were obviously older, rain-filled bomb craters, some dating back a decade or more, others created just the day (or night) before. Occasionally, smoke from burning truck carcasses, trophies from the American airstrikes the night before, brought the truck war to an unmistakable reality. If it wasn't Hell, it was a cousin.

On the eastern side of the valley in front of the Nails was a second, parallel, and much taller mountain range with another set of karst formations. That range extended as far as the eye could see. In fact, the second set of mountains extended all the way to the sea. Those mountains were entirely in North Viet Nam. The vision in front of the pilots explained vividly why the flat rice fields of the Laotian valley under them were so important to North Viet Nam. Infantry could travel south through the mountains, but heavily loaded trucks needed flat land to run. Laos was flat. North Viet Nam was not. It was that simple. And it was the *raison d'être* for the first of the Laotian Secret Wars, the Truck War.

To fight the war, Ho Chi Minh needed supplies: food for attacking troops, guns and ammunition, medical supplies, building materials for underground storage, truck parks, and living quarters for the construction crews and truck drivers. The Ho Chi Minh Trail was a living, breathing organism solely dedicated to reuniting Viet Nam.

The flat land on both sides of the trail was heavily forested. This gave the North Vietnamese a big advantage. Triple canopy jungle on both sides of the valley hosting the trail allowed for almost uninhibited activity under the trees: truck parks, R&R centers for the southbound troops, hospitals, maintenance garages, communications centers, and fuel depots.

The Ho Chi Minh Trail had a mysterious aura about it caused by the shroud of dust which hovered nearly a mile high over the entire 50-mile length. The result of continuous bombing 24 hours a day, the haze layer was visible from 20 miles away and would have aroused anyone's curiosity since it looked so out of place against the backdrop of lush green jungle on both sides capped by clear blue skies above. Flying into the haze meant leaving clear air, and safety, far behind. It was as if one were flying into a time warp. The trail's reputation among Southeast Asia pilots was legendary. Other than the bombing of Hanoi and Haiphong Harbor, nothing matched the ferocity of gunfire. Unlike North Viet Nam, getting shot down on the trail was often the kiss of death, and pilots knew it. There were no TV cameras to record Americans captured, such as those in North Viet Nam, and therefore no propaganda value; there were no friends, no sympathizers, and no safe havens. Prisoners were too much of a burden. What little active agriculture remained was suspected to be entirely communist: Pathet Lao or North Vietnamese cultivation.

Thatcher, without waiting for instructions from Sam, started jinking the O-2, constantly changing course in small but random turns intended to prevent the gunners below from getting an easy shot. It didn't require dramatic movements because the anti-aircraft fire usually came up from 5,000 feet or more away and took a minimum of five seconds to reach the aiming point. A random series of slow turns would place the aircraft at least a few feet away from the trajectory of the shells. Very few missions did not experience anti-aircraft fire, and pilots thinking they had been spared probably weren't looking behind or above the aircraft. The O-2 looked like a speck to gunners below, but there were usually multiple guns shooting clips of seven to 20 shells depending on the size of the gun. Pilots who didn't return were often the ones who slacked off the jinking to take a picture, scratch an itch, or who got distracted reading a map.

Sam hit the intercom button and asked, "By the way, did you ever put in airstrikes in Sector One on your previous tour two years ago?"

Thatcher wiped the sweat dripping from under his helmet before answering Sam's question. "Getting through the mountains from North Viet Nam to South Viet Nam has always been a challenge because we had unilaterally avoided bombing North Viet Nam after the division in 1956. Ho Chi Minh never accepted the division of his country and started the reunification in steps. The pipeline for supplies and troops into South Viet Nam became known as the Ho Chi Minh Trail. Sector One was the first entry point for the troops and supplies but later they developed passes farther south at Mu Gia and Ban Karai and rarely used Sector One. That's because they could stay in North Viet Nam longer before entering Laos since we had quit bombing the North. Laos was only in play because it was flat and trucks could run far easier at night."

Sam interjected, "The grunts in South Viet Nam have found huge underground tunnels that link everything from ammo supplies to hospitals and truck parks. We're finding more and more stuff underground all over the trail."

The headsets of the O-2 pilots crackled to life and the history lesson was suspended.

"Nail 79, Boomer 20 and 21 inbound with 28 Mark 82s each, 30 minutes play time."

"Roger that Boomer. Meet us at the Dog's Head."

Sam made the return call as the O-2 reached the dirt roads coming out of North Viet Nam on the far side of the valley they were traversing. The roads, little more than crude dirt trails, snaked along the flood plain of the Ngo River which twisted here and there even though the things which once caused it to twist were long gone.

Ban Laboy Ford, at the literal border between North Viet Nam and Laos, was a part of a river loop resembling the profile of a dog's head, which is what the pilots named it. The surface for hundreds of yards on either side of Dog's Head was surrounded by remnants of rice paddies long abandoned. It looked like the landscape of the moon, cratered by years of bombing, devoid of vegetation, and powder dry.

The tree lines on either side of the valley/flood plain were as much as a mile apart in some places, only a few hundred yards in others, depending on the terrain and the jungle, which was gradually being bombed away. The edges of the jungle were defined by huge masses of trees lying scattered and splintered, obviously the battleground between something trying to hide and something trying to kill. Typically, the anti-aircraft guns were hidden close to the jungle's edge, although many were hidden in caves at the base of the karst formations; these were usually rolled out after dark unless a daytime airstrike was initiated. In this case, the RF-4 infrared photos of the target showed the guns were protected by extensive camouflage netting and not in caves.

So far, there was no gunfire. Nevertheless, Thatcher intensified the jinking, banking erratically left and right never allowing the plane to hold course for more than a few seconds at a time. The AAA in this area was especially heavy and could reach well over 18,000 feet. The O-2, only 5,000 feet above the ground, was a tempting target, but the gunners hadn't sensed hostile action yet. They would be advertising themselves as a target if they did.

Always turning, never in a predictable pattern, Thatcher maneuvered the O-2 over the valley to a river abutting the mountain range on what was the far side of the trail. The land around the river formation was encircled by dozens of huge bomb craters filled with aquamarine water. In fact, there were craters on top of filled-in craters. They were obviously past attempts at bombing the fords which, in many cases, were successful. Bomb craters in Laos dated as far back as the French, after WWII. But, it was also apparent the North Vietnamese had relocated the road a few meters away or hauled in dirt and resumed operation. Much of the work was done at night or under cloud cover when possible. Bulldozers were often used, and FACs that found and directed airstrikes on dozers were given a few extra pats on the back at the nightly parties at the Nail Hole.

Sam pointed out of the right window. "See the pool in the right in the middle of the Dog's Head? Photo recon shows at least one gun, maybe more, a few meters north of there in those bushes. It's probably radar controlled, so there may be a control van hidden there as well. It will be impossible to see, though. They've got it covered up with camouflaged netting and leaves."

The Dog's Head was well named. It could have been the profile of almost any dog. The river was about 50 yards wide and had no visible current. Thatcher looked intently through his binoculars, but Sam was right. The camouflage was perfect.

Thatcher pointed to a spot on the river a few hundred meters south of the Dog's Head. "Is that where Baker 22 Bravo was rescued?"

"Hell yes, how'd you know that?"

"Underwood and I met him at the Cam Ranh Bay Officers' Club two days ago. What a story! There was still a cut on his nose from the bailout. He told me the Nails played a big role in his rescue. He described the piece of karst and the river. His description was pretty accurate. I recognized it easily."

Sam responded. "The Nail putting in the airstrike where Baker 22 got hit put in several more airstrikes on guns using what aircraft he could get after the shootdown. He's rotated back to the States, so you won't meet him. But several more of our guys provided constant aerial surveillance, locating additional guns and directing airstrikes when the Sandys didn't have a fix." Sandys were the A-1s from NKP who used the Sandy call sign when operating on rescue missions.

During regular nighttime missions, when they normally flew, they used the call signs Hobo or Zorro depending on their squadron. The discussion between Sam and Thatcher was interrupted by the Marine A-6 flight.

"Nail 79, Boomer 21 and 22, two A-6s with 28 Mark 82s each. We're overhead and have you in sight. O-2 circling left over the river."

Sam answered, "Roger that. Target is a gun complex, probably a 57mm with four 37mms around the main gun. Now let's give ourselves the advantage of surprise. Instead of smoking it, which would wake 'em up, I'm going to describe where that bastard is. This should be easy. Do you see about where the tip of the dog's ear would be?"

"Affirmative," radioed the flight leader.

"Drop your entire load right there and they'll never know what hit 'em," Sam chuckled.

"Fifty-six Mark 82s? Do you know what kind of a hole it's going to make?" A Mark 82 was a 500-pound bomb, the most common used on the trail.

"Damn right I do! I expect to see hell when you're finished."

"Roger that Nail. That's exactly what you'll see. Are we cleared in hot?"

"Go get 'em tiger. We'll be holding east at 6,500 feet."

"Boomer flight is in hot." The A-6 flight leader and his wingman came in a few seconds apart, vapor streaming off their wingtips as they rolled inverted and pulled the noses of their planes down steeply.

"Our Willy Pete would just wake 'em in time for the A-6s," drawled Sam over the intercom to Thatcher. "We'd be safe, because they wouldn't give their position away for something as small as an O-2, but the A-6s would catch hell. Going against a gun is tough work, and surprise is the best tactic I've found. If the first pass doesn't kill the gun, you better believe the next pass is going to be like flying into a wall of lead. When you have a couple of pros like these Marine pilots, it's one pass and haul ass on guns. Coming out of the sun is another good choice."

Thatcher double-clicked his mic again to acknowledge the last comment and watched intently as twenty-eight 500-pound bombs separated from each of the twin attack jets. The bombs hurtled down as the jets pulled up hard and broke left. Seconds later, 56 enormous explosions sent shards of dust spiking up from the earth. A huge orange fireball roiled up through the huge black cloud of dust. The shock wave of the bombs physically shook the O-2, flying a mile high and a few thousand feet away. There was only one problem, as far as Thatcher could see. The explosion was at least 400 meters to the north of the target, completely outside the Dog's Head.

"What the hell, over?" shouted Sam into the radio.

"Beggin' your pardon?" replied the Boomer leader.

"You're 400 meters north." Sam's voice displayed his obvious displeasure.

"Bullshit. That dog ain't got an ear left."

"Negative, Boomer. You're 400 meters north. I will admit it's about normal for you guys, but hell, man that was a gun. You could have at least put your coffee cup down and used two hands."

Boomer lead responded and he wasn't happy. "North my ass, Nail! You bastards are drinking too much Wild Turkey down there at the Nail Hole."

"Is that you, Mike?" asked Bad Sam. "For your information, Air Force pilots drink Black Label. We also wash our hands before we piss, not after. That's so we don't contaminate our organ. You swabbies drink shaving lotion and have to wash your hands after you piss because you piss all over yourselves. Which is what you did on that drop."

"Hell, Sam, I didn't know it was you. Did you change your call sign? You weren't Nail 79 the last time when we hit that gasoline pipeline. Boy, we still talk about that one back on the boat. But you are getting on in years, and if I'd known it was you, I would have adjusted a few hundred meters knowing you're too old to see shit anyway. But c'mon Sam, we wiped out the damned dog's ear and everything around it."

"I told you to hit the tip of the dog's ear." Sam was exasperated.

"And that's exactly what we did. What kind of dog do you think it is, anyway?"

"It's a damn Beagle you asshole. Didn't you see the nice square jaw line?" Sam was getting more agitated.

"Beagle my ass! It's a German Shepherd."

What followed might be described as a pregnant pause. By the time the reality hit, Sam was laughing so hard he couldn't talk. He motioned toward the boom mic on Thatcher's helmet, so Thatcher called Boomer flight lead. "Well, Dorothy, I guess we're not in Kansas anymore."

"I guess not, Nail. Merry Christmas. See you next time."

Thatcher looked over at Sam, who was already looking at Thatcher. "Did you remember it was Christmas?"

"Hell, no! I can't even remember what month it is." Sam grunted.

On the ground, Sgt. Ca, the North Vietnamese gun crew commander who scored a hit a few days earlier on an O-2, for which he was promoted to Sergeant, had been caught completely by surprise. There was no rocket to mark a target, and no airplane circling above the intended target. His gun crew hurriedly manned their gun and began to punctuate the blue sky above the haze layer, first black puffs from the 37mm anti-aircraft guns, then occasional white puffs from the 57mm weapon. He was shooting at the O-2 since the A-6s were out of range and heading home to their aircraft carrier. In less than 30 minutes, the A-6 pilots would be eating pancakes and drinking coffee on their aircraft carrier.

Thatcher took back the controls and intensified the jinking as he headed for the North Vietnamese side of the trail, where mountains and jungle promised a reprieve from the guns underneath. Once out of range, he turned west toward NKP, crossing the trail at a spot where trees were more abundant and the chance of a clear shot for gunners would be less likely.

Sam triggered his mic, "How about celebrating our victory today at the Officers' Club for lunch?'

"Sounds good to me."

The return flight was uneventful. Leaving 5,000 feet above the ground, the air became progressively warmer as the O-2 descended after crossing the last ridge of karst. It was in the mid-nineties, at noon. Bad Sam handled the radio transmissions and Thatcher flew. After unstrapping and squeezing out of the door with their parachutes still on, they started looking over the plane. Sure enough, there were some small punctures in the wing, evidence of shrapnel damage from anti-aircraft guns and a North Vietnamese gunner's dashed hopes for another victory for Uncle Ho.

The following day, the TUOC briefers, who always drew a grease board cartoon based on some previous day's screw-up, drew a cartoon of Snoopy wearing pilot goggles and sitting on a doghouse, propellers front and rear, shaking a fist and saying, "Henceforth, the Dog's Head is that of a Beagle."

Thatcher and Bad Sam returned the parachutes, survival vests, .38 caliber pistols, AR-15s, helmets, and water flasks and caught the TUOC Trolley to the Officers' Club.

6

Let's Do Lunch

Super Thai placed the rolled-up washcloths in the steamer and left to begin supervising the staff setting up the evening tables. The NKP Officers' Club was decorated for Christmas, even though most officers didn't pay much attention. It was just another day at war. Super Thai's position as hostess was the result of her command of the English language, which was primitive but sufficient to the task. Her delicate fingers placed the decorations precisely in place on each table as a Philippine rock band practiced American rock songs on the stage. They were trying their rendition of "Proud Mary" but were having trouble pronouncing their R's. It sounded as if they were singing, "Lolling on the Liver."

Like many Thai women, the thought of marrying a GI was enticing to Super Thai, whose real name was pronounced 'Sonni'. Her motivation was economic. Northern Thailand was a place of excruciating poverty, which overwhelmed the hopes of even the most optimistic. She spent less time than most girls thinking about it, though. She made a good living at the base, and one day when the Americans left, as everyone knew they would, she would have enough saved to move to Bangkok. The war had been very good to her. She began bussing tables but perfected her English rapidly, moving to the position of hostess within three years of her arrival. She supported her mother and father and three younger siblings.

The officers all thought she was a prostitute, an assumption she encouraged for two reasons. First, in Thailand a prostitute was not the pariah one would be in the Western or Middle Eastern countries. The Southeast Asian attitudes were much more liberal in that regard, and a young woman who could support her family sleeping with men, discreetly and selectively, was not always looked down upon. But second, and more importantly, Sonni knew something about Americans they would never admit themselves. Most of them were very decent men, and if they thought she was not a prostitute, they wouldn't pay her much attention. Less attention meant less tips. She once listened to a rather intoxicated colonel explain the peculiar American custom of treating a whore like a lady and a lady like a whore. From that point on she flirted outrageously, and her tips skyrocketed.

Bad Sam and Thatcher disembarked from the TUOC Trolley after a 10-minute ride. Thatcher swung the door open, leaving the afternoon heat behind them, spilling the bright afternoon sunlight into the cool, red carpeted interior of the Officers' Club. Solid mahogany, not paneling, adorned the walls, and many of the tables were already taken, mostly staff officers wearing khakis instead of flight suits. Bad Sam entered first with Thatcher following. As their eyes adjusted to the light, the hostess approached and bowed with her hands in typical Thai greeting position, fingertips together, hands under the chin. She wore traditional Thai silk dress, tightly fitting and decorated lavishly with embroidery, in this case tropical birds of paradise. She was not what most men would call beautiful, but was more of a caricature, excessively long nails painted a bright, flaming red, and black hair piled almost a foot high and sporting some very long bamboo sticks through the middle in random directions. She was six feet tall but probably weighed no more than 100 pounds.

"Captain Thatcher," Bad Sam announced with mock fanfare, "I want you to meet Super Thai, the most beautiful woman in all of Southeast Asia."

"*Sawatdee-kah*, Ted."

Thatcher mirrored her bow, but not as low, indicative of the social stature customs of the East, and responded in a low voice, "*Sawatdee-krap*, Sonni. How have you been?"

"Fine. I wonder if you come back."

Sam didn't say anything. He didn't have to. As he turned and stared at Thatcher, his eyes said it all.

"Sonni, we would like a table away from the crowd, if you please," Thatcher said.

Sonni bowed and led the way to the table farthest away from the other occupied tables. She handed them menus, motioned for a waitress, and left. Sam was staring at Thatcher, waiting for an explanation.

Thatcher let him twirl in the wind for a while, pretending not to notice that something strange had just happened. Finally, he laughed, "Sam, don't read anything into it. That's how she increases her tips."

"Well, she didn't flirt with me." Sam was grinning.

"How many times have you eaten here?" Thatcher was grinning right back.

"Just twice. I don't eat. I drink."

"Well, now you have an excuse."

Sam re-directed the conversation. "Maybe I do. Now, have you ever heard of Cricket West?"

"Sure I have, the war between the Pathet Lao communists, and the Laotian monarchy, sometimes called the second Secret War or the People War. Nothing much has changed since my last tour, according to my conversations with the Intel guys at Bien Hoa. Raven FACs handle the People War; they get to wear civilian clothes and fly unmarked O-1 Bird Dogs as low as they want. They don't have to shave or say 'sir' and there aren't any real markings of rank. They have two operations, one in the far north of Laos bordering China in the territory called the PDJ, or Plaine des Jarres. There was also an operation across the Mekong River from NKP in the Panhandle. Kind of pathetic isn't it? Two secret wars butting up against each other in one small, formerly peaceful country. The Truck War and the People War."

Thatcher paused for a moment, collecting his thoughts, and then continued his commentary.

"Except for the Ho Chi Minh Trail in the east, Laos is supposedly under the control of King Sisavang Vatthana. He occupies a throne established hundreds of years before Europeans even knew Laos existed. But the Chinese and Pathet Lao are never going to be content until the monarchy is abolished and they're in control."

Thatcher and Sam paused to place their orders with a waitress who had been waiting patiently. Then they continued.

Thatcher picked up the conversation, "I'm surprised the king's still here."

"Well, he is, but it's not looking good." Sam answered. "Three Nails out of the 20 pilots here are flying part time in the People War in addition to our trail missions. I'm one, and one is leaving. We support the Laotian Army and answer to the CIA. Those missions are on a volunteer basis. I'd like to recommend you for a slot given your interest and past experience. About 20-percent of my missions are Cricket West and flown with a Laotian paratrooper in the right seat. The Laotian's we fly with are called X-rays. Since we take off from Thailand, we don't wear civilian clothes or fly unmarked airplanes like Raven FACs do. It doesn't mean much if you're shot down because they'll kill you anyway. The Laotian paratrooper who will fly with you in the right seat will validate targets. In other words, he assures us we're shooting at the bad guys. The good news is you get to fly as low as you want. Are you interested?"

"Hell yes! I have some friends flying the Raven mission, including the guy who trained me my first summer at the Zoo, Paul Bartram. You might have heard us talking about him last night in the Nail Hole. He was the hard ass who always had a smile on his face.

I know of other Air Force buddies who were, and maybe still are, flying that mission. They don't have a one-year tour like we do; theirs is indefinite. They can stay longer if they choose. They live full time at the so-called secret bases in Laos."

Sam continued, "In the western portion of Laos, where you will fly, the AAA is 12.7mm machine gun category, not the usual 37 or 57mm fire we get over the trail. But it will kill you just as fast because you're lower and closer. So, don't think it's a milk run just because it's not the trail."

Thatcher smiled. "Well, the twisted prop mounted on the Nail Hole wall as a trophy came off an O-2 flown by my best friend on my first tour here. It was the result of a 12.7 that was still in use back then. I notice there are still no props on the wall from the larger calibers, 37mm and up."

Sam laughed. "A 37mm wouldn't just twist a prop, it would tear the engine off."

The two Nails took a long time eating lunch. Like two Vikings around the campfire, they talked, told war stories, shared jokes, lied about their female conquests, and gradually formed a bond that would grow stronger over the next year and last a lifetime. They finally headed back to the Nail Hole. The ambience of the Officers' Club evaporated immediately as they walked out the door. An OV-10 buzzed over the club, inbound for landing. The war was back on. They caught the TUOC Trolley and in ten minutes were back at the Nail Hole. Sam disembarked first and headed for his room.

"I'm taking a nap. How about you?"

Thatcher shook his head. "No. I'm meeting Bill Stancil here in ten minutes. He's taking me to the Green Beret Compound for some sort of ceremony."

"Well, be careful. Those guys are not all that tightly wired. I think they like to eat snakes."

Thatcher laughed. "I tried some smoked rattlesnake one time at a barbecue in Arizona. It wasn't all that bad."

Sam grinned. "These guys don't smoke the snakes; they bite the heads off and eat them alive."

"Good thing I'm no longer hungry. Great lunch. See you later Sam."

"Later. You did good today. Thanks for the stories of the old days."

"Nails were shit hot then, Sam, and they still are."

7

Snake Eaters

Thatcher entered the Nail Hole. He was alone except for the cat curled up on the bar sleeping. Bill Stancil entered a few moments later, his perpetual grin in place, sandy brown hair neatly combed, and sporting his best flight suit, the one without wine stains.

"How's it hanging, Ted?"

"Short, shriveled, and leaning to the left." Bill laughed. After a few backslaps and good-natured insults about who was the ugliest, they headed for the door to catch the TUOC Trolley to the Green Beret compound.

"Ted," Bill Stancil, shouted over the noise of the open-doored step van, "this operation you're going to see is super-secret, so bear that in mind. We don't have any ground troops in Laos. So, officially, these guys are not there. They are cream of the Green Beret crop, and they have probably the highest casualty rates in the war. Quite frankly, I don't know what motivates them. They are dropped by chopper on a mountain peak somewhere near the trail and quietly make their way down and get to work. They are inserted where there may be activity we Nails can't see from the air. A lot of North Vietnamese activity is underground in caves that have been expanded into truck parks and storage facilities. Heavy Hook captures a few of the stragglers and interrogates those using

73

Montagnards who speak the language. This information is funneled back to our Intel guys and that's where we get a lot of our target direction. You will be hitting targets these guys found that you and I would have never seen from the air."

"And your job?" Thatcher already knew the answer, but he asked anyway.

"My job is to use all the airpower we have to protect them. On the Ho Chi Minh Trail, they're almost always in trouble sooner or later. You may be called if I'm not available and you're close, so the guys you're looking at here today may be on the other end of a radio one day and you may be the only way to get them home safely. We don't bring many in here, especially the younger pilots, because security and good judgement is critical. Consider yourself honored."

"I do. Before I lose my nerve and back off from saying this, I'm proud of you. They picked the right guy for this mission."

"Ted, every mission over here is important, none more than the others. If you can kill more trucks, these guys you meet today will be that much safer, not to mention the grunts in Viet Nam. We're all fighting for each other, and that's probably true in any combat situation."

A few minutes later, they disembarked at the gate of a fenced-in compound surrounded by coiled barbed wire. A six-foot-two, 230-pound giant, whose arms were as big as oak limbs, stood guard. He was carrying a Swedish Sten Gun and had an assortment of things hanging from his belt, all looking dangerous. Thatcher recognized a few: hand grenades, but not the U.S. kind, a knife the size of a small machete, and an assortment of pouches. Since the compound they were inside was inside the perimeter of a heavily guarded U.S. Air Base in Thailand, Thatcher assumed the Green Berets trusted no one. He made a mental note not to make any sudden moves.

As they passed through the gate, Thatcher noticed weight benches with what looked like six or seven railroad wheels on each end of the bars; Heavy Hook team members were actually lifting them into the air. Thatcher tried not to look at them and followed his old pilot training classmate through the door of the one-story concrete block building, once again enjoying the blessing of air conditioning.

Inside, an animated conversation was taking place. One speaker was a 30-year-old man wearing dungarees and a T-shirt. He was a few inches over six feet and well-muscled, but not as bulky as the other Heavy Hook members. He was clutching a tabletop microphone in both hands; on the other end of the conversation was a voice coming from a speaker. The voice came from an obviously out of breath and very animated individual.

"Head for high ground," commanded the man in dungarees. "We've already scrambled the Jollys. ETA is 30 minutes. Stay in touch with the Nail and call me whenever you can but don't stop moving."

As the call ended, he turned to Bill Stancil and shook his hand. "Bill, we're glad to have you here and we're looking forward to the ceremony. As you can tell, we've got a team on the run, but what else is new? It's getting worse day-by-day. Who's the ugly guy with you?"

"This is Ted Thatcher, a pilot training classmate and the second-best pilot in our class."

Thatcher grinned and held out his hand. "Ted Thatcher, Nail 79. Thank you for inviting me. He tells me not many people get to see the inside of this place."

"Well, let's just say we don't have time for guided tours, but if Bill says you're OK, you're OK. He has done a hell of a job for us and, quite frankly, he hasn't been given much time to come up to speed. Things are heating up out there, so you may get a call one day as well. Let me also say you wouldn't even be in this compound if he hadn't given you the highest marks. The nature of our business makes us a little paranoiac. So, make yourself at home, and know you're among friends."

"Thank you, sir."

Bill Stancil led Thatcher to the next room which was a bar/lounge area, concrete block walls painted beige, a corrugated metal ceiling unpainted, and a few neon lights to enhance the ambience. They ordered two beers. The cans were placed on the bar by another gorilla who Stancil introduced as Mako. Four other Heavy Hook members were there drinking a beer; Stancil introduced them to Thatcher as an old friend from pilot training. When he told them Thatcher might very well be the FAC responding to a call for assistance if the designated Nail was not available, they warmed up immediately and insisted on paying for the beers. The two Nails thanked them, took a hard pull from the beers, and they all moved to an old wooden table.

"Are you using landing lights at night or are you still looking for new ways to show off?" Stancil asked. "My buddy here landed a T-38, a supersonic trainer we called the White Rocket, at night, in the rain, without landing lights. Do you ever think about that late at night Ted?"

Stancil was not bringing the event up just to make conversation. The T-38, the Air Force top-of-the-line trainer, was called the 'White Rocket' by those who flew it because its short, stubby wings meant that the only way to keep it flying without stalling was to go fast; it landed nose high at 100 miles per hour. A night-time, no-light landing in the rain was tricky, to say the least. In fact, none of the instructors in the squadron could ever remember it happening before.

"It was a piece of cake compared to playing poker with you! Now, how about another beer? I'm still thirsty. You're treating me like a cheap date."

"No time for that. The ceremony is about to begin. Now comes the hard part. You have to hit the 55-gallon oil drum over there behind the bar with your empty beer can. If you miss, the bartender gets to hit you on the arm." Stancil and his friends were grinning; Thatcher was looking from the trash can to the bartender and back again. Thatcher said a short prayer and then hit the oil drum with a hook shot. Thatcher and the other Nails as well as the Green Berets would be praying a lot in the coming year.

The crowd moved outside where there were about ten other beefy guys dressed in assorted camouflage apparel, none of it regulation. The commander of the unit stood in the center. He motioned for Stancil to join him, and as he did, he pulled a Green Beret out of his back pocket. Putting his arm on Stancil's shoulder he began the ceremony.

"This man has earned the respect of all who have worked with him. He embodies everything this Green Beret represents. Bill Stancil, I'll ask your back-seater, Sergeant Mrozek, to make the presentation."

The sergeant, dressed in jungle fatigues, stepped forward, saluted, took the Green Beret, turned, and placed it on Bill Stancil's head. Then in a move Thatcher did not expect, but would never forget, Bill Stancil's beefy, back-seat Green Beret companion grabbed Bill's head in his two huge hands and kissed him right on the mouth.

Stancil broke out in a laugh and the other Green Berets came up and proceeded to squeeze the breath out of him, each one whispering something in his ear as they slapped him on the back. It was a memory that would never dim for Ted Thatcher. One of many Thatcher would never forget in his year fighting a war which seemed to have no end.

8

Spotting Artillery

Bad Sam was relieved to be flying a Cricket West mission the day after his dinner with Thatcher at the Officers' Club. The Cricket West program was a part of the second Secret War, the 'people war' in which the United States was supporting the benevolent 1,000-year-old monarchy in Laos. For Cricket West missions, a Laotian Army officer, code named 'X-Ray', flew in the right seat as a target validator. The Laotian X-Ray in Sam's O-2 for the day was Lt. Tonsonnai, a handsome Lao with black hair and pearly white teeth constantly on display. Tonsonnai was a personable, energetic officer with an incredible resume. He was with a major Laotian infantry operation several years ago that had gone south, which is to say it was a complete disaster. He spent two days running through the jungle before reaching safety. Tonsonnai volunteered for the Cricket West program, determined to keep on fighting, but recognizing American air power offered a lot more to the Laotian cause than infantry operations.

Unknown to most Americans, President Eisenhower selected Laos, not Viet Nam, as the 'line in the sand', the place America would attempt to prevent communism from enveloping all of Southeast Asia. He created a separate army and air force financed and run by the CIA, the spy agency's first experience with its own army. The current king and his royal family were revered by the people of the Elephant Kingdom, the name by which Laos was known. The Prime Minister, Prince Souvanna Phouma, ruled the western part of the country bordering Thailand with great diplomacy and strong support, although his half-brother, Prince Souvanavong, had broken ranks with the rest of his family and turned to the communists in an attempt to overthrow his father, the king. Although not directly related to the communist threat in Viet Nam and elsewhere in Southeast Asia, there was some commonality, primarily China, which was a source for weaponry and financing for all things communist.

This day, Bad Sam and Lt. Tonsonnai were looking for signs of an enemy incursion near a small village close to the Mekong River. Reports indicated some stolen rice and other suspicious activity. Although the Cricket West operation was technically not related to the interdiction campaign on the Ho Chi Minh Trail farther to the east, the two geographic spheres paralleled and sometimes overlapped each other. Sam was excited by Cricket West missions because the punishment by the Air Force for getting hit by small arms fire was waived. The punishment was variable, depending on the circumstances, but a small arms hit was often cause for disciplinary action because there was a mandatory altitude minimum of 5,000 feet AGL (above ground level) on the trail. Since Cricket West missions were ostensibly flown off the trail, where there were no big guns, small arms hits were not punished. And further, since the Cricket West area was an ill-defined area west of and abutting the trail, he could fly much lower and pick up some juicy targets, even on the western boundary of the trail itself. As Bad Sam flew over a remote landing strip, one of many that served the Royal Lao outposts, Tonsonnai began speaking to a ground unit on the VHF radio.

"Captain Sam," he reported after his conversation with the ground troops, "bad guys attack village two clicks northeast from here, army wants us to spot artillery." His face displayed concern, and his voice a sense of urgency.

"*C'est vrai?*" asked Sam, reverting momentarily to French. He was surprised by the request. He learned how to direct artillery fire in FAC training at Hurlburt Field in Florida but had never done so. On the Ho Chi Minh Trail, his normal place of business, the only artillery was anti-aircraft, and he was always on the receiving end of that.

"*Oui. Le Pathet Laotien a détruit tout le riz dans le village.*"

"Why would they destroy all the rice?"

"Bad guys." To Tonsonnai, the worst curse to put on anyone was to call him a bad guy.

Sam answered in French, "*Dis-lui qu'on est en route.*" ("Tell them we are en route.")

Sam spoke French with a Midwestern accent, but the X-Rays who flew with him appreciated the effort.

"*Mais oui.*"

Sam wheeled the O-2 around 180 degrees and pushed up the power. Fifteen minutes later, they arrived over a village where the ground was as white as snow. A whole year's rice crop spilled on the ground, wasted out of nothing but meanness. It made Sam sick. It was a typical Laotian village with dirt paths between thatched-roof houses. In the center was the ubiquitous Buddhist Temple, its gold-leafed roof sparkling in the morning sunlight.

"*Ou le batards sont?*" ("Where are the bastards?") Sam asked the Laotian artillery officer on the ground on the VHF radio. Sam didn't speak fluent French, but the Laotians taught him a few phrases for typical or recurring situations. This was one phrase he used often since the war in the western part of Laos was the People War, not the Truck War, and there were a lot of bastards.

"*Dans le bosquet d'arbres au nord du village.*" answered the officer.

"What did he say?" asked Sam, not as good at understanding French as speaking it.

"In the grove of trees, over there." Tonsonnai pointed.

Sam spotted the grove of trees and flew over it at 1,000 feet, but the canopy was too dense to see anything. He pulled off to one side. "Tell them to fire when ready," he told Tonsonnai, reverting to English.

The artillery piece was located on a road on the opposite side of the village, but in line with the village and the grove of trees. Sam didn't know what size the gun was because he never paid much attention to such things in training. A puff of smoke announced a round was on its way, and Sam watched the trees intently. Nothing happened. As he turned the aircraft around in a steep turn, he saw smoke arising between the houses in the village. "Damn," he said to himself.

"*ARRÊTER! ARRÊTER!*" Sam shouted over the radio.

Tonsonnai was telling the artillery crew to cease fire in Laotian, as well, but the artillery crew appeared to be laughing. Sam was disgusted. A quick pass over the town showed the round had not hit anything of substance. Probably a water trough at most. But why in the hell did they find hitting their own village so funny?

He told Tonsonnai to adjust the fire 500 meters to the north and the next round splintered a tree near the grove. Sam made a low pass but saw nothing. The Pathet Lao weren't stupid enough to hang round close to a village they had just raided, and Sam knew the artillery show was just that, a show. He told Tonsonnai to advise the gunners they killed five bad guys and headed east, hoping to find something to restore his honor.

That evening, after awakening from his nap, Sam headed for the Nail Hole. He put on his best flight suit, the one without wine stains, and ran his fingers through his hair, the only real grooming he ever did. As he entered, the cloud of cigarette smoke, the clink of glasses, and the animated discussion signaled a normal evening. That meant no one was missing or lost that day, at least so far. Tonight, the specialty on the Akai reel-to-reel tape deck was Hank Williams who was singing "I can't help it if I'm still in luuuv with you."

He sidled up next to the crowd at the bar and ordered a beer. The topic for the evening was when in the hell was the war going to end. It was almost always the topic.

"Soon," opined one of the navigators. "How can it go on? The trucks are multiplying like a fungus. We kill one and two take its place. We need to declare victory and leave."

"Have you guys thought about Super Bowl IV? I'm betting on Minnesota."

The speaker was one of the New Beans who arrived just after Thatcher. The other Nails looked at him with a mixture of incredulity and disgust. Who gave a crap about the Super Bowl?

9

Farm Boy

Captain Ted Thatcher took off at daybreak on a cool morning, by Thailand standards, clear and about 60 degrees. It was his twentieth mission on his second tour. His first month had only been semi-productive because the monsoon rains cancelled missions or degraded visibility more than half the time. Today, however, it was clear. He headed for the trail around the Chokes, a place in the valley where several dirt roads came together for a few hundred yards due to a constriction in the terrain. Normally the trail was more than a mile wide. Although he had been briefed on several targets and assigned Navy air, he didn't expect to find anything. The Navy A-4s were probably launching at that moment, and since the aircraft carrier they were on, the *Kitty Hawk*, was only about 50 miles east at Yankee Station, they would be there in a matter of minutes. Thatcher felt a particular bond with that carrier: he sailed on it for a week on an exchange visit while a cadet at the Air Force Academy. The carrier then had been cruising up and down the California coast for 'carrier quals,' qualifying Navy pilots for carrier duty. Now it was cruising up and down the coast of Viet Nam and he would be directing those pilots against enemy targets on the ground. "Small world," mused Thatcher.

83

There were small outcroppings of karst with caves housing guns in the Chokes and they were very active at night because of the convergence of roads, but what came out of the north at night was almost always gone by daybreak, hidden under the triple canopy jungle on both sides of the road network. Still, it was a good place to start. Occasionally, trucks bogged down and were good targets the first thing in the morning along with the road crews trying to haul them into the trees.

The haze of the trail looked artistic in the early morning light, not unlike an Impressionist painting. Out of the tragic stories of combat in any war were often found sprinkles of beauty or humanity: the poppies of Flanders Fields, the haunting melody of a harmonica on a Civil War battlefield, a gorgeous sunset over North Vietnamese mountains accentuated by streams of red tracers. Perhaps, thought Thatcher, it was God's way of saying, "I'm still here."

Thatcher was sorry he hadn't borrowed Roger "Mad Dog" Brown's famous tape recorder. A little Mozart would have been appropriate. Roger was the only Nail who figured out how to splice in a tape player to his O-2 so he could listen to the "1812 Overture" while shooting Willie Petes at trucks on the trail. He was a virtual fountain of creativity. Roger paid for some of this creativity, however. In his first year, his First Class, or senior, Element Leader at the Academy, aka 'The Zoo,' was Paul Bartram, who was constantly inventing new punishments for Roger's creative misbehavior.

Bartram was an Iowa farm boy and as plain as a homemade bar of soap. He looked and sounded like a hayseed, slow of speech with a deep, Mid-western drawl that masked an IQ of 140. He was not mean, like some of his classmates, but came from a background where obedience to the rules was taken for granted. The discipline of the Academy wasn't much of a departure from his Iowa boyhood. But Roger Brown didn't make sense to Bartram. Roger was, to put it mildly, not too interested in perfection. If Roger's bed wasn't completely square and blanket pulled tight enough so that a dropped quarter didn't bounce, what did it matter? Even though Bartram was constantly prescribing grueling punishments, such as 200 pushups or 100-yard run with an M-1 rifle held overhead, Bartram seemed to have a twinkle in his eye when sending Roger off on another gut-wrenching disciplinary maneuver. There was a bond between the two, although no one, including Brown or Bartram, knew why.

Thatcher was drawn out of his musings by the voices crackling in his headset.

"Nail 79, Derby flight inbound with two A-4s, eight Mark 82s each."

"Roger that Derby. Just find the air bursts." The guns around the Chokes opened up early this morning. Thatcher wondered what they were hiding. He was jinking the O-2 like a dove on opening day of dove season. Growing up with North Carolina cornfields all around him taught Thatcher a thing or two about avoiding hostile fire. Doves characteristically flew in erratic patterns, constantly banking or twitching, slightly left or right even while maintaining a straight course. It wasn't unusual to shoot one or two boxes of shotgun shells to get the limit of 12 birds. And getting hit by the spent pellets raining back to earth from other hunters wasn't unusual either. With a dozen hunters all shooting upward, that was common; the pellets were harmless unless one was looking up. The dove metaphor wasn't lost on Thatcher. He laughed at the spectacle of his reversed role. He didn't know it then, but he would never dove hunt again after this second tour. He would lose his appetite for killing things, especially flying things.

It didn't take long to find what the guns were protecting. A bulldozer was trying to hide in the shadow of some rubble near a small karst formation. It had been clearing the road from the bombing the night before. Judging from the burned-out truck carcasses scattered around, it had been an exciting night indeed.

"FAC's in sight." Thatcher looked up and saw the A-4s circling.

"OK. Let's try two apiece. Hit my smoke. I will be east over the trees. Target is a bulldozer at 950 feet. Confirm FAC in sight."

Thatcher rolled his O-2 up on one wing, rolled wings level as the nose dropped 60 degrees, hit the thumb button on the right side of the yoke twice, a second apart, and watched as two white phosphorus rockets screamed down toward the bulldozer below. He pulled up and over the trees on the North Vietnam side of the trail. The rockets impacted with two brilliant white clouds, 10 meters apart, and easily visible from a mile or more away.

"Bulldozer is between the smokes. Smokes are ten meters apart. You're cleared in hot. I'll be east of the target." Thatcher radioed.

The A-4s called in hot and rolled in seconds apart, one after the other. Navy A-4s were as good as they get, and the leader's bombs were just to the side of the dozer. The dozer stopped moving although it wasn't destroyed. The bombs probably killed the driver. The wingman, taking a cue from lead, hit the dozer directly and it literally disappeared. What was left was a hole full of metal scraps that would never be put back together again.

Knowing they didn't have much fuel, as a rule, Thatcher directed the A-4s to hit the road on either side of the crater they had created to make moving the carcass of the dozer harder and the road impassable without a second dozer to clear the rubble.

"Shit hot, guys! You can add a bulldozer and a 20-meter road cut to your score cards; that will stop a lot of trucks tonight and the guys in the trenches down south will appreciate it. By the way, you're from the *Kitty Hawk*, right?"

"Roger that Nail. Why do you ask?"

"Because I got to sail on your boat when I was on an indoctrination tour sponsored by a little school in the Rocky Mountains."

"Oh crap. Is your football team still trying to find the end zone?"

"Next time you have the opportunity, grab one of those hops to NKP and I'll buy you a beer at Nail Hole. We can debate that in a more liquid setting."

"Sounds good to us! Have a good day. And thanks for that nice target. Maybe that will win the war." Sarcasm had been developed to an art form by trail pilots. Thatcher laughed to himself and double clicked his mic, shorthand for acknowledging a transmission.

As they pulled off and headed for the carrier, Thatcher reminisced about his appointment to the Naval Academy. He had applied to both Air Force and Navy; Annapolis accepted him first, sending telegram after telegram four days in a row asking him to confirm acceptance of his appointment. Since his father died flying for the Army Air Corps in China in WWII, he couldn't bring himself to accept a Naval Academy appointment and wondered why he even bothered to apply. When the Air Force appointment came a week later, he breathed a sigh of relief and headed for Colorado Springs. *Could have been flying A-4s,* he thought. True, but who was commanding who that day? Sam was right, he was a god.

"Nail 79, Hillsborough." The call from the daytime airborne command post was unexpected.

Thatcher switched over to the VHF radio, "79."

"Nail 79, we have a Raven down somewhere west of you. He's near the old tin mine. He's on guard."

Thatcher keyed the mic and answered, "Nail 79, roger that. I'm headed west. Have the Air America helicopters launched?"

"Will in about ten minutes."

Ravens were the bravest of the brave in Southeast Asia. They were shot down more than any other group of pilots because they flew low in support of Laotian ground troop activities both in northern Laos, in the *Plaines des Jarres*, and in the southwestern part of Laos between the Thai/Laotian border and the Ho Chi Minh

87

Trail, where the People War was raging. Thatcher switched over to guard channel, the channel reserved for emergencies. At 5,000 feet above the ground, his reception was good even though he was at least ten miles away.

"Raven, this is Nail 79. I'm headed your way. Give me some coordinates."

The voice answering was raspy, out of breath.

"Nail, I'm hiding in a clump of trees north of the tin mine about 400 meters. There's a ZPU in the area somewhere. That's what got me so be careful. I'll let you know if they're shooting at you."

A ZPU was an old anti-aircraft gun based on the Soviet Union 14.5mm heavy machine gun. It entered service with the Soviet Union in 1949 and was used in over 50 countries worldwide. Because it was old, the rifling in the barrels was worn and it sprayed the shells almost like a shot gun. Ironically, that increased the lethality, especially to slow, low-flying aircraft.

"I'm only five minutes out. Keep your head down."

It would be hard to describe the feelings a downed pilot would have in circumstances such as this. The feeling of the air blowing out of the aircraft vents only moments before, although warm, would be like a cool breeze compared to the stifling tropical furnace of a Laotian dirt carpet. Furious insects attacked in swarms, the sun beat down unmercifully, and thirst, not even a consideration in the aircraft, instantaneously became a major factor. Fear of death, something attending all soldiers in war, was magnified exponentially on the ground for pilots with no friends anywhere near to commiserate or share the danger. Pilots in that situation experienced a sense of dread that could never be explained or understood by those who had not been there.

Thatcher firewalled the throttles and used his excess altitude to max out the airspeed. After ten minutes, that seemed like an hour, Thatcher finally had the tin mine in sight. It looked like any open pit mine in the States but apparently had been abandoned. He remembered it well from his first tour, when it was still in operation. The weathered, ramshackle wooden buildings were falling apart now, and there was no sign of life anywhere. The morning light was still casting long shadows from the buildings and the sun was not so bright that tracers wouldn't be visible, which they were in a few moments. The Raven called Thatcher on his survival radio.

"Nail, I see you. I'm at your two o'clock about 300 meters."

The breathing over the radio was heavy with fear, not an unreasonable condition for anyone in such a predicament. Thatcher knew of FACs landing to pick up Heavy Hook teams under emergency conditions but finding a flat area to land would be tricky in the terrain under him. Rice paddies, although dry at the time, were full of ditches, and the tree lines crisscrossed everywhere.

"Hillsborough, where are choppers?" Thatcher was on normal trail frequency, not the guard channel the Raven was on. The Raven couldn't hear the conversation.

"Nail 79, they're airborne and about 20 minutes from you."

"Roger that, Hillsborough."

Thatcher switched back to guard channel on UHF.

"Raven, choppers are on the way."

The O-1 Bird Dog of the Raven appeared to be unscathed, sitting in the middle of a rice paddy which was dry and brown, much like a Kansas wheat field. Thatcher suspected the engine had been hit and the Raven glided to a landing, not a problem at all in the Cessna O-1 with its excellent handling characteristics at slow speed. Ravens had a long-standing tradition of gliding to a landing as opposed to bailing out. Some Ravens didn't even carry parachutes; some didn't bother with seat belts. The O-1, despite its lack of speed and armor plating, was as good as a parachute if there was a suitable landing field.

"Nail, they're coming after me." The voice was understandably hyper, and Thatcher, already at an adrenalin peak, was searching frantically for the downed Raven.

"Raven, I see them, but I still don't see you. I don't know where to shoot. I might hit you."

"I'm in a clump of tall weeds, about 100 meters east of my plane."

The voice was Midwestern, shaky, and quite unforgettable. Oh my God, thought Thatcher. I know that voice. He picked out the clump of weeds and flew over the position low and fast to be sure he had the pilot's position.

"You have me Nail and they're shooting at you."

"Don't give up Raven." Thatcher got a sick feeling in his stomach. The situation looked hopeless. Thatcher pulled up steeply, kicked hard left rudder, and came down in the opposite direction. He started shooting rockets wherever he could see the dark uniforms of the Pathet Lao. They scattered into bushes and rice paddy ditches as they saw him arrive. The chance of hitting a running soldier with a rocket was slim, but he hoped it might at least slow their advance. He kept firing rockets wherever he saw the enemy soldiers, but they were swarming everywhere; he ran out of rockets in a few minutes but continued to make feigning passes. The ploy didn't last long. The dark shadows flitted ever closer to Paul Bartram, the Air Force Academy cadet who trained Thatcher when he first arrived at the Zoo. Streams of red tracers were intersecting in the shallow ditch where he was hiding. Thatcher was swooping ever lower, and the dull thunk of rifle bullets hitting his aircraft were getting more frequent. He started shooting his AR-15 out of the right-hand window, holding it with one hand, but it was futile, and he knew it.

"Raven, the Jolly Greens are almost here," he lied. But the lie didn't matter. There was only silence. Paul Bartram was dead.

* * *

The Nail Hole that night was the usual raucous place. Thatcher entered and joined Roger Brown, Mark Tinga, and the carnation-loving navigator, Steve Johns at the bar. Jimmy Durante was singing "I'll Be Seeing You" from the Akai tape deck and the smell of steaks from the barbeque pit was wafting throughout the room.

Thatcher looked at Roger, not knowing what to say about Paul Bartram, the element leader for both of them their first summer before they even took off their civilian clothes. He was the one who taught them how to salute, how to stand at attention, how to march, how to eat. In short, he was the one who turned them into Air Force Academy cadets. Thatcher knew how Roger challenged Bartram the first summer they were there by refusing to toe the line, and how the punishments meted out by Bartram were never done out of malice, but with a sense of paternalism and a half-hidden smile. Thatcher also knew the two of them became good friends after Roger's freshman year ended and Roger was welcomed as an upperclassman.

"What the hell's wrong with you?" asked Brown. "You look like someone's died."

"Someone has," Thatcher was unable to hide his emotions, his voice wavering.

"Who?" Roger Brown, normally the most jovial person in any crowd, became serious.

"Paul Bartram."

A long silence followed. "Who told you?"

A few more moments of silence followed as Thatcher fought to maintain control. Finally, he took a deep breath and spoke. "No one told me. I was there."

Thatcher recounted the events, leaving out nothing.

Brown was impassive. He finished his beer and went to the bar for another. After taking a long drink, he asked "Do you remember the time I didn't have my shoes polished just right?"

Thatcher managed a feeble grin. "What do you mean, you didn't have your shoes polished just right? You never polished your shoes just right. But the night you're talking about I was watching you two out of our dorm room window. He must have run you up the Hill 100 times."

"More like 150. But what you left out was that I was carrying my M-1 over my head."

Thatcher told the story to the pilots gathered around.

"The Hill was a grassy knoll 150 feet long, 50 wide, and with sloping sides about 30 feet high and obviously not a natural hill. It was in back of the two-acre terrazzo assembly area where all 24 squadrons of the cadet wing formed up for marching to meals or parades. No one knew why the Hill was there. It was probably excess dirt left over from construction, but it was great for dishing out punishment for minor infractions. Running up and down a few dozen times, especially carrying an M-1 Rifle, would take the starch out of anyone, no matter how fit or how tough. And believe me, Roger owned the record for minor infractions. He never did learn to polish his shoes. Roger ran the marathon, and so running up the Hill was just practice for him. Bartram tried his best to get Roger to holler uncle, but Roger just kept on going."

It would have been a funny story under other circumstances, but the death of a Raven, a brother FAC, made the group somber. No one spoke for a few minutes. Then Roger raised a glass. Everyone followed suit.

"To Paul Bartram, Raven One Two."

"To the Raven!" they shouted in unison.

They downed their drinks and broke their glasses on the floor of the Nail Hole.

Years later, Ted Thatcher and Roger Brown would remember this tragedy, whenever they met at reunions or spoke by telephone. In a list of things, they would remember with pain from this insane war, this would be near the top of the list. Adding to the poignancy of the tragedy was the realization that it was a mission in which both secret wars overlapped at one time and place. Thatcher was on a truck-killing mission over the Ho Chi Minh Trail when the call came that a Raven engaged in the People War was in trouble. His efforts to save Paul Bartram were unsuccessful, and the airstrike he directed over the trail, like all missions over the trail, was inconsequential; the bulldozer he destroyed was replaced in 24 hours. The Viet Nam War was lost before it ever started.

10

Night Mission

Night missions comprised half of all Nail missions but contributed more than 75% of the BDA (Bomb Damage Assessment). Trucks on the Ho Chi Minh Trail were forced to traverse rutted dirt roads and experienced frequent mechanical breakdowns. Overcoming these problems during the day, when they were visible, was suicidal for both the truck drivers and the maintenance crews, so they were always hidden under trees or other camouflage. That's why day missions for the Nails were based more on intelligence reports from Green Berets, acoustic sensor readings, and personal knowledge from previous missions. Finding a truck park hidden in trees or under a karst ledge was not a high probability exercise from the air.

Although more lucrative because trucks had to use headlights, night missions from the Nails' perspective were also more dangerous because the intensity of gunfire was incredible, unceasing, and any number of other adjectives that described danger on the highest scale. Gunners could operate in the open at night with freedom to walk around in the dark without any chance of being seen until they opened fire with their anti-aircraft guns. Even then, their tracers didn't start to burn until they were a few hundred feet in the air, and a Nail trying to guess the exact location of the guns on which to direct a counter strike was usually not successful on the first attempt. Since the primary targets were trucks in any event, the anti-aircraft gunners operated with impunity most of the time.

From the aircrews' perspective, the prickly feeling on the back of the neck on night missions started well in advance of reaching the trail. A Nail night crew of pilot and navigator/strike control officer could see the tracers from 20 miles away, tracers from the guns that would soon be directed at them. There was ample time to think about the wife and kids back home on the flight out. The sweat stains on the aircrew's flight suits were a mixture of that realization as well as the tropical heat of Laos. But, as with daytime airstrikes, nervousness usually disappeared after the action started and the adrenalin kicked in. The hundreds of tracers, in a perverse sort of way, resembled a field of red flowers against a black backdrop.

Stan Barwick took off at 2100 hours and crossed the fence outbound with Gary Pearsall in the right seat, considered one of the better navigators. They headed for Sector III and leveled at 7,000 feet, the evening air cool and refreshing. Barwick was a captain, or perhaps a major. Short and unshaven, he never acted the least bit nervous heading into combat. He rarely read his mail and especially avoided anything official. Most of his contemporaries were wearing the gold oak leaves of a major, but he either hadn't received an official promotion letter or had ignored it. Perhaps the most unmilitary in a group of officers that seemed to relish the rebel image, he didn't pay much attention to anything relating to regulations or other official business. He read a great deal, particularly about eastern religions. He thought about becoming a Buddhist monk, but didn't know how to go about it. He thought about Zoroastrianism and Taoism as well but didn't know how to sign up for those religions either. He made up his mind to look into them on his return to the States. The war diverted his attention from mundane things; it gave him a unique perspective on life. Existence was reduced to a simple concept. People were trying to kill him, and his job was to kill them first. There was a certain balance, a perspective about everything which made sense to him. A Yin and a Yang. The killing wasn't at all personal. If an ammunition truck blew up, he envisioned the driver floating away to heaven. Therefore, he was not killing but releasing. At least that's how he described it to his squadron mates in the Nail Hole after he'd had a few. And that was often. He was hoping he might release a few spirits this very night. Not surprisingly, most Nails thought he was nuts and if it weren't for his impressive kill statistics, he would have been in a psychiatrist's office back in the States.

Gary Pearsall, on the other hand, was tall, always well groomed, and 'had it together.' He read classical literature, played the piano at least as well as Thatcher, and was not only a gentleman but one with a high truck kill record. It was a perfect night for hunting because it was a perfect night for running trucks. Good weather was required to see the trucks; the North Vietnamese, in a bizarre twist of fate, required good weather to make the roads passable. There were about two months of the monsoon season which made the roads impassable to trucks and the visibility was so bad pilots couldn't see their wingtips. And for those two months, no one died. At least not in combat.

Secretary of Defense McNamara had come up with what he considered a brilliant plan for tilting the advantage to the pilots. He ordered acoustic and seismic sensors dropped by A-6 aircraft along the heavily traveled portions of the trail. Everything military must have a code name; the code name for the sensor program was Igloo White. Disguised to look like shrubs, the sensors emitted radio signals any time a truck drove by. Since they were spaced evenly, the signals could be used to calculate the speed of the trucks. This information was fed via satellite to a giant computer complex at NKP, which then ordered computerized bomb drops by Marine EA-6 attack aircraft. Weather, and the North Vietnamese, could be defeated by computers! Computers, McNamara reasoned, worked in manufacturing plants, so of course they could be programmed to destroy trucks in the jungle. The jungle was just a big manufacturing assembly line with dirt roads in the place of conveyor belts and trucks in the place of eggbeaters or vacuum cleaners! It was that simple, he thought.

It was uncertain how many trucks were killed by this strategy, but Nails often found themselves in a crescendo of bomb explosions from the A-6s whose aircrews were not on the Nails' frequencies. These aircraft were piloted by humans but controlled by the auto pilot which in turn was controlled by Igloo White computer operators at NKP. Of course, mistakes weren't supposed to happen, but war is hell as Sherman once opined. Consequently, Nails looked for friendly fire from above as well as hostile fire from below. Very few Nails went back to the States without at least one recurring nightmare in which the night-shrouded jungle below their aircraft erupted in an inferno of bomb explosions from the A-6s out of nowhere.

In another interesting development, the North Vietnamese figured out what the sensors were for and often relocated them. As a result, thousands of air strikes were put in on nothing but trees because the sensors were moved far away from their original locations, to cattle pens, to the huts of the North Vietnamese Trail workers, or taken by truck drivers as souvenirs. During their indoctrination briefings, Nails got to hear a recording of a Vietnamese man and woman having sex in their hut recorded by a relocated acoustic sensor. The NVA also hung cricket boxes on the acoustic sensors to further confuse the listeners. This night, Barwick and Pearsall were pre-briefed on sensor activity in one specific area and headed for those coordinates.

Barwick and Pearsall had flown together before and developed an excellent sense of crew coordination. The way Nails hunted truck at night was crude, but effective. Usually, two A-1 Skyraiders would rendezvous with the Nail FAC, following the FAC's shielded red-blinking tail beacon, visible only from above. The navigator focused a hand-held starlight scope which he used to find the headlights of trucks. In the O-2, there was no window on the right side of the aircraft and the scope actually protruded into the slip stream. The scope looked like a short, fat telescope with a light amplification mechanism that displayed the ground in a green and white picture with the resolution of an old-fashioned TV screen.

Moonlit nights gave better resolution than black nights. Truck headlights showed up as bright green dots or streaks on the scope and the terrain appeared in graduated shades of green. Once the trucks had been discovered, the navigator, using simple hand signals, would direct the pilot until the aircraft was directly over the convoy. In an O-2, he would then jerk his left hand, thumb down, since the pilot was sitting to the left of him. In the OV-10, it required a verbal command since the navigator sat behind the pilot. Either way, the pilot would toggle a drop of a ground flare.

When the ground flare hit the ground it ignited; in a minute or so, it glowed a brilliant red like a truck flare on a highway. The navigator, using the radio, directed the fighters circling overhead in the attack, being very careful to assign roll-in and roll-out headings to prevent a mid-air collision. It was crude, but thousands of truck kills, the vast majority, were accomplished this way.

Trying to stop hundreds of trucks dispersed over 100 miles of twisting, often tree covered, dirt roads at night using handheld starlight scopes was, as the war in South Viet Nam confirmed, an exercise in futility. As soon as an airstrike began on one convoy, hundreds of other trucks hiding under the trees elsewhere began rolling with virtual assurance they would not be attacked, at least in that sector. So, in a perverse way, dozens of other trucks were given *carte blanche* to proceed on down the trail with impunity. Since there were Nails hunting in all sectors, if trucks did get a free pass in Sector II, sooner or later they would end up in Sector III or even in South Viet Nam, where additional attacks would be waiting.

Strike reports were misleading in terms of total material escaping destruction. If truck kills went up, it could represent a small percentage of an increased traffic count, not a decrease in cargo reaching South Viet Nam. No one, except Ho Chi Minh, could calculate the percentage of traffic reaching South Viet Nam but Robert McNamara ultimately learned about the flaws in his statistical process control system the hard way.

Nighttime attacks were dramatic, to say the least. Dozens of anti-aircraft guns opened up as soon as the first bombs went off. Since the gunners couldn't see blacked-out aircraft, they fired in pre-arranged patterns designed to get maximum exposure of a given airspace. President Nixon had announced publicly he would not bomb the North after 1969. The North Vietnamese, to show their appreciation, tripled the concentration of guns in Laos, with flak reminiscent of WWII raids over Germany. Red balls, streaking skyward, could be seen for 20 miles or more all along the trail at night.

At the southern end of the trail, which extended well into South Viet Nam, larger and more vulnerable C-123 flare ships called Candlesticks, and C-130 gunships, called Spectres, were used in lieu of Nail-directed fighters. The anti-aircraft fire there was less intense so larger aircraft could survive. Candlestick navigators used even larger night vision scopes and directed A-1s, like the Nails did, only from open cargo doors. C-130 Spectres fired 40mm recoilless rifles from the cargo doors. They were able to fly in a computer directed orbit and fire continuously from 360 degrees.

On a clear night, Nails could see the flares and tracers in the south from 50 miles away as well as the North Vietnamese flak coming up toward the gunships. Every clear night there was a constant stream of red balls going up and red balls going down. The gunships flew at or near 12,000 feet. At that altitude, the anti-aircraft fire was at its range limit, so unless it hit its target, most of it exploded based on the fuse settings, adding brilliant white starbursts in the sky to the red tracers. Most battle damage to the larger aircraft was not fatal; there was occasional damage, but usually the cargo aircraft were not incapacitated. The Nail O-2s and OV-10s, on the other hand, would almost always be uncontrollable with a direct hit due to their much smaller size and lower altitudes.

Barwick and Pearsall were entering this inferno, accompanied by two A-1 Skyraiders, Hobo 21 and 22, orbiting above. It was usually cool at night, and this night was no exception. A pleasant 70 degrees made the nighttime flight more than comfortable. It wasn't long before Pearsall, eyes glued to the starlight scope, tilted his left hand to the right, and Captain or Major Barwick banked slowly in response. Pearsall motioned for a drop by jerking his left thumb down. Barwick triggered the switch, watching as the first ground flare fell away. Pearsall motioned again for another drop and Barwick again responded. This would give the A-1s two points to use both as directional indicators and as a measure of distance. Barwick wheeled the aircraft around to a reciprocal heading and Pearsall began directing the A-1 attack.

"Hobo flight, there are ten trucks between the marks. We'll be holding well to the west at 6,000."

"Roger that Nail."

It took a few minutes for the A-1s to get into position, but as the leader's first napalm canisters hit, the splash of fire from the jellied gasoline extended well over 100 feet along the ground, illuminating the string of trucks and immediately engulfing two of them in a brilliant sheet of fire. Hobo lead had hit the tail end of the string, and his wingman, Hobo 22, followed up a minute later setting three more trucks ablaze at the front of the convoy, blocking the rest of the convoy from moving.

With the drop of the first canisters, all hell broke loose as 23mm guns (dozens of small red tracers), 37mm guns (seven sizable red tracers), and an occasional 57mm gun (one big red tracer), spit out their deadly strings that snaked up from the ground. Tracers arched through the sky from every conceivable direction. Gunners had nothing to lose by firing even though they couldn't see a target. If nothing else, they distracted the Nails and the strike aircraft they were directing. If the anti-aircraft gun crews missed their targets, the rounds self-destructed at a predetermined altitude a few thousand feet higher than the Nail aircraft in sparkling airbursts any Chamber of Commerce would be proud of on the Fourth of July. That prevented the explosive rounds from falling back to earth, endangering the gun crews.

Pearsall gave a hand motion for a turn to the right and then gave the next drop command, "Hobos, come in from the south and hit 200 meters east of the burning trucks. There are several more trying to hide in some small trees there."

"Roger that Nail. Two, you take the lead on this one."

"Zorro two, roger, in hot."

The Skyraiders' second drops were made easier this time because fires from the first drop allowed clearer aiming points. On the second round they hit pay dirt as ammunition trucks trying to hide in the small clump of trees exploded in multiple orgasms of self-destruction. Other trucks, perhaps carrying food or medical supplies, were set afire by their exploding convoy partners and soon 12 trucks were burning furiously below. The Zorros continued their attack for several more passes.

Tracers were zipping by the O-2 constantly, but Barwick paid them no attention except to bank slightly one way or another if a stream of tracers appeared fixed on the windscreen. The O-2 was not specifically the target because it was black and invisible for all practical purposes. But the dozens of guns below were shooting in all directions hoping to hit something or at least discourage more attacks. The 'ripping' sound shells made as they passed the open window on the right side was comforting in a way to Barwick, the would-be Buddhist monk, who considered them the shrieks of dying evil spirits. Navigators had mixed opinions of Barwick. Some thought him a few tacos short of a Mexican mini-platter; others, like Gary Pearsall, welcomed the occasion to fly with him. He was, if nothing else, calm under pressure. Other pilots, especially the younger ones, tended to rip the wings off airplanes, figuratively speaking. But, on a few occasions, evading flak resulted in out-of-control airplanes. Pilots known to yank and bank abruptly under fire were often the ones who never returned from missions.

Pearsall flew with one O-2 pilot who panicked and yanked the airplane into an inverted spin. In the daytime this was a tricky recovery, but at night it was a ten on the difficulty scale. At night, there are no visual references to the ground, horizon, or sky. The correct recovery procedure is to punch off the rocket or flare pods, pull the yoke full back until the aircraft rights itself into a normal spin, kick the rudder opposite the spin, wait one full turn, and then pop the yoke forward. If everything goes as planned, the plane will emerge nose down in a steep dive. Of course, one should mention this maneuver is done entirely on instruments since there is no ground reference at night. Recovery from the dive is a matter of pulling back pressure on the yoke without exceeding the G-force limit of the aircraft. In the case of the O-2, the limit was 3.7 G's, or 370% of the normal force of gravity. The night this happened to Pearsall, the G-meter was pegged at the maximum, meaning no one knew what the stress level was. The return flight was the longest, quietest flight he'd ever been on, with pilot and navigator watching each tremor of the wings, wondering if they were going to come off.

"Nail, Zorro lead, we're out of nape, but we have guns. Got anything else?"

"Let's get some anti-aircraft guns. Watch for the flashes below." Barwick turned on the O-2s navigation light and the red rotating beacon, defeating the purpose of the airplane's flat black paint job. These were always turned off before reaching the trail on night missions to prevent detection. After a brief pause, the gunners below reacted with gusto to this obvious challenge, throwing everything they had at the twinkling red and green lights looking so out of place on the black canvas backdrop of the night. Red tracers filled the inky blackness of the Laotian night. The Skyraiders dove toward the flashes below, their miniguns spitting streams of tracers at the gun flashes below.

"Break right!" screamed Pearsall over the intercom. He had spotted streams of tracers headed toward his side of the plane, but Barwick, seeing tracers approaching from the left side as well, rolled the aircraft up and over on the left wing to reduce the profile of the O-2. He let it float long enough for the twin streams of anti-aircraft tracers to zip by on each side. Cutting the lights off, he rolled wings level, pulled the nose of the airplane up, and reversed course. The A-1s did some apparent damage on their strafing run on the guns. There were numerous secondary explosions observed by the FACs and after the Zorros exhausted their remaining ordnance, everyone headed home. The entire mission would be logged as four and a half hours, take-off to landing.

"Good work, Hobos!" Pearsall radioed. "I count 12 trucks and four 37s killed. The war should be about over."

"Don't you wish, Nail," replied Hobo lead. "You guys have balls of brass. Hope your life insurance is paid up."

Pearsall the navigator put the starlight scope back in the bag. When he finished, he triggered his mic and spoke slowly and calmly, "I wish you wouldn't do that." He meant turning on the lights, inducing the gunners below to fire at a visible target just to satisfy the lust of a few A-1 drivers for an additional target. Barwick didn't answer, lost in meditation and gazing at the stars overhead.

Stars which had been there for millions of years. Stars that had cast their light on everything that ever happened on earth. Stars that witnessed the formation of the earth, the creation and destruction of dinosaurs, the Ice Age, the fall of Rome, the raids of the Norsemen, the night he and Jenny Sue had gone all the way in her father's Nash Rambler at the drive-in movie. Life was good. Twelve trucks.

As they cleared the mountains west of the trail and started their descent, a rising full moon became visible over the horizon. Building up a little airspeed, Barwick pulled the nose up smoothly until the bottom of the full moon filled his windscreen and then did a slow roll, perfectly outlining the moon before settling back to the descent. Pearsall looked over at him and keyed his mic, "Feel better?"

"Hell yes."

Barwick and Pearsall entered the Nail Hole just after midnight and the party was going strong. The Hobos Pearsall directed were already there. The A-1 pilots came over, slapped the two Nails on the back, and used the traditional compliment to Nails who had performed well. "You Nails is shit hot!" Another Hobo with a guitar was holding forth on a bar stool, barely stable from too much alcohol. His raunchy lyrics were causing waves of laughter. After pausing for another swig from his beer bottle, he broke into a favorite of the all the pilots at NKP, the "Hobo Song," sung to the Johnny Cash tune, "Folsom Prison Blues."

I see those tracers comin',
Their hosin' me again,
I'm a supersonic Hobo,
And I'm rollin' in from ten.

With CBU and rockets,
I'm gonna have some ass,
But in my G-restricted aircraft,
I'll only make one pass.

I'm on a super-secret mission
And my sump light just came on,
I'm pullin' all the handles,
My centerline is gone,

I'm RTB to home plate,
I'm playin' with my wheel, [the elevator trim wheel]
A Raven FAC goes by me
Just like I'm standin' still.

I'm a gray-haired fighter pilot
And I'm spoilin' for a fight,
But I think that only Blindbats
Were meant to fly at night.

When I die and get to heaven
St. Peter I will tell,
I've been a Fightin' Hobo
I've served my time in Hell.

11

Damn Those 23s

After returning to Laos for his second tour, Thatcher had met Major Khampat, the senior Laotian Officer assigned to the Nails as a target validator and liaison officer on special missions related to the 'People War' in Laos. They formed a warm relationship and spent many quiet moments together in the Nail Hole before and after missions. The major often took Thatcher on the Mekong River ferry to Savannaket, the Laotian town across the Mekong River for lunch. The western portion of Laos bordering the river was still safe, and the people were loyal to the king. However, just a few miles to the east, the Pathet Lao communists had assumed control of the country and the king had no control. All visits by Americans in the safe areas close to the Mekong River were done in civilian clothes, of course, to comply with the Geneva Convention.

Cool under fire, Major Khampat displayed an unflappable demeanor cultivated over years of fighting the Pathet Lao communists as an infantry officer. Short by American standards, but with a humble manner and perpetual smile, he was the antithesis of the brash swagger of the typical American combat pilot. The People War in which he and Thatcher were engaged, the other Secret War, started at the end of WWII. The Americans fighting in Laos would go home if they survived a year. The Laotians would fight the remainder of their lives. There was no R&R, no leave, no brass bands welcoming them home. They were home.

Major Khampat's FAC unit consisted of two infantry officers, Lt. Boun Thang and Lt. Tonsonnai, veterans in the ground war against the Pathet Lao. Early one morning the major met Thatcher at the Nail Hole and they caught the TUOC Trolley to the Operations Center for a briefing prior to launching a Cricket West mission. Since there was no precise line of demarcation between the NVA-dominated Trail territory in the east (the Truck War) and the Pathet Lao territory in western Laos (the People War), the action was often indistinguishable from the standpoint of a Nail flying over the fuzzy boundary. Where potential civilian impacts were at stake, the Laotian officers, such as Major Khampat, exercised absolute authority to determine friend or foe. They could authorize airstrikes on the fake villages used to hide radio transmitters, house armed troops, truck drivers, and other NVA/Pathet Lao supported activities.

Today's mission objective was to take out a North Vietnamese radio transmitter in one of the fake villages on the boundary of the Ho Chi Minh Trail, one which probably had supplies hidden inside the half dozen straw huts. Gardens and other non-military improvements on the boundary of the Ho Chi Minh Trail were meant as a disguise, but the real evidence was radio transmissions being made on a frequent basis from the straw-thatched structure. Triangulated by EC-47s, electronic spying aircraft which were converted WWII "Gooney Birds," the signals confirmed this was the headquarters of a Pathet Lao battalion.

As Captain Thatcher and Major Khampat flew over the structure at 6,500 feet, there was no sign of activity anywhere.

"Major Khampat, okay to bomb?"

Even though it was the assigned target, anything that could possibly be civilian needed a Laotian officer to approve it.

"Yes. This should not be here." A peaceful little cottage had no business being right on the edge of the Ho Chi Minh Trail. It wasn't long until the scheduled Navy A-4s checked in. Laotian X-Rays had absolute authority to bomb anything off the Ho Chi Minh Trail since it was their country.

"Nail 79, this is Canvas flight, east of you at 12,000. Four A-4s with eight Mark 82s apiece."

"Roger that, Canvas flight, this is Nail 79. Target is a communication center in a fake hooch. I have you in sight now, I'll mark the target and pull off west over the karst. You are cleared in hot once you confirm FAC in sight. Break toward the mountains on the east side of the valley. Let's drop everything on the first pass and expect heavy ground fire." Thatcher rolled in, fired a Willy Pete at the structure, and pulled off to the west over the mountains. Within seconds, the marking rocket sent a brilliant white cloud into the air from the front yard of the hooch.

"Hit my smoke." Thatcher made the call as he was pulling up and rolling west.

The lead A-4 called in, "Roger that. Canvas 1 in hot, I have your smoke and FAC is in sight."

Lead rolled in, followed in close succession by the other A-4s each calling FAC in sight. Canvas flight's A-4s all had direct hits, destroying everything in the compound including the companion sheds and infrastructure. Secondary explosions and thick curls of black smoke, normally associated with petroleum products and not rice, billowed up from bright orange flames within a matter of seconds, confirming the Intel report. Anti-aircraft fire immediately punctuated the blue skies with black, puffy clouds, another confirmation this was a military target of some value.

"They're shooting at you Canvas," Thatcher radioed.

The A-4s rolled aggressively left and then right and left again as they pulled off the target. This was standard procedure, and the A-4s were out of range before the AAA smoke dissipated.

Thatcher remained over the mountain ridge to the west, both to keep clear of the A-4s and to avoid the fury being unleashed from below. Within minutes, an RF-4 reconnaissance pilot called in.

"Nail 79, this is Atlanta 22, watching over your strike at 12,000. Can I take a picture? I have you in sight and I'll come in from the south and break east."

"Affirmative Atlanta. The A-4s are heading back to the ship, so you should have a clear path in a minute. Lots of guns in the area so keep it moving."

"Roger that."

From their new perch above the mountain ridge, Thatcher and Major Khampat, who were enjoying the A-4 show, prepared for another round of AAA fireworks. They weren't disappointed. Atlanta 22s RF-4 swept down at an impressive airspeed 500 feet above the ground taking the pictures. The pilot pulled up steeply and the guns opened up one more time. The pilot radioed Thatcher with some surprising information.

"Nail, there's a gas pipeline in one of ditches down there."

"A pipeline? Are you serious?" Thatcher, using binoculars, had glassed the area over well before the strike but had not seen anything like a pipeline, although his view had been obscured by the black smoke from the previous strike. The rice paddies below looked like Grandma's quilt after a few glasses of schnapps, with ditches laid out in a random pattern. From 5,000 feet, the pipeline was invisible.

"Absolutely. I'll mark it for you."

The RF-4 came in from the opposite direction, but this time he wasn't 500 feet above the ground, he was about 100 feet and doing 500 knots. In the middle of his run, a white cloud appeared right on top of a ditch. Atlanta pulled up vertically, jinking vigorously, as the gunners below reacted to this insulting display of arrogance. The flak was more pronounced than before, the previous airstrike having caught some of the North Vietnamese gunners napping.

"I have your mark, Atlanta. How in the hell did you do that?" Thatcher asked.

"That, my friend, is a flash bulb we use for night photography. I always wanted to be a fighter pilot, but they stuck me in this impotent crate and doomed me. I haven't been able to kill anything. When my kids ask me what I did in the war, what in the hell am I supposed to tell them? That I took pictures? Now I can tell them I was also a FAC!"

"Well, the next time you have the opportunity to land at NKP, please come by the Nail Hole and I'll personally pin our highest decoration for valor on your flight suit. It's a pair of brass balls on a red, white, and blue ribbon. Comes with all the booze you can drink."

"Damn, my kids will be so proud. Have a good day, Nail. And watch those 23s."

"Roger that. Have a good day Atlanta."

Thatcher turned to Major Khampat. "Did you follow him Major Khampat?"

"Yes. Pipeline for gasoline. We kill?"

"Yes, but our rockets aren't enough. We need bombs. I'll call the airborne command post."

"Okay."

"Hillsborough, Nail 79, I have a POL pipeline at my last target coordinates. Got anything I can use?"

"Nail 79, affirmative. We'll divert some F-105s your way with Mark 82s."

"Great. ETA?"

"Ten minutes."

"Thanks."

"Major Khampat, this is turning out to be a good day." The major gave the thumbs up he had learned from his American friends.

The pilots of the Thunderchiefs were the top of the line in Southeast Asia, honed by the experience of bombing Hanoi and the port at Haiphong. The missions there were so hazardous that 100 missions earned a 100-mission shoulder patch, a badge of honor more cherished than the Distinguished Flying Crosses and Silver Stars they all received as well. It also earned a trip home. Even though many of the current pilots in the 105s arrived after the bombing of North Viet Nam was suspended, they still benefitted from the experience passed down. Thatcher's T-38 instructor pilot at Moody Air Force Base was a 105 pilot, shot down and rescued on his third mission over the trail in North Viet Nam. Thatcher's class of student pilots commissioned a shoulder patch for their instructor's flight suit reading, "3 missions over North Viet Nam." He never wore it but was amused by the gesture.

The F-105 leader checked in, "Nail 79, Taper flight, four 105s with 18 Mark 82s each."

"Taper, glad to have you in the area. Very active 23s and maybe some 37s we haven't heard from yet, so we need a quick drop on an east-west POL pipeline and then recommend strong evasive maneuvers breaking north. The pipeline is in a ditch. I will mark the target with two smokes and move south at 6,500 feet. One pass, haul ass. Break north."

"Roger that."

"Okay. Let's get to work. Nail 79 is in hot with two smokes."

Thatcher rolled in using a Split S maneuver. It was a half loop, beginning at the top of the loop. This required raising the nose to bleed off airspeed to a near stall, rolling the O-2 upside down, and pulling back hard on the yoke. When the nose was pointed straight down, Thatcher fired two rockets, one after the other. He carefully pulled the nose back up to level flight, now heading in the opposite direction. He was careful to keep the G meter under the max allowable 3.7 Gs. The maneuver was prohibited in the O-2, because of its G force restriction; inexperienced pilots had ripped the wings off trying it. In high-performance airplanes, a

Split S was not a problem, and every Air Force pilot learned the maneuver early in jet training. Experienced O-2 FACs used this maneuver when they were in a very high threat area, as in this case. Gunners normally were caught off guard by the maneuver since their target changed directions 180 degrees during the attack. Nails in the OV-10s, developed specifically as a FAC aircraft, didn't have to worry about overstressing their aircraft. The G limit of the OV-10, depending on weight and configuration, was at least double that of the O-2.

The rockets impacted about 100 meters apart. The white plumes produced two distinct results: First, the F-105s knew which ditch held the pipeline and its orientation; secondly, the gunners opened up like angry hornets. At first, Thatcher was the target, but the F-105s soon got their share of the attention after they dropped. The 105s, commonly called Thuds, were right on target, not surprisingly.

The Thuds had rolled in, one after the other, in quick succession, much closer to each other than other attack aircraft. Their experience was developed in the North Viet Nam bombing campaign, now suspended, in which the following aircraft could divert quickly to any guns firing on the aircraft in front of them. The four 105s hit the pipeline in quick succession and the result was like a small volcano erupting. Orange and black flames curled hundreds of feet in the air. Black smoke swirled higher and higher, looking like a giant black snake. Based on the size of the fire, it looked like a lot of gasoline was burning. Thatcher wondered how many Marines were saved by the lucky break in finding and destroying this major trail pipeline. He didn't have much time to think about it though. The 105 flight leader called.

"Nail, they're shooting at you."

The transmission came from Taper lead. Thatcher expected gunfire and had never stopped jinking but assumed it would come from the same guns that hosed down the A-4s. Bad assumption.

Flak was coming from every quadrant. He increased his jinking and headed for the mountains to the east. Reaching safety, he and Major Khampat looked at each other, grinning. They knew they had cheated death once again and, in the process, inflicted serious damage on the North Vietnamese fuel capability. There was no doubt what they destroyed would be replaced, probably within a few days. But, perhaps, a few grunts in South Viet Nam might find temporary relief from the mortar and rocket attacks. Trucks carrying ammunition to the battlefield would be stalled for lack of fuel. But not forever.

There was one more footnote to the day's events: When Captain Thatcher and Major Khampat landed 45 minutes later at NKP, the crew chief opened the door for them. They crawled out, removed their helmets, and began unstrapping from their parachutes. The crew chief cursed and with faked anger asked them, "What in the Hell have you done to my airplane?" When they turned and looked at him, his right hand was inserted into the bottom of the left wing, up to his wrist. The shrapnel hole conveyed a message to all: if the anti-aircraft shell had been a few inches higher when it exploded, the fuel cells within the wing would have exploded and the mission would have ended ... differently. As it was, the large piece of shrapnel that punctured the wing fell away with no serious structural damage. The captain and the major would re-fly this mission and others like it, many times at night as they grew older.

The Nail Hole was quiet when Thatcher got off the TUOC Trolley. Roger 'Mad Dog' Brown was eating boiled eggs and watching the news on TV. President Richard Nixon named diplomat David K. E. Bruce to head the U.S. delegation to the peace talks in Paris with North Vietnam and the Viet Cong. They both laughed, knowing there wasn't a chance in hell the North Vietnamese would ever negotiate anything meaningful.

"How'd you do today?" asked Brown.

"Hit a tank farm and a POL pipeline. Bastards put a shrapnel hole in my wing."

"Doesn't it just piss you off when they do that?" Brown was laughing.

"It does. Makes me feel unwelcome."

"Maybe we should leave." Brown stuffed the whole egg in his mouth.

"Maybe we should. From what they we're seeing on TV it looks like that might be a reality in the near future."

The two pilot training classmates continued their discussions, reminisced about pilot training at Moody Air Force Base, and were still there late that night as the Nail Hole became, once again, an oasis in the middle of a war that seemed to have no end.

12

MiG

Mark Tinga, Nail 52, was proud of his Indian heritage. His father was a construction worker who specialized in assembling the huge girders of skyscrapers, walking on thin ribbons of steel hundreds of feet above the ground. But he died of pneumonia, incurable by tribal medicine and unseen by the white doctors whom his father would have never consulted.

Mark excelled in reservation school and got an appointment to the Air Force Academy. After graduation came pilot training. Like most pilots, he wanted, more than anything in the world, to fly fighters. When Mark and his classmates graduated three months later, the only openings were in bombers, cargo, and tanker aircraft. Mark took KC-135 aerial refuelers, but like most pilots, refused to give up his dream to fly fighters.

When he walked onto his first base in North Dakota, he went immediately to the personnel office and volunteered for Viet Nam in any fighter available. He was told that because of the Air Force investment in his KC-135 training he couldn't leave North Dakota for at least a year. So, he waited. At the end of the year, he was promised an F-100. After his belongings were packed and was on the way to Luke Air Force Base in California, he received a telegram with two names on it, one advising some major he was to report to Luke AFB for training in F-100s. The second name was Mark's. His orders were revised. He was to report for training in OV-10s at Hurlbert Field, Florida. Air Force politics not only screwed Mark, but the name of the guy who did it was on Mark's orders. He was probably the son of a politically connected father, Mark surmised. Mark redirected his household goods shipment, resigned his commission effective two years hence when his commitment was up, and got commode-hugging drunk.

Since becoming a Nail at NKP however, Mark learned F-4 pilots had essentially become bomber pilots since the air war over North Viet Nam had ended. They took off, flew at high altitude to a target marked by a FAC's smoke rockets, dropped their bombs on the smoke which marked targets they often could not see through the trees, and in mere minutes headed back to base, often without really seeing the results of their efforts. That certainly didn't diminish their bravery in any way, but it did remove most of the satisfaction of being a hunter: the thrill of the hunt, the satisfaction of finding the prey with nothing but one's own powers of observation, and the moment of truth as the trophy was added to the game bag through a carefully placed shot. As a Nail, however, Mark got to spend hours hunting, probing the trail, memorizing every twist and turn. Like his ancestors of old, he knew when something was out of place, even if it appeared normal. It might be a clump of bushes, normal in every respect, except, it hadn't been there the day before. Because of his keen powers of observation, Mark was killing trucks and guns at a rate faster than anyone in the 23rd TASS. Whether it had anything to do with his Indian heritage he didn't know, or care. All he knew was he was having more fun than he had ever imagined.

There were two choices for FACs in terms of finding targets. First, they could follow the leads of the target planners at NKP who analyzed everything from infrared photography to the reports of SOG (Special Observation Group) units on the trail. While well intentioned and competent, the planners were no match for the fluid nature of events on the trail. Trucks or supplies there yesterday were not likely to be there today. The brilliance of the North Vietnamese leaders, beginning at the top with General Giap, would ultimately win the war. No one knows how many airmen lost their lives in Laos thinking they were bombing trucks hidden in the triple canopy jungle, but who were only bombing yesterday's truck parks surrounded by today's anti-aircraft guns. 'Tree Parks' was a Nail term for sites that once had demonstrable value, such as trucks, supply stashes, or fuel farms, but which had been abandoned due to the NVA practice of rotating their inventory frequently. Since trucks were usually hidden under trees, sometimes the only way to discover their presence was to blow the trees away.

The second option open to FACs was to find their own targets. In a high-threat anti-aircraft environment, this could be accomplished more safely from the mandated 5,000 feet above the ground using binoculars, lots of jinking, and lots of patience. In Mark's case, flying high was too unproductive and he was not patient. His motto was "Patience Hell!" He perfected ways of getting lower, sometimes right on the treetops without getting hit. He would sneak around a hill or karst formation from the opposite side of the target at tree top level, engines at flight idle to reduce noise, grab a quick peek under the canopy of trees or into the mouth of a cave, gun the engines, and then zoom back around the hill before gunners could get the muzzle covers off their guns. To hide the anti-aircraft guns effectively, they were usually placed at the base of the mountain near the trail and could not effectively shoot toward the mountain.

Normally, Mark's sneak peek tactic worked, but it wasn't perfect. He landed his planes on four separate occasions with battle damage. Fortunately, and as strange as it may seem, Mark was always lucky enough to get hit by shrapnel from 23mm or 37mm flak guns. A direct hit from small arms fire, and he would have been washed up.

A bullet hole from a rifle would have been a sign announcing, "I flew a little too low today." Upon landing, the evidence could result in disciplinary action. A direct hit from an anti-aircraft gun, on the other hand, could be fatal because the warheads were mini-bombs, steel casings filled with gunpowder and a detonator fuse. There might not be an airplane left to leave. Shrapnel hits, however, were a common occurrence because of the high volume of anti-aircraft fire at all altitudes over the trail and weren't even questioned. Most of the FAC aircraft had a few metal patches on the skin of the planes because most FACs had been hit by shrapnel which left jagged holes, not neat round circles.

Late one afternoon, Mark completed his preflight and was soon circling his favorite hunting ground, Ban Karai Pass. This was one of the most heavily traveled passes allowing the trucks access from North Viet Nam into Laos only 12 miles from the DMZ and South Viet Nam.

"Hillsborough, Nail 52. I have a gun; anything extra for me?"

"Negative, 52. The F-4s for your fragged target are inbound now. You can use your judgment on how to split the ordnance."

The fragged target was a pre-arranged target selected by intelligence teams based at NKP. It was a suspected truck park just south of Mu Gia pass, close to the dirt road right on the border of North Viet Nam and Laos, about ten miles north of Mark's current position. Mu Gia Pass was famous among Southeast Asia airmen because it once was the main pass from North Viet Nam into Laos. Demonstrating its strategic importance, Nails had designed a shoulder patch for their party suits depicting red tracers crossing in midair with the words, "Ski Mu Gia Pass" emblazoned in silver thread on a blue background. Ban Karai Pass to the south, closer to South Viet Nam, had eclipsed Mu Gia in traffic, but Mu Gia was still very much in play. Target selection for any given day was often based on sensor readings from either acoustic or seismic readings.

They could be useful if fresh, but Mark didn't give a damn about a sensor reading: he was looking right at an anti-aircraft gun, a confirmed sighting. Nevertheless, he had no choice but to make the rendezvous with the fragged fighters, but he made a mental note to come get the gun later. He headed for the pre-planned target at Mu Gia. It took a few minutes to reach the target coordinates but he couldn't see anything through the trees. The only option was to probe around the triple canopy jungle using the F-4 Phantom's Mark 82s, 500-pound bombs. A secondary explosion, or a truck uncovered by the first blast, would confirm the Intel.

"Nail 52, Bobbin 20 flight inbound to your location. Two Fox 4s. Eighteen Mark 82s each."

"Roger Bobbin. Call FAC in sight."

"Roger that, Nail. We have you now. OV-10 circling left over Mu Gia."

"OK. Targets at 2,500 feet. Suspected truck park. No wind. Heavy threat area. Six apiece the first pass. South to north. Break toward your pencil."

Mark's terse instructions gave the Phantoms the roll-in heading and the target's elevation. The comment about the pencil, which was in the left shoulder pocket of the flight suits, told them which way to break coming off target without alerting any gunners who might understand a few words of English that the F-4s were breaking left coming off the target. Mark didn't tell them there was not a high probability of hitting anything on the first pass because he was guessing. He was intentionally withholding 12 bombs per plane to use on the confirmed gun at Ban Karai after the fragged target was hit. As he was speaking, he rolled inverted, pulled the Bronco's nose down, rolled out wings level, and fired a single Willy Pete at the brown earth 3,000 feet below his aircraft. He then pulled back up to 5,000 feet and off to the east across the border into North Viet Nam.

"Hit my smoke."

After a minute to align with the target, the lead F-4 called in, "Lead's in. FAC in sight."

"Cleared hot," Mark radioed back.

"Two's in, FAC in sight."

"Cleared hot."

The standard air strike procedure for fighter bombers, absent any other instructions from the FAC, was to roll in one after the other, adjusting their bomb drops as necessary to ensure total target coverage. Another advantage was to allow the second or succeeding aircraft to hit any guns showing up as the lead aircraft dropped. More than two passes were begging for trouble since the gunners below could adjust their fire as well. Often the FAC would simply command, "one pass, haul ass." In this situation, there was a good possibility of hitting something simply because Mu Gia Pass was a choke point. It was a narrow, constricted pass where a lot of trucks and supplies were invariably hidden nearby; a few bombs might uncover something hiding in the weeds.

F-4, F-4, fly so fast. Can't see shit, can't hit your ass, Mark sang softly to himself, as he did whenever he worked F-4s, his envy boiling over.

The lead F-4, Bobbin 20, did a fair job. His projectiles hit only 25 meters from the smoke, enough to damage, but not destroy, any unhardened target, had one been there. Their plumes of dust spiked skyward, followed by rolling flames and black smoke which quickly dissipated. The second F-4, Bobbin 21, which should have adjusted his release based on the lead's bombs, rolled in too quickly and hit the same spot. Mark wasn't surprised. Wing men were often a little light on hours, and the demands of the Viet Nam conflict required sending them into combat far earlier than usual. Several had flown into the ground on night bombing runs. The daily Snoopy cartoon on the bulletin board at the Operations Center once displayed a macabre sense of humor. "Put the next F-4 three clicks north."

Snoopy the cartoon FAC sitting on his doghouse was grinning, but it was only funny to pissed-off Nails like Mark.

"All right," Mark radioed. "Let's try one more pass. Six apiece, 100 meters north of your last drop."

The F-4s rolled in again. Flak intensified, which it normally did anytime an attack was occurring, and the sky was soon filled with black puffs of smoke. The puffs numbered from seven to over a dozen telling Mark both 37s and 23s were opening up. The noise of the OV-10 engines precluded hearing air blasts. However, experienced FACs always looked up as well as down, knowing that often the only clue they were being shot at were the airbursts above them.

Mark's cavalier attitude suddenly took a sharp turn, "Bobbin 21's hit!" screamed a frightened F-4 pilot over the radio. "WE'RE ON FIRE. PUNCHING OUT!"

Mark wheeled his plane around and caught sight of two parachutes deploying on the North Vietnamese side of the target. Both the front and back-seater of the second F-4 made safe ejections. Their aircraft, missing one wing, hit the ground with a large explosion amid a huge cloud of dirt. The parachutes were good news, so far, in a very tense situation. Mark had seen aircraft going down with no chutes, a sickening sight to FACs anywhere in Southeast Asia. The first time it happened to him, he choked up, something he never admitted to anyone. This time, he felt a temporary sense of relief, but there was much work to be done. He got right to it.

"Hillsborough, Nail 52. We have an F-4 down near Mu Gia. Two good chutes." The call was made on his UHF radio to the airborne command post; simultaneously, the lead F-4 was broadcasting the same message on guard channel. This channel was specifically reserved for emergencies, but Mark didn't use it because he was already talking to the only person who could help, the battlefield coordinator at the airborne command post, Hillsborough.

"Nail 52, Hillsborough. Roger. I'll divert another flight of F-4s from a strike in Sector III. Scrambling Sandys and Jolly Greens now."

"Roger, Hillsborough. Please send Nail 24 up from Sector III until the Sandys get here."

"Roger that Nail."

Mark was watching the two chutes descend and could see they were the targets of massive gunfire. Airbursts were turning the blue sky black. Occasional puffs of white smoke indicated even heavier guns. He used the distraction of the gunners to begin searching for their locations, and after ten minutes found what appeared to be a complex of guns, probably four 37s surrounding a big gun, probably a 57mm radar guided gun in the center. As usual, the guns were well camouflaged with netting and vegetation in the tree line just off the main body of the trail. The intense gunfire left puffs of smoke and gave them away. Mark couldn't wait for something to throw at them. So, he didn't. He rolled in and fired a salvo of white phosphorous rockets at the installation.

"52, Nail 24 overhead at 6,000. Good hit. Probably killed the gunners but not the guns. I've got it marked."

"Roger 52. Good to have you here. Let's do what we can to locate the other guns before the Sandys get here."

"Roger that."

"Nail, this is Bobbin 20. We still have five minutes of playtime and 12 Mark 82s."

"Roger that Bobbin. Let's keep you in reserve in case we need some quick help on the ground."

Mark didn't know if a battalion of troops would charge the pilots but guessed they probably would observe their landing area and wait until nightfall. Five more minutes wasn't much of an advantage, but it was better than nothing.

The F-4 pilots finally landed, their parachutes deflating rapidly in the still hot air. One landed on one side of the North Viet Nam border, one in Laos. The lead pilot called in on his survival radio.

"Nail, Bobbin 21 Alpha. I'm going to try and make it to the small karst formation to the north of me. There're guns all over the place. It sounded like constant gunfire all the way down." The voice was strained, reflecting obvious pain and barely disguised fear. Alpha was the call sign for the front seater, the pilot. Bravo was the backseat pilot.

"Bobbin 21 Bravo, are you on?" Mark could see the backseater. He had discarded his parachute and was running uphill on ground devoid of all vegetation from years of bombing. Heading for high ground was a bedrock principle of escape and evasion. He didn't answer Mark.

"Nail 52, Bobbin 20: I'll monitor Bravo from up here so you can concentrate on Alpha."

"Roger, 20. Sandys should be here soon. I'm going to drop down a little and see what I can. Watch for the guns."

"Roger that. You better jink like a hummingbird."

"Yeah, like a shitting hummingbird."

Mark dropped down to 2,000 feet above the ground, twisting and turning his OV-10 aggressively. Calming himself, he keyed his mic. "Bobbin crew, don't worry. The whole damned Air Force is on the way. There are two of us overhead now and the Sandys will be here in about 20 minutes. Two more F-4s have been diverted as well. Bobbin 21 Bravo, you OK?" He was being far more optimistic than he really was.

"Roger, Nail. Don't know what hit us. I'm heading for trees uphill of me. I'll try to get to ... Alpha ..."

He almost used his front-seater's name over the radio, which was a no-no, but caught himself in time. While he waited for the rescue team, Mark thought briefly of how disappointed he was at not getting an F-4 assignment out of pilot training and then realized how ridiculous those thoughts were. It could have been him on the ground. No helicopter could possibly survive in this environment. It was going to take a lot of work to get these guys out. The next ten minutes were spent gun hunting, but the gunners were not cooperating; they undoubtedly knew what was coming next. A nice fat target called a Jolly Green Giant helicopter.

"Nail 24, got anything?"

"Nothing. They're holding their fire for you know what."

"I know. I figured that out too." The Nails continued circling, flying at different altitudes in opposing directions to confuse the North Vietnamese as much as possible. After ten more minutes with no confirmed targets, the lead F-4 pilot called.

"Nail, Bobbin 20 is bingo fuel. Have to RTB. What can we hit before we go?"

"Bobbin, let's cut the road north of the crew in the event they're here overnight. The pass there is in a narrow V shape 500 meters long with steep slopes on either side. I won't mark it because it will just give them advance notice, but you can't miss it. That will delay North Vietnamese ground troops from just swarming in. Do your best."

"Got it. Bobbin 20 is in hot."

The drop was perfect. Dirt showered down the steep slopes, effectively blocking the road at the narrowest spot at the North Viet Nam/Laotian border. It would require several hours of work to make it passable. It had been cut hundreds of times during the war, but the NVA had dedicated an entire road crew permanently to the pass to ensure it would never be closed for long. Bobbin 20 jinked aggressively as the pilot pulled off the target and headed back to base, the black airbursts of anti-aircraft fire providing a frame for the picture the FACs were watching.

"21 flight, see you guys back at the bar. Now keep your head down and do what the Nail tells you to do."

"21 Bravo, roger that sir," the F-4 back-seater transmitted on his survival radio to his departing flight leader, his voice even more raspy.

Bravo 21 Alpha, his voice strained, signed off, "21 Alpha."

* * *

Ace Faircloth, the most experienced A-1 pilot at NKP on search and rescue efforts, was playing with the mixture on his Pratt and Whitney R-2800 radial, not satisfied with the sound of the big engine. With an aircrew down, he wanted confidence he wouldn't have to divert his attention to problems of his own. It seemed to smooth out and he looked away from the Jolly Green Giant in front and to his left to briefly check on his wingman, Otto Krug. Otto gave him a thumbs up and he nodded back. Another Jolly Green and two more A-1s were holding 1,000 feet higher and to the rear of the lead flight. Still more were on ground alert at NKP waiting for a follow-up call. Ace knew how much danger he would be in, but it wouldn't compare to that of the Jolly Greens. Hovering over the Ho Chi Minh Trail was not far off the scale from pure suicide and Ace had the highest regard for those crews. It was his intention to keep them out of harm's way as much as possible, a difficult task over the Ho Chi Minh Trail in any situation, but especially at Mu Gia Pass.

"Nail 52, Sandy lead. We're one out."

"Roger Sandy. F-4 crew down at Mu Gia. Heavy triple A. I have some fast movers inbound diverting from Sector Two. Your discretion."

"Roger, 52. I have you in sight. I'll assume command. Please stay above us and mark the guns when I call for it."

"Roger that."

Mark called the Bobbin crew on guard channel. "Bobbin crew, Sandys are about here. Hold tight."

"Roger Nail." Both pilots answered almost simultaneously. The downed pilots sounded, for the first time, relieved.

"MIG! MIG! JOLLY GREEN 1 HAS BEEN HIT. GET DOWN JOLLY GREEN 2. GET DOWN!"

The voice of Sandy 3, one of the A-1s, was as high pitched as a man's voice could get. Mark Tinga wheeled his OV-10 around in time to see a Jolly Green Giant falling like a popped balloon on fire and a MiG 21 circling back to the rescue teams a half mile away. The remaining helicopter, Jolly Green 2, was nose low, diving for the trees, while all four Sandys were trying to maneuver around to keep the MiG in sight. As slow as they were, there was no chance of getting a shot, but they did their duty to try to protect the remaining chopper.

"JOLLY GREEN 1 JUST DISAPPEARED! OH MY GOD! IT JUST DISAPPEARED! STAY DOWN 2! TURN AROUND AND HEAD BACK!" Whoever made that call did not identify himself, but it could have been anyone, understandably hyper, as were all the crew members involved.

The MiG 21 swept by Jolly Green 2 and the A-1s and headed back in the direction of the OV-10s. At the high speed it was traveling, there was no way for Mark to attempt a shot with a marking rocket, although he toyed with the idea. He watched as the sleek silver jet sliced through the air a few hundred feet away.

The MiG pilot turned his face toward Mark, held his glance for a few seconds, and then disappeared in the distance. Mark clearly saw the pilot's face and blue helmet insignia.

While the A-1s were surrounding Jolly Green 2 and heading toward NKP, staying low over trees, Mark took a deep breath and tried to regain his composure. His heart was nearly pounding out of his chest. There were still two pilots on the ground and the sun was low in the sky. Another rescue attempt would not be feasible until the next morning.

"Bobbin 21 crew, I guess you heard." Mark's voice was somber. The message was unmistakable.

"Roger Nail. I'm sorry for the crew." The pilot's voice disclosed the pain from a broken leg.

"They were the bravest of the brave, that's for sure. But you guys are right up there with them. We're going to go to work now to give you a little security for the evening, so keep your heads down."

The two Nails worked on the gun positions with several flights of fast movers who showed up ten minutes later. As they directed the last of the ordnance in the most logical places the enemy might be hiding, Mark called them one last time.

"Bobbin, we can't work anymore. It's getting dark. Turn your radios off to conserve the batteries and turn them on when we buzz you in the morning. Bury yourselves if you can and don't move after dark."

"Wilco Nail. Thanks. Bobbin 21 Alpha."

Bobbin 21 Bravo, the backseater, did not respond, probably still scrambling for a safe hiding place.

* * *

The next morning, the MiG Cap, a second flight of F-4s, which should have been routinely in place the day before, was now in place: four F-4s with air-to-air-missiles with four more holding higher. As the sun rose, the Sandys swept down over the last position of the Bobbin crew. They could see nothing. No radio transmissions were ever received. Mark Tinga, Nail 52, orbited high and outside the flight pattern of the Sandys watching for any signs of hostile activity while the Sandys did their work. For the rest of his tour in Laos he would revisit this site when time permitted, never giving up on the possibility the Bobbin crew might have survived.

After the war, the family was notified by the Department of Defense that no evidence of survival was ever found, suggesting the crew was captured and killed. On the trail captives were too big a burden in most cases. It was also possible the crew members decided to shoot it out rather than be captured.

Later that day, as the sun was setting, and the Nails were migrating to their watering hole, Mark Tinga entered and saw Thatcher sitting on the sofa, watching the Nail Hole cat playing with the Nail Hole mouse. He plopped down, obviously exhausted or depressed or both, next to his classmate from the Zoo.

"You ain't gonna believe what happened to me yesterday."

"Try me. Where you're concerned, I could believe almost anything."

"I was putting in two F-4s on a fragged target at Mu Gia, right at the Pass when a MiG popped out of nowhere and shot one of them down."

"Are you shitting me! A MiG? What kind?"

"Twenty-one."

"Did he come after you?"

"Hell no! Bastard must have been doing 400 knots. I think he wanted me to tell the story—maybe to send a message that the party is over."

"Well, the party is just about over, so he sure wasted a lot of gas. Did you give him the Nail signal for go screw yourself?"

"I wasn't sure if it was in good taste. After all, we are officers and gentlemen, or did you forget? And it dawned on me he might take it personally. I think he was just making sure I saw him. He could have shot me down too, easily, but he wanted a witness. He wanted to make sure someone could tell the story. And he won. Here I am telling the story. I will never forget that look as long as I live."

The two classmates sat here for a long time, not speaking; they didn't have to. In just a few months, they had amassed a lifetime of stories, months which seemed like an eternity, memories which would keep them awake late at night well into old age. The Nail

Hole filled up gradually through the night and everyone wanted to hear the story firsthand, so Mark told the story again and again.

* * *

A few weeks later, another contingent of A-1 and Jolly Green Giant crews from NKP launched a super-secret rescue attempt at Son Tay Prison Camp in North Viet Nam to rescue U.S. POWs held there. All the personnel at NKP were alerted and met the returning crews and the Green Berets that attempted the rescue at the flight line. The mission was unsuccessful although there were no casualties among the rescue team. Despite the intelligence reports, the prison camp was empty. American policy planners, already straining to justify continued American presence in Viet Nam, were facing two more high-profile disappointments to add to the continued domestic turmoil over the war.

This was a poignant moment in the Viet Nam War. In one respect, it symbolized the end was very near. The most powerful nation in the world had once again exhibited an incapacity to achieve an objective despite its unlimited resources. Its best military men could not return their brothers being kept prisoners in inhumane conditions. No one knew just exactly how or when the final shoe would drop, although among the Nails there was no doubt it was imminent. Nails had a very special vantage point: being the farthest north of any FACs in Viet Nam, they could see the futility in trying to win an unwinnable war. They had a front row seat to the guns, troops, and supplies heading to South Viet Nam. They reported it daily. The question was, were the politicians in Washington reading the reports?

13

The Last Time Ever I Saw Your Face

The week after the MiG incident, Captain Roger "Mad Dog" Brown was loitering over Ban Karai Pass in Sector III as the sun was hovering just over the horizon in the west. Sunsets over the trail were, in many respects, a conundrum. The beauty of the sunsets was enhanced by two things. The first was the profusion of lights and shadows. The peaks of the mountains and karst formations created a vision artists would have both loved and hated. They would have loved the incredible diversity of the formations. The tall, thin spires were adorned with hundreds of small pools of water sparkling on the tops and sides of the karst. As the sun set, the sparkles reflected the sunlight in a constantly changing kaleidoscope of color, like a prism dividing the light into its color spectrum. Artists would have hated it because the change occurred so swiftly that trying to capture it on canvas it would have been impossible. And in just a matter of minutes, it was gone, and the Laotian night assumed control.

Mad Dog had been directing an assortment of Navy attack aircraft on tree parks for most of the afternoon. He was frustrated at the lack of visible damage on all the strikes and assumed the lack of results was not due to faulty Intel, but the time lapse between the sightings and the planned strike. His last target for the day was in a superb location for a truck park, lots of trees nestled up at the base of the karst formation providing cover for the North Vietnamese trucks. After directing two passes by Navy A-7 attack aircraft, on his last directed pass and to his surprise, the attack aircraft hit pay dirt. Secondary explosions lit up the shadows in the jungle below as the bombs ignited trucks loaded with ammunition, ammunition destined for the grunts in South Viet Nam. Orange flames leapt into the air and were soon superseded by a roiling cloud of black smoke.

As expected, anti-aircraft guns for a mile around responded, spitting out a fireworks finale of dozens of strings of red tracers, each string seeking out the metallic flesh of Roger's O-2. Fortunately, each string missed and the seven shells of each string hungrily seeking an aluminum feast self-destructed in an orgy of sparkles momentarily lighting up the dark jungle below. In the waning sunlight, the red tracers became even more visible and therefore easier to evade. Roger was at the sweet spot all FACs loved: a defined and visible target, dim light to make the AAA visible and easy to avoid, and strike aircraft with play time and plenty of ordnance. His adrenalin was pumping like a fire engine at a three-alarm fire. After a hard pull to the left to avoid yet another string of red tracers, Roger directed the second aircraft to move to the right of the last strike, still visible by the light of fires on the ground. As the second set of bombs exploded, so did the AAA. Up came more strings of red tracers from another set of guns aimed directly at Roger's O-2, still visible to the gunners in the waning light. The A-7 pilots, circling a few thousand feet above Roger, were enjoying the show.

"Nail, you *are* aware they're shooting at you?" The lead A-7 pilot's voice displayed a little sarcasm.

Roger came right back, "Well, I'll tell you what, there's a gun 150 meters to the right of the fire you just started, so let's give *you* a chance to enjoy the attention. Go get him cowboys. I'll be holding west at 6,000."

"Roger that Nail. Get the hell out of the way and watch some superb airmanship. We'll be departing south after this drop for our cocktail hour, so have a good evening."

Roger, an electrical engineering graduate, had connected a tape deck through a jack to his aircraft intercom. He only turned it on when there was a certain poignant moment in a mission.

This night had poignant written all over it. He turned on the cassette and put in a Roberta Flack tape. Flack, he mused, was particularly appropriate this night because the flak from the guns was intense. Several more strings of tracers spit out of the gun barrels below, the red tracers burning in a few seconds after the muzzle flash. Roger loved music, especially when destroying things. Sometimes he played the "1812 Overture" and sometimes Stravinsky. Tonight, however, was Roberta's night. This was his wife, Bobbi's, favorite performer. "The first time ever I saw your face ..." Roberta sang.

When they'd met, the mutual attraction was immediate and powerful. Bobbi was not only beautiful, but also extremely bright, an obvious attention-getter to any red-blooded American boy. She was equally impressed with the handsome Air Force pilot. As he finished pilot training, she was graduating from a small local college with a degree in interior decorating. They hadn't spent much time together, but after one year, the passion reached the boiling point and they got married. At his first base in North Carolina, they spent every spare moment getting to know both the Outer Banks beaches and the Smoky Mountains. Without warning, he was added to the Palace Cobra list, a list of SAC pilots selected for assignment to Southeast Asia. While he was reminiscing, he observed continuing explosions below which were indicative of a major ammunition cache.

"Way to go, Navy. Almost as good as the Air Force."

"Nail, need we remind you of the football score this past fall?"

"Blind luck," answered Roger. "Besides, 48 to 45 isn't exactly a blowout. The next time you get a chance, get an overnight at NKP and I'll teach you how to drink. I understand you don't have bars on that barge you call home. I promise we won't step on your fingers after you pass out."

"Sounds like a challenge. We'll look for an opportunity. Have a good night."

Roger gave the A-7s their BDA and bid them farewell.

"Hillsborough, this is Nail 73, I've got secondary explosions at the last target." He broke hard to the right to avoid yet another string of tracers coming from directly below.

When he'd told Bobbi about his assignment to Southeast Asia, she flung a fit. "You son of a bitch! You told me you wouldn't volunteer!" She'd thrown something then, an ashtray he seemed to remember. He broke hard to the left then too. She was always throwing things. Explaining that he didn't volunteer didn't seem to register.

"Nail 73, do you want additional ordnance?"

"Roger that, Hillsborough."

He snapped the aircraft to the right as the intensity of ground fire picked up. He was grateful it was dusk. The worst clips, in any lighting conditions, were from behind the aircraft. Unless the pilot maneuvered constantly, it was easy to be shot down from behind.

Bobbi hit him in the head from behind once, with an umbrella. He'd been grateful they weren't in the kitchen where the wrought iron skillets were hanging on a ceiling rack.

"Nail 73, this is Sandy 3 and 4, Mark 82s, Funny Bombs, pistols."

Shit hot, thought Brown. Hillsborough gave him the A-1 Skyraiders that always launched from NKP just before sunset. They were there with the Jolly Greens in case of a last-minute bailout on the trail. When there were no bailouts, and it was too late to do anything about it if there were, the Jollys went home, and the Sandys were allowed to expend their ordnance with any FAC who with a target. Funny Bombs were particularly effective weapons against the cold steel of anti-aircraft artillery. They were magnesium bombs with thermite initiators. When they first hit the target, there was a small flash which soon turned into a bright white bubbling mass of molten metal. Within a few minutes, the mass melted anything it touched including gun barrels, ammunition, or artillery carriages. Pilots had to be careful not to stare at the hellish scene because it would ruin their night vision. The A-1 'Pistols' were .50 caliber machine guns, Mark 82s were 500-pound bombs that would leave a hole in the ground 20 feet wide and ten feet deep. They A-1s may have been old and slow, but they were flying munition warehouses.

The funny thing about Bobbi was how her sweet side was so different from her hostile persona, Roger mused. He reminded himself to look up 'persona' when he landed—he liked the sound of the word, but, after all, he was an electrical engineer, not an English major.

"Sandy, arm your Mark 82s. I'm going to give you two Willy Petes; walk the 82s from one smoke to the other." He armed his master switch, selected a rocket from the left outboard pod, and pulled the nose of the O-2 up to about 40 degrees to bleed off speed while rolling left, and then down.

How could she be so sweet one minute and such a bitch the next? He hit the trigger on the yoke and launched the rockets. Showers of sparks screamed out of the rocket tubes under the wings, not as visible during the day, but dramatic at night. Brown tightened his stomach muscles slightly as the O-2 strained under the maximum allowable 3.7 G pullout which was far harder on the plane than its pilot. Roger and other O-2 pilots, trained in jets with 7 G capability, hated the lack of more "G" capacity of the Skymaster. More than one O-2 pilot came back missing a few rivets in the wings. In fact, since there was no way to determine why O-2s disappeared when they did, it was always written up as flak damage. While that may have been the norm, breaking too hard to miss the flak might very well have been the cause on more than one occasion.

Roberta felt the earth moving in her hand.

The white phosphorus rockets made the earth move too. The white plumes were clearly visible in the waning light and the gunners below reacted with fury, spitting out another string of red tracers. From Brown's altitude 4,500 feet above the ground, there was ample time to avoid the gunfire with minimum maneuvering. As with other experienced Nails, he knew a miss was as good as a mile; as long as the tracers appeared to be moving in any direction on his windscreen, they were not on a collision course with his O-2. If they were stationary, they were, and breaking in an appropriate direction was the correct course of action.

The white plumes of the last Willy Petes were now large and easily visible, even in the dark. "Hit my smoke," Roger told the A-1s. "I'll be east over the trail. Break to the karst coming out." Brown favored the A-1s on the pull off from the target. If they got hit, they would be in the safest bailout area.

"Roger that. It is Sandy lead is in hot."

No marriage was perfect, but damn I tried. He'd bought her a Golden Retriever puppy for her birthday. She treated it like a child, cuddling it every morning for 15 minutes, talking baby talk to it, dressing it up for Halloween as a witch. I wish she could have treated me like the dog.

"Nice drop, lead. Sandy Two, extend that line."

She used to pin earrings in the tufts of hair behind the dog's ears or put Easter Bunny ears on the dog and then laugh for hours.

Even more explosions followed the initial blast of the bombs, leading Brown to conclude there was indeed a very large staging area. The initial explosions were near the edge of the tree line. He guessed, correctly the supplies or trucks, or both, extended into the trees toward the base of a large karst formation riddled with caves. No surprise there. It was uncommon to find guns anywhere near an open space.

He watched the drop of the second A-1 with continued satisfaction, as the secondary explosions continued.

Why did you bother coming to Hawaii for my R and R? What a hell of a place to ask for a divorce. Why not just write me a Dear John like most unhappy women? I went to Hawaii to get screwed, and I sure did.

He jinked hard to the right to avoid yet another spray of red balls from a 23mm gun. Along with other Nails, he hated 23s more than any other gun in the NVA arsenal even though they were the oldest guns of the large caliber anti-aircraft artillery. Their barrels long ago lost their rifling from years of use, first against the French and now the Americans. As a result, they sprayed the shells. Larger guns sent the clips up in a straight line. Miss the first one and the rest would follow in the same path. Not 23s, which were more like shotguns. If that were not enough, they fired 20 or more shells at one burst as high as 10,000 feet.

What I'll miss the most about you is the Bobbi who was so innocent she couldn't tell a joke without destroying the punch line. You would get so tongue tied the group you were telling the joke to would laugh until they were in spasms.

It was dark now. Roberta was saying the moon and stars were the gifts you gave to the dark and endless skies as the air was filled with strings of tracers. The hornet's nest awakened earlier was approaching the furious stage.

"Assholes," Roger muttered under his breath. "Sandys, I have another 23. Let's try some Funny Bombs on him."

"Roger that, Nail."

Brown repositioned his rocket switches to all four pods, and as he rolled the O-2 over to the left and down, he began to salvo all the rockets remaining since he was low on fuel and wouldn't need them anymore for marking. They lit up the trail and even after the blast from the impact died down, the huge plume of white phosphorous smoke was still visible under the quarter moon. The gun he picked out was slightly to one side of the smoke, and it made the tragic mistake of marking its position in relation to the smoke by opening up one last time. For the A-1s, it was like shooting fish in a barrel.

Roberta sang, "I knew our joy would fill the earth, and last till the end of time, my love."

The muzzle flashes were clearly visible to the Sandys and they dropped one Funny Bomb each. The gun stopped firing. As the magnesium of the Funny Bombs was ignited by thermite initiators, they began to boil like a scene from hell. The white-hot inferno grew and grew, too bright to look at, melting everything it touched. Ammunition began cooking off, sending Roman candles into the night air.

"And last till the end of time," sang Roberta.

The Sandys' blue-tinged exhaust flames were visible as they pulled up hard and headed for home, tracers from other guns following them all the way.

Reminds me of your incredible temper, mused Brown. *I will have to say one thing, though my darling. If I had missed the hell, I would have missed the heaven too. It was worth it. I hope you find happiness.*

"Enjoyed it Sandys. Stop by the Nail Hole and I'll buy you a beer."

"You're on, Nail. Good work."

Roberta sang, "The last time ever I saw your face, your face, your face, your face, your face."

After landing, Brown joined the nightly party at the Nail Hole that always began around suppertime and continued until nearly morning. The daytime FACs began grilling steaks on the barbecue pit starting around sunset and wouldn't stop until last of the night flights checked in. Poker and bridge tables were fully staffed, and war stories filled the air. A war novel could have been written with nothing but a few nights there with a tape recorder.

Brown was the last daytime FAC to land, and his description of the Funny Bomb attack was greeted with back-slapping and a few free beers. Brown joined a table of Nails who were still eating. Later, the Hobo pilots, flight suits still drenched with sweat, entered to a burst of cheers from the Nails and the party shifted into overdrive. Brown, true to his word, bought them all drinks for the rest of the night. At ten cents a drink, his total outlay was $3.20 at night's end.

"What's been your experience with the trail traffic?" asked one of the newer Nails, Capt. Howard "Howie" Zeller, as he sidled up to Roger. "Are we making a difference?" Like most New Beans, Howie was not just asking to be polite; he was trying to ascertain just what the odds of dying were.

"Well, we're killing more, but it's just an indication there are more trucks to kill. And anyone who's been here almost a year, like I have, will tell you this is a screwed-up war. I don't know how many trucks I've killed, but I suspect you could fire a Willy Pete at any clump of trees bordering the trail and hit something."

Zeller pressed the point. "Is there any hope of winning this war or are we fooling ourselves?"

"Howie, your definition of victory needs to be surviving for a year. This war was lost before it started. In a few months, we'll be begging the North Vietnamese for terms. And, if I don't miss my guess, they aren't going to give us crap. What I don't understand is how in the hell we got here to begin with. What exactly did Kennedy, Johnson, Nixon, and McNamara have in mind? Why don't we ask Thatcher? He's the expert."

Ted Thatcher was playing the piano and suggested they ask Don Jefferson to pull out his guitar. The song, which was the answer to the question, was sung to the tune of "Both Sides Now." It was an especially appropriate song for the sweat-stained night crews:

Layered decks of strata cue
A nine-eighths cover hides the view.
It's overcast above them too.
We've looked at clouds that way.

They're Popeye now at seven five
Climbing, turning in a dive,
It's vertigo we must surmise.
We've been in those clouds too.

Hey Moonbeam, this is Nail 83,
This turbulence is killing me.
There're no trucks here that we can see.
Request we RTB . . . right now.

Nail 83 please standby one,
Request you check out 601
That Boomer flight is almost done.
He must get bombs away.

Moonbeam, Moonbeam Nails 83
I don't believe you're hearing me
My TACAN's out, I have to pee,
I guess you don't know clouds . . . at all.

The question of winning the war was answered with this song, lots of alcohol, and another four hours of war stories as the Nail crews continued to arrive from the night missions.

14

The Old Man and the Trail

Lt. Col. Melendez took off at 0600, his OV-10 thriving on the cool air of a Thailand morning. The new Squadron Commander had never been in combat until this tour, and this was his first solo mission. His predecessor, Lt. Col. Everen, completed his tour with the respect of his squadron through fair management and a respectable number of combat missions. Melendez was a handsome man with a ready smile and sturdy build. He might have been a football player, but no one asked him if he was, and he never mentioned it.

Lt. Col. Melendez's few checkout missions were with seasoned veteran pilots in the 23rd, but there were no particularly exciting air strikes. Today, he was hoping to achieve the Nail equivalent of a birdie on a golf course: Finding his own targets and coming back with some confirmed BDA, or Bomb Damage Assessment. One thing every Squadron Commander faced in combat was the inevitable suspicion by the junior officers that the Old Man had picked a milk run. Col. Melendez was determined to put their suspicions to rest on his first solo mission. There were Squadron Commanders who became famous for being combat leaders, Air Force commanders such as Jimmy Doolittle and Actor Jimmy Stewart. Col. Melendez was not so naïve as to think he would become famous, but he sincerely wanted to earn the respect of his squadron, so he knew he would have to work hard to achieve respectable results.

There was no one benchmark to surpass. The fluid nature of combat over the trail offered numerous opportunities for respectability. A large number of truck kills, for example, perhaps ten or more on one mission. Destruction of an anti-aircraft gun complex was a particularly admirable achievement. Guns were often grouped in clusters to take advantage of a single aiming radar, and killing several guns at once, especially if they were all firing, was right at the top of the testosterone scale.

This was the setting which Squadron Commander Lt. Col. Melendez found himself in 1970, on a June morning. As he reached his cruising altitude of 6,500 feet, he pulled out his binoculars and began scanning the terrain below him in Sector II. That's when he lucked out. He was flying almost straight and level, using his binoculars to scan the terrain below. Flying straight and level over the Ho Chi Minh Trail was not dissimilar to walking across the middle of Fifth Avenue in New York City reading the newspaper at noon. He was taught never to stop jinking by his checkout pilots, but in his desire to show his worthiness, he violated the rule. Sure enough, a five-gun complex, one 57mm radar guided gun with four smaller 37mm guns, reacted with gusto to the opportunity.

If there was a Vietnamese word for 'plum,' this was one. They all opened up on cue and Lt. Col. Melendez found himself in the situation he had been looking for—a chance to impress the troops back home. With the noisy turboprop whine of the engines of the OV-10, the Squadron Commander couldn't hear what O-2 pilots heard on a regular basis through their open window on the right side: a characteristic sound like sheets ripping. But he did feel a dull thud in his belly tank. He broke hard to the right, before the guns could reload. He headed to safety over the mountain range on the

NKP side of the trail, checked his instruments and flight controls, and found nothing awry. Still uncertain, he called the FAC in Sector III, Tex Robertson, and arranged a rendezvous over the mountains to the west, toward NKP.

Anyone getting hit over the Ho Chi Minh Trail faced a number of potential outcomes. The trail, by nature, was a life or death environment, and death was a very real possibility. Death wore many faces. The pilot/crew could be killed immediately. AAA could be instantaneously lethal because most of the projectiles were not just large lead bullets. They were little bombs. If they hit something, they exploded. If they didn't hit anything, they exploded at or near the peak of their trajectories and the shrapnel might hit something if close enough, such as a cockpit window, an engine, a wing, or a flight control surface.

Lt. Col. Melendez didn't know what damage had occurred, but he did know bailing out over the Ho Chi Minh Trail was a form of Russian Roulette. Some of the most dramatic stories from the Laotian war were the survival accounts of downed airmen. Baker 22 Bravo was such a man, as was Bat 21. But the most heartbreaking stories were of pilots who ejected over Laos, were captured, and taken to the inhumane prisons in North Viet Nam, such as the Hanoi Hilton. Many of them were given up for dead by their families and friends since no one knew where they were. Often, pilots shot down over Hanoi or Haiphong, were paraded in front of cameras for propaganda purposes so their families at least knew they were alive. Not so the Laotian captives. So, understandably, Lt. Col. Melendez breathed a sigh of relief as he made it safely over the mountains.

After some very anxious minutes, Capt. Robertson arrived at his Squadron Commander's location and flew all around the OV-10.

"Colonel, you have a hole the size of a golf ball in your belly tank and fuel is streaming out. Punch it off."

The Squadron Commander punched off the tank, watched it drop away, and headed back to NKP, his reputation established, and legacy assured. He had faced death and prevailed.

Later that evening, the 'Old Man', as military commanders the world over are often called, couldn't buy a drink at the Nail Hole. Ted Thatcher bought him the first one.

"Colonel, from what Tex told us, you've found one hell of a way to locate a gun complex. My hat is off to you, sir!" He was smiling, of course.

The squadron commander laughed. "Ted, everyone needs a lesson in humility from time to time. I got mine early, and if nothing else, maybe the New Beans after me will hear my story and pay attention to you old heads. And by the way, didn't you and Major Khampat come back with a hole in your wing last week? Was that your lesson?"

Thatcher laughed. "Touché, colonel, touché."

Colonel Melendez would never know why the tank didn't explode, but when the lights went out at night, he would never forget the beast he faced. Before his tour was over, he would compile a respectable resumé, but he would live the rest of his life hearing a dull thud in quiet moments, especially late at night when there were no distractions. And the airmen he commanded would experience their own quiet moments the rest of their lives, some hearing a dull thud, others enveloped in a spray of red tracers, and still others seeing human beings swallowed up in an orange splash of napalm. General Sherman was right. War was, and always would be, hell.

15

The Second Kick of a Mule

Mark Tinga came back from Bangkok after a one-week pass after the MiG incident, pissed off and ready to kill something. The first morning after his return, he met the TUOC Trolley and 30 minutes later, briefed and fully suited for combat, he pushed the OV-10 engines up to takeoff power. The morning air was crisp, a blessing in the otherwise tropical climate of Thailand, but Mark knew it would be hot and humid on his return. He headed to the mountains near Ban Karai pass, the southern-most pass on the border between North Viet Nam and Laos. It was a favorite hunting area of his. His specialty was anti-aircraft guns. For some reason, killing guns gave him a special thrill. Perhaps the adrenalin rush knowing guns, unlike trucks, offered a visceral challenge. Killing a truck was like stepping on a worm. Killing a truck was like stomping a snake.

This morning he surveyed the jungle below him, asking himself, "Where would I put an anti-aircraft gun to get maximum exposure to the aircraft trying to kill me and at the same time not making me too visible?"

In the triple canopy jungle of Laos, it was an easy question to ask, but a hard question to answer. Leaving the mandated safe altitude of 5,000 feet above the ground, Mark once again applied his solution to the problem of finding guns by dropping down to tree top level on the mountains abutting the trail and then skimming down over the trees toward the flood plain below. He pulled the power back, keeping the engine noise to a minimum, hoping the surprise element would assure his safety.

This was completely against all the rules, but normally the tactic worked because of the element of surprise. He often got a peek at a gun under camouflage netting invisible from a few thousand feet higher. Usually, the gunners were caught by surprise and were either unable to get off a quick shot or incapable of aiming accurately. This morning his system did not work. As he completed his first pass, he applied full power and headed back up the slope of the mountain to reach a safe altitude. Of course, nothing was ever safe over the trail, and a very well camouflaged 23mm gun hidden near the base of the mountain proved the point. Mark's OV-10 became an airborne scrap yard. It was hard to tell where he got hit because both engines quit and none of the controls worked. Both stick and rudder were useless. His ejection occurred so fast that later he could not even remember it. So much for the bad news. The good news was he was close to the trees. Within less than a minute he was perched in the top of one.

Nail 76, Jim Russell, was flying Sector II the same morning and was surprised to hear Mark's voice on guard channel.

"Where in the hell are you?" he asked. "I saw you less than an hour ago in briefing."

"East of the Chokes. You'll see the chute in the trees. But be careful. There's a 23 almost on top of me."

Mark's voice was amazingly calm. Even he thought so. He did feel somewhat protected because he couldn't even see the ground as high as he was in the tree.

"Roger that," replied Russell. "Let me get on the horn and get the Jollys airborne. Call me when you hear my engines."

"Roger that." Mark took off his flight helmet and, in an attempt, to secure it to a branch, he dropped it. He was amazed he never heard it hit the ground. Camouflaged as it was, he didn't worry about it giving his position away.

The sound of an O-2 soon announced the arrival of Nail 76.

"I have your chute right in the top of a tree. Rescue is on the way. I'm not going to get too close to avoid giving your position away."

"Roger, 76. The 23 that got me is in the trees almost right under me and just off the trail itself. He's well camouflaged, so be careful."

"I think I have him. His camouflage netting was blown away when he fired. I'll mark it for the Sandys as soon as they arrive. Your chute is real visible from the air so they won't have any problems seeing you."

Within 45 minutes the two A-1 Sandys were overhead with two additional Sandys orbiting a safe distance away in formation with the rescue choppers. Jim Russell gave the Sandys a briefing on the situation and the approximate location of the gun. He suggested they come in from the sun and then marked the gun with a Willy Pete, breaking 90 degrees from the roll-in heading, jinking vigorously, like a bat. The gun opened up, confirming its location, and within seconds the Sandys killed the crew with cluster bombs followed by napalm, which caused the gun and its ammo to explode. No other gun crews volunteered to expose themselves. Mark's pickup went uncontested. It was one of the shortest SARs on record.

Later that night in the Nail Hole, Captain Tinga was the toast of the Nails, who always celebrated the return of one of their own. Thatcher walked up beside his Academy classmate at the bar, grinning.

"Well, Mark, are you trying to win the Medal of Honor or something? I know you well enough to know you weren't at 5,000 feet."

"No comment." Mark grinned.

"Tell me about it." Thatcher once faced off against Mark in intermural rugby at the Zoo, and he knew how tough he was.

"Okay. I knew there was a gun there because the little bastard hosed me down a few days earlier on a fragged truck park mission. I assumed he was somewhere at the base of the mountain where he was supposed to be. He wasn't. The sneaky little bastard was 100 feet out on the trail with nothing but a bush hiding him. That should be against the rules. So, I thought I'd clean his clock. But it didn't work out the way it was supposed to. There was no option. Both engines were hit, so I punched out. I landed in a tree way high above the ground. How high I don't know, but I dropped my helmet and never heard it hit."

"I talked with the Sandy pilots," Thatcher laughed. "Apparently they got him for you."

"That pisses me off. I wanted to go back and clean his clock."

"Now, now, Mark. There are a lot more guns out there for you to play with. Maybe this is a sign you need to take up something a little less dangerous than gun hunting." Thatcher was smiling. "There's an old saying my grandfather used when I was young: 'You don't learn anything from the second kick of a mule.'"

"Maybe not, but you and I both know this war will be over soon and I don't know what in the hell I'm going to do. I'm not going back to KC-135s and I sure don't want to end up selling life insurance."

"Well. For now, maybe you should think about buying some. Come on. There's a hell of a poker game going on over there. Maybe if you lose some money, you'll feel better."

"OK by me. It'll give me a chance to kick your ass again like I did in rugby we played at the Zoo."

Thatcher smiled but didn't answer because Tinga kicked everyone's ass in rugby. The night went quickly, and the two friends continued their banter until the Nail Hole party ended late. It might be more accurate to say it paused and resumed 12 hours later. Nail Hole parties never really ended.

16

Miracles Do Happen

Captain Tex Robertson launched his OV-10 at daybreak for Sector III. His flight suit was already drenched in sweat—Thailand could be hot even in the morning. His fragged target was one mile south of Ban Karai Pass coming out of North Viet Nam. This was one of the major entry points of supplies from Laos into South Viet Nam and therefore one of the most heavily observed and bombed, both by B-52s and FAC-directed airstrikes. Roberson loitered high and east of the target, which was in triple canopy jungle interspersed with the typical outcroppings of karst at random intervals. He was over North Viet Nam in his holding pattern although the border was indistinguishable in the jungle below. At the exact time specified on his strike plan, four Navy A-4s called in to establish contact.

"Nail, Zebra flight, four A-4s with eight Mark 81s each. We have you in sight. Anytime you're ready."

"Roger that. Target is a truck park; elevation is 800 feet. Give me two apiece on the first pass. I can't see what the hell is down there, but the AAA will probably be intense, so I will smoke the target and get out of your way. I suggest mixing up the delivery if you know what I mean."

What he meant was changing the roll-in and roll-out headings on each pass so the gunners couldn't draw a consistent bead.

Nail 33, like most FACs, hated these invisible targets selected by infrared photography or observations from Heavy Hook operatives on the trail because he couldn't see them through the foliage, but the known quantity of guns in this particular area was indicative of something important. Robertson rolled in and fired two Willy Petes, one seconds after the other.

"Zebra flight, you're cleared in hot. Those smokes are 100 meters apart for reference. Call FAC in sight. I'll be moving north."

"Roger that Nail. Zebra 1 is in hot, FAC in sight."

At four second intervals the other A-4s rolled in. The Navy and Marines often attacked in formation. The Air Force, especially the F-105s, rolled in almost immediately, one after the other, so the succeeding members of the attack could alter their drops to hit any anti-aircraft guns shooting at the lead aircraft. There were advantages to both tactics, but the experience of the flight leader was always the deciding factor.

The A-4s hurtled downward in trail formation, one after the other, at a 60-degree angle. With a background of lush green jungle below, it was an impressive sight, one Tex Robertson and other FACs never tired of seeing. Imagine a front row seat to a display of incredible power, not just from masses of steel and aluminum hurtling toward earth in a choreographed performance of incredible precision, but the finale of a huge fireball accompanied by a shock wave that jostles the FAC aircraft a few thousand feet away. As the fireball subsides, a cone of gray and brown dirt spikes upward like an ice cream cone before collapsing in an orgasm of brown dirt and splintered trees in an immense crater that wasn't there seconds ago. As the strike aircraft pull off the target, wisps of vapor trail from their wing tips as they twist and turn in unpredictable patterns to confuse the gunners below.

"Nice drop Zebra. I don't see anything, but you were right on my smoke. Try 200 meters to the east."

"Roger that Nail."

Robertson was probing, and with nothing to go on but the initial target coordinates, he was using his best judgment on where the jungle might be hiding something. He selected a typical area at the base of a karst formation about 200 meters to the east of the initial drop. Up until that moment, there had been no flak—welcome news, or non-news as it were. That's when all hell broke loose. Red tracers engulfed his aircraft and he heard and felt the distinct hits of anti-aircraft shells. The OV-10 was controllable, barely, but it wasn't going anywhere. One engine was toast, and the other was damaged, barely turning. The ailerons didn't work, so the only control was the rudder, which allowed Robertson to keep the wings level long enough to punch out, which he did, all in a matter of seconds. As his parachute opened, he tried his best to steer away from the danger below, but the best he could do was to aim for the upslope of the mountains on the North Vietnamese side of the strike zone.

The parachute snagged some bamboo as he landed. He quickly detached himself, fell about three feet, and began running uphill. He took his survival radio in his left hand and pulled out his .38 caliber revolver from the shoulder holster with his right hand.

As he continued his climb up the steep slope of the bamboo-cluttered mountain, his wind gave out and he realized he needed to hide. Too many smoke filled nights of boozing in the Nail Hole took an early toll. And he didn't even smoke. The clusters of bamboo were about 20 feet in diameter and interspersed along the slope of the mountain. *Just pick one and crawl inside,* he thought.

The bamboo was so thick, the best he could do was squeeze in with the left half of his body. He turned on his survival radio and immediately heard the Zebra flight leader trying to contact him on the guard frequency.

"Zebra, this is Nail 33. I'm okay. Can you see any bad guys?" He was wheezing heavily. "I'm about 200 feet up the slope from my chute."

Zebra 1 answered. "Not from where we are because we don't want to get too close and give your position away. We see your chute. We have about ten more minutes of playtime, but another Nail is inbound. Sandys are being scrambled now."

Zebra 2 came up on guard channel, "Zebra 1 and Nail, I may have a fix on the gun. It's about 500 meters from the chute and out on the flood plain behind some camouflage."

"Nail, Zebra 1. Do you want us to take it out?"

"*Hell* yes. Go for it."

"Roger that. Keep your head down."

Zebra 1 called his wing man, "Zebra 2 you have the lead."

"Zebra 2, roger that."

Zebra lead was hoping the gunner would be stupid enough to fire on Zebra 2 and give away his position; he was. As Zebra 2 pulled off the target, the gunner opened up even before the bombs hit. The bombs were 20 meters away from the gun, close enough to kill the gunners but not destroy the weapon. The other A-4s, having a specific mark, were shooting fish in a barrel. The gun was obliterated.

"We got him Nail. Stay off the radio. We have to head back to the ship. But help is on the way."

"Roger that. Good work on the gun." Robertson tried to sound calm, but his voice wavered, disclosing his lack of bravado. He was not as frightened as he was before the A-4s killed the gun but was far from relaxed. Further transmissions were not only a waste of battery power, but also a potential hazard for any direction-finding equipment the NVA might have. Robertson continued catching his breath and trying to remember his survival training. Nothing came to mind except hiding.

Memories came flooding back about the Negrito tribesman at Jungle Survival School in the Philippines. He and other members of the Viet Nam-bound airmen were taken to Clark Air Base for briefings on the Viet Nam situation and a two-day course in jungle survival. There, after a helicopter ride into the middle of the jungle, an Air Force master sergeant gave the inbound airmen a course in how to survive in the jungle. A short and very dark Negrito tribesman was his assistant. The Negritos were pygmies, and what was survival to Americans was daily living to the Negritos. The sergeant explained how accomplished the Negritos were at hiding in the jungle. During WWII, the Philippine government wanted to use Philippine soldiers to guard the newly constructed Clark Air Field. General MacArthur wanted to use Negritos. The decision was made to do a test: Philippine soldiers would guard Clark Field for one night, but if the Negritos could infiltrate the base, MacArthur would win. At first light, the Philippine officials were bragging that no intrusion was made. MacArthur's staff officers asked them to look at the shoes of their guards. Every guard's shoe was marked with a white 'X' in chalk. The debate was over. Negritos would guard the base.

The survival instructor asked them to close their eyes for one minute. When he asked them to open their eyes, he gave them 20 minutes to find his Negrito associate. The group fanned out in the jungle clearing they were standing in, and gradually expanded their search area to well over 100 yards but returned empty handed. After admitting defeat, the Negrito emerged from leaves nearly under their feet, smiling with the few teeth he had left. He wasn't three feet from where he was first standing. The demonstration left its mark.

Tex Robertson tried to put his training to use. He tried for several more minutes to squeeze into the clump of bamboo next to him, but the canes were so close together, no amount of effort worked. As he was trying for a third time, he heard a whistle and saw a line of NVA soldiers in uniform slowly marching up the hill, line abreast, straight toward his position. He gripped his revolver even more tightly in his right hand, squeezed as far as he could into the bamboo, and resigned himself to his fate. He didn't know whether he would surrender or fight it out. Only God knew.

As the line slowly advanced, he froze, expecting the worst, but not knowing exactly what the worst was. Was it capture and torture? The Hanoi Hilton? A summary execution? It didn't take long for the NVA officer in charge, who was blowing a whistle and carrying a pistol, to climb up the steep slope to the opposite side of the bamboo stand, which was about ten feet in diameter. He looked up through the gaps in the bamboo, made eye contact with Nail 33, and paused. Robertson was shaking so hard he doubted he would even hit his adversary if he fired. He was surprised by two things: the man was a regular, uniformed officer, and he was young, probably not over 20. Later he would come to understand the Vietnamese had been fighting this war, in one form or another, since the end of WWII. There were no old officers, except for those in the headquarters units.

The eye contact seemed like an eternity, but after what was probably just a few seconds, the officer abruptly turned, blew a series of calls on his whistle, and headed back down the slope. His troops followed and they disappeared in a matter of minutes.

Nail 33 was submerged in a sea of emotions. Relief was immediate, although he wasn't out of danger yet. He was still deep in enemy territory. Bewilderment was not far behind. What just happened? And why? Did his enemy suffer from poor eyesight? Fear of being shot himself? Pity? Nail 33 would spend the rest of his life wondering. He would later suffer from PTSD, although he didn't know then what it was. And he wouldn't be alone.

And now, where in the hell were the Jolly Greens? The A-4s, true to their word, stayed around for as long as they could, but their sound had faded long ago. As the NVA advanced up the slope of the hill, Robertson had turned down his radio volume to avoid giving his position away. He turned it up ever so slightly and immediately heard the chatter of the rescue team on guard channel.

"Sandy Lead, Nail 33."

"Nail 33, give me a five second hold on your radio."

Robertson complied by holding the transmit button.

"Nail 33, got a fix. Stay off the radio until you hear us overhead. We're about ten minutes out."

Fifteen minutes later, the Sandys roared over and around the jungle surrounding the downed pilot, his parachute snagged in the trees and visible from the air.

"Sandy Lead, you have no idea how good you look from down here. I'm not hearing any gunfire, but I can't promise anything. Some Navy A-4s got the bastard who got me, so that may be it."

"Well, just to make sure, we're going to sprinkle a little popcorn around just to make sure. Keep your head down."

The A-4s dropped CBU 29 in the area around the pickup point, but at a safe distance from Robertson. The thousands of stainless ball bearings covering the ground neutralized most of what or who might have been hiding in the weeds, giving the Jolly Greens time to affect the rescue. Robertson wondered if this was a clue as to why the North Vietnamese officer decided to leave as quickly as he did. He may have had previous experience with A-1s and CBU.

"OK, Nail. Pop your smoke."

Robertson pulled the ring from the red smoke canister. Red smoke almost boiled out immediately; and he tossed the canister 20 feet away down wind.

As soon as he saw the first wisp of smoke, Sandy Lead cleared the lead Jolly Green rescue chopper to Robertson's position. Within minutes, Nail 33, face smeared with dirt and flight suit soaked with sweat, was surrounded by medics in the helicopter who gave him water and conducted a quick physical. In 45 minutes, he was met at the NKP flight line by a huge contingent from the base, especially Ted Thatcher, his squadron mate from the Academy.

At these events, which occurred once or more a week at NKP, the honoree, regardless of the unit he was assigned to or the airplane he flew, would be sprayed with champagne and embraced by those who rescued him along with his brothers who were not in the air. Later, Robertson got totally plastered at the Nail Hole, nearly squeezed the breath out of the Sandy and Jolly Green crews again and ended the evening by throwing up on the Nail Hole lawn. Just another day in the life of the Nails.

17

A Visit from Group Headquarters

Roger Brown awoke at 0500 for a 0600 takeoff. The weather was good, and early morning air was refreshing, although it wouldn't last much longer, the tropics being the tropics after all. Brown was fragged to fly with a staff member from Bien Hoa, a Captain Powell. He hadn't been told what the purpose of the flight was, but assumed it was some sort of information gathering exercise to pump up a resumé. After a few boiled eggs and some coffee at the Nail Hole, he caught the TUOC trolley to the flight line. As he walked into the briefing room, he met the visiting captain.

"Hi. I'm Roger Brown. Nail 73. Welcome to NKP."

"Glad to meet you Roger. Art Powell. I hope you don't mind taking a staff weenie along for a ride."

"Not at all. My pleasure. Where you from?" Roger was being extra nice. He was characteristically a little sarcastic. Being nice was strictly an act.

"Buffalo, originally. No comments please."

"Why, what a strange thing to say?" Roger was smiling. "Where'd you go to pilot training?"

"Laredo. How about you?"

"Moody. Valdosta, Georgia. You've heard of it, I'm sure. Clouds, rain, real instrument flying, and stuff like that."

"Okay. Rub it in."

Texas and Arizona flight schools were well known for lack of real weather to practice instrument flying. The standard joke was that every time a cloud appeared there were a few mid-air collisions because every pilot wanted some real weather time. The staff officer seemed pleasant enough and after the briefing they suited up and headed for the flight line.

After a 30-minute flight, and some personal comments about where they went to school and previous assignments, they leveled at 6,500 feet and Brown started jinking the O-2 and glassing the trail below.

Captain Powell keyed his microphone. "How about letting me show you a few of the tricks we use down south?"

Roger removed his hands from the yoke, holding them momentarily in the air to confirm he was no longer flying. Powell cranked in some right rudder trim and negated the trim by over-correcting with left aileron. The O-2 was flying wings level but slightly skewed, with the nose pointing a few degrees right of its actual flight pattern.

"This is a way to give the impression the airplane is flying in one direction when its actual flight pattern is a few degrees left of the actual line of the fuselage."

The staff officer was smiling, obviously pleased with his trick, which may have worked at low altitudes where gunners might have been somewhat misled, but at a mile high, the orientation of the fuselage was not evident to ground gunners. The flight pattern was evident not from the direction the plane was pointing, but from the simple observation of a spec moving through the sky. Within a few minutes, something was making noise as it passed by the open window of the O-2. It was the sound like sheets ripping, which, in the absence of any laundry at 5,000 feet above the ground, was a clue anti-aircraft shells were passing close by the open window and probably all around the O-2.

Small arms fire, which is what the staff officer was used to, was not a factor on the trail. Large anti-aircraft shells took several seconds to reach the desired altitude and were fired ahead of an airplane's course, not at the airplane itself and certainly not the way the nose was pointing. Brown assumed control rather abruptly and began jinking aggressively toward the nearest tree line. The staff officer, turning a little pale, didn't object and observed passively as Brown assumed control. No one spoke.

After Brown re-trimmed the O-2, the radio crackled.

"Nail 73, Hillsborough."

"Hillsborough, Nail 73."

"Nail 73, your fragged flight of two F-4s with Papa Whiskeys is inbound to you now."

Papa Whiskey was a code name for Paveways, 500-pound Mark 82s with laser homing bombs controlled by the F-4 crew and used for precision airstrikes on targets that required precision within a meter or two. They were often used on cave entrances where a hit a few meters to one side with conventional bomb drops might not damage the cave at all. But the primary targets this day were guns. Dropping bombs on an anti-aircraft gun emplacement was near suicide anyway if the gun was active, but Paveways allowed one F-4 at a higher altitude to 'light' the target with a laser operated by the back-seat pilot. That F-4 did not drop the bomb. It could be circling a relatively safe distance away. The second aircraft, the one dropping the bomb, could be less accurate than normal. His job was to drop the bomb from a safer altitude, but within an envelope, and monitor it as it flew itself to the heat generated by the laser light from the first F-4. The bomb had a sensor located on its nose controlling small, movable fins on the nose of the bomb. The accuracy was incredible, a few feet at most from a few thousand feet away.

"Cisco, Nail 73. Target is a gun emplacement near the base of a karst formation. I'm glassing it now, but the camouflage is excellent, so it may take two passes to knock the camouflage off it. If the first pass doesn't kill it, you'll need a second, but the blast should at least disable the crew. Your second pass should be on a clearly visible target. I will mark the target and pull off north. You need to come in from the east and break south. We'll see what happens before the second round. But let's not play all our cards yet."

"Roger that Nail. Waiting for the smoke."

Brown rolled in and fired a Willy Pete. The rocket hit and the smoke grew into the normal white mushroom shape.

"Cisco, the gun is about five meters left of the smoke and hidden behind a small bush. You're cleared in hot."

The F-4 making the drop rolled in and dropped. The bomb hurtled earthward and impacted exactly where it was supposed to. The gun was obliterated and a large crater marked its grave. Brown flew over the hole at 5,000 feet to confirm the kill. As he did, two additional anti-aircraft guns suddenly appeared from the base of the karst, but 50 meters farther to the left side, and began bracketing his O-2 with ribbons of scarlet tracers. The guns were clearly visible now but hadn't been seen before. That's when the light came on for Brown. They had emerged from the left of the cratered area from a cave where they hid during the day, a very common situation on the trail. Anti-aircraft guns were frequently moved, and wheeled carriages were standard on artillery pieces the world over.

Brown's passenger from Group Headquarters screamed at Brown to get the hell out of there. Brown was already in a 90-degree bank left pulling 4Gs and ignored his distraught expert. He radioed the F-4s once again:

"Cisco Flight, there are two additional guns about 50 meters west of the destroyed gun. They were in caves and wheeled out. They're firing, so be careful. You won't need a mark because they're not camouflaged." For no apparent reason, Brown started humming

"As the caissons go rolling along." Brown's passenger stopped screaming and appeared catatonic.

The F-4 Phantoms responded immediately and in two passes destroyed both the second and third anti-aircraft guns. The first gun was firing as it was hit; the second gun's crew was apparently killed by the blast on the first gun and their gun was then destroyed with another Paveway without any further resistance. The Phantoms emerged unscathed, a miracle considering the wall of lead they flew through. As Brown slipped back to the west over the mountainous karst formation, he gave the F-4s their BDA. "Cisco Flight, you destroyed three 37mm guns despite intense anti-aircraft fire. All gun crews killed. I salute you brave sirs. Great performance."

Cisco Lead came on the radio in response. "Nail, I return your compliment with the classic Ho Chi Minh Trail cheer. 'You Nails is shit hot.'"

"Well thank you sir. I hope we meet again under more liquid circumstances."

Lead double clicked his mic, and the Phantoms were soon a faint smoke trail in the azure blue skies over Laos.

Brown spent the next hour and a half reconnoitering the karst ridges on the trail, always jinking, always looking behind as well as ahead and above the aircraft and below it. After making a few notes about other potential targets, he called Hillsborough and told the operator he was RTB. Brown's passenger, clearly shaken, didn't speak for a while. After they were safely over the mountains heading west, he managed a weak, "Good work."

Brown nodded and added a little right rudder and left aileron to make him feel at home. Arriving at the Nail Hole just in time for Happy Hour, Brown found the party in high gear. Killing anti-aircraft guns with Funny Bombs was the equivalent kicking the winning field goal at a high school homecoming football game. The absence of a special thank you from the homecoming queen was replaced by free drinks all night from his fellow Nails, many of whom faced those very guns on previous missions. Of course, it wasn't a perfect substitute, but it would have to do—until his year in Hell was over.

Mark Tinga was the first Nail to greet Roger that evening at the Nail Hole. Roger related the story of the 'trick maneuver' of the staff officer to him and to some of the other Nails nearby and everyone got a good laugh. Mark put his arm around Roger. "Roger, not many guys have the oranges to do what you did. By the way, you're not trying to break my gun kill record, are you?"

"Mark, you're so far ahead that no one could stop you. There aren't enough Willy Petes left in Viet Nam to mark that many targets."

"You are just too kind," Mark laughed. "But what are you doing insulting a staff officer from Headquarters? You're going to give Nails a bad reputation."

"Mark, there is an old saying I once heard from my grandfather: 'Never spit in another man's face unless his moustache is on fire.' It was and I did." The laughter from the nearby Nails was both predictable and loud.

The Nail Hole party that night went on as usual, but the fun was coming close to an end.

18

Night Flying the Hard Way

Bad Sam was hung over. It was almost 1600, and all he could remember was killing 27 trucks the night before with Big Jim. Big Jim was the major nicknamed 'Gorilla' who loved playing bumper cars with other inebriated Nails using seat cushions from the sofa when he'd had a snoot full. But when Sam checked the flying schedule this evening, his hangover pain increased even more. He was scheduled for another night mission, but this time with the navigator no pilot wanted to fly with, Major Stanley Kratz.

Major Kratz had the lowest truck count of any navigator in the squadron. He was a slight, balding man with stooped shoulders, not at all the picture of an Air Force warrior. In the Nail Hole, he was the wet blanket of the party, always complaining about something, never boisterous, and never happy about anything. Navigators, as a rule, liked the pilots they flew with, and took great pride in BDA, which for them was primarily truck kills and guns since there wasn't much else to see at night. Extra points were awarded for tanks, fuel trucks, and anti-aircraft gun emplacements, double that for hitting a gun in the act of firing. But Kratz never seemed to find anything to kill. The pilots that were unfortunate enough to get him on a mission would spend hours flying around in circles, following his hand signals, but never getting a drop signal, the left thumb down motion by the navigator whose eyes were glued to the starlight scope in the right hand. The point system for nighttime kills was rather crude, and the actual point total seemed to get skewed in direct proportion to alcohol consumption, the lateness of the hour, and the phase of the moon. But it served a purpose: competition always increased effort and improved results, in life and in war. The world's sports industry was based on the same concept.

Pairing Kratz with Sam, who had one of the highest hypothetical average point counts in the squadron, was either someone's idea of a joke, or the Squadron Commander's idea of improving total kills by plugging holes in the offensive line. It was an admirable management tactic, but Sam didn't give a crap about management goals. He would have killed trucks if no one was even keeping score. Nevertheless, it was what it was.

Kratz didn't like the war and he let it be known. He didn't fulfill his obligations as a crew member for reasons of conscience but because of spinelessness. Every time he flew, he was given an opportunity to save American soldiers fighting in South Viet Nam. That's why Nails fought. Instead, he skirted the edges of the trail where the gunfire was sporadic and the probability of finding targets was slim.

None of the pilots and navigators liked the war. They knew it was not only a hopeless cause, but of questionable justification. Any Nail who ever stepped into the cockpit knew he might not come back. But they were Air Force officers, and they understood clearly the oath they swore to serve their nation. The Nails with the highest BDA were often those who gravitated to the areas with the most gunfire because they knew the trucks were there. Stan Barwick, the pilot who often thought about becoming a Buddhist Monk, opened the door to the Nail Hole. Unlike Sam, who was looking for a light breakfast after a late-night flight and a late awakening, Stan was looking for an early lunch before taking off on an afternoon trail mission. The two began eating peanuts and cracking boiled eggs.

"How'd you do last night?" Barwick asked Sam.

"Twenty-seven. Three convoys coming out of the mountains east of Tchepone. How about you?"

"Eighteen trucks and two tanks. And I was on the last flight of the day schedule. I found them right at sunset. Have you noticed the increase in truck traffic over the last several months?"

Barwick poured each of them a cup of coffee from the pot Sam had started when he entered the Nail Hole earlier. Sam took a light sip of the hot black coffee. "Hell yes. We are in for something big, and it won't be long. There's no way we can continue with the troop withdrawals in the South and the increase in truck traffic from the North. We're on some sort of collision course, and it won't be long in coming. I've only got two months left on my tour, so I won't be here for the end, and I'm glad. It ain't going to be pretty."

"What's crystal ball say?" Sam spoke while still trying to get the little pieces of eggshell off his egg. His fingers were shaking so badly from his bender the night before he was having trouble, so Barwick gave him a peeled egg and took Sam's half-peeled egg.

"Kind of obvious," Barwick answered. "The acceleration in traffic and the increase in gunfire is getting to the point where we'd be idiots to think SAMs aren't far behind. I don't know about you, but I see the curtain starting to come down."

"Well, let's make sure it doesn't hit us on the head on the way." Sam washed down the egg with a swig of coffee, the cup trembling in his hand.

"Have you ever figured out what in the hell we're doing here?" Stan was being serious, not caustic. And it was a question Nails asked each other frequently.

Sam was not an academic by any stretch, but he was a lot smarter than many gave him credit for. "I think a few politicians think Viet Nam, like WWII, was a fight between good and evil. Kennedy, Johnson, and finally Nixon wanted to be like Eisenhower, a real

164

hero who turned out to be a great president. We could call it the Savior Complex. But Viet Nam is not Japan or Europe, and Ho Chi Minh is not Hitler. According to Thatcher, Ho Chi Minh was our ally in WWII. He says a lot of the war is about rice. North Viet Nam doesn't grow it very well."

Barwick washed down the last part of his egg and then answered. "Well, I didn't know that, but I don't disagree. I was a music major, so I'm not much on world history, but I have never figured out why the United States government thinks this place is worth thousands of American lives, not to mention the thousands more wounded. It's one thing to help someone who has been invaded by another country, but in this case it's the Vietnamese who were invaded, first by France and now by us."

Sam pushed his bar stool back and got up. "The only problem I see is that you and I aren't in charge. Well, thanks for helping an old man with his boiled eggs. You flyin' again today?"

Barwick swallowed his last bite and then answered, "Yep! And then I'm headed for Bangkok for three days after I land."

"Well, have a good time. See you when you get back."

"How about you, Sam?"

"Drew Kratz for tonight's mission." Sam's disgust was not hidden.

"Well, good luck. I've never killed a truck with him."

Sam smirked. "Well, tonight he's going to kill some trucks. I've got a plan."

* * *

Sam went back to his room, got a good day's sleep, and later that evening met Major Kratz at the TUOC briefing room. Kratz was a slightly built man with thinning gray hair and a permanent look of suspicion or perhaps distrust. His eyes never seemed to stay focused on one thing very long—they darted around like ping pong balls on a table. When Shakespeare wrote, "Cowards die many times before their deaths; the valiant never taste of death but once," he must have known a Stanley Kratz. Sam was known to be slightly less poetic: he suggested Kratz just didn't have the oranges for combat. After the standard briefing, he and Kratz walked out to their black O-2 and met the crew chief. After a standard preflight, they strapped on their parachutes as the sun was going down on a beautiful, clear evening at NKP. They didn't speak more than a few words through the briefing which was fine as far as Sam was concerned. He started the engines and after taxiing and taking off, he spoke to Major Kratz over the intercom.

"Well, Stanley, what say we set some records tonight?" Sam was grinning his famous Bad Sam grin, a combination of mischievousness and sarcasm.

Kratz didn't say anything, but looked over at Sam from the right seat, expressionless.

Within 30 minutes, darkness set in; Kratz took the starlight scope out of the bag and started warming it up, looking out of the open window on his side of the plane. He scanned the terrain below and motioned for a right turn to Sam, using his left hand. Sam complied, and rolled out when Kratz held his hand up level. The twists and turns continued for over 20 minutes with no indication from Kratz he saw anything. Sam slowly reached up to the armament panel and flipped the outboard drop switch on the left side of the O-2. He then hit a button on the yoke which released a parachute flare that Kratz would not see from the right seat until it ignited, after about 15 seconds later. Parachute flares came in an aluminum box about three feet long and five inches square. Because they were not aerodynamic, they tumbled as soon as they were dropped. A parachute popped out after a few seconds, a bright white flare then ignited below the chute, and the ground 5,000 feet below was illuminated well enough to see with the naked eye. Parachute flares were optional, depending on pilot preference. The normal night marking devices were red ground flares. Sam ordered parachute flares loaded on his O-2 for good reason. With them, the pilot and the navigator could see the trucks below, something not possible with red ground flares. There was one drawback: the gunners below knew someone was trying to kill their trucks. As usual, they opened up with a barrage of anti-aircraft fire aimed in all directions since they couldn't see who dropped the flares. The range of the shells was over two miles.

Kratz reacted with shock. "What in the hell did you do? I didn't call for a flare drop."

Sam rolled the O-2 up 60 degrees on the right wing and looked out of the window on Kratz's side of the airplane. It was apparent they were over jungle covering rugged mountains, at least a half mile from the trail.

Sam triggered his intercom. "Tell you what Stanley, since there aren't any roads down there, there won't be any trucks. Let's see if we can find some guns."

He turned on the navigation lights, a bright red rotating beacon on the tail, a red light on the left-wing tip and a green light on the right. The gunners cut loose. Tracers burned a fiery red path toward the airplane from the east, from the trail. Sam avoided them easily since they were relatively far away. But it had the desired effect. Kratz screamed so loud he didn't even need the intercom to be heard.

"What in the hell are you doing. Are you crazy? Turn the lights out!"

"Tell you what, you find me a truck, and I'll turn the lights out."

"There aren't any trucks here!" shouted Kratz.

"Then take me to where they are." Sam's voice was completely calm.

"Okay! Turn east!" His voice was raspy, desperate.

Sam turned east. He left the lights on and continued to dodge the flak. Sam was perhaps the most experienced pilot in the squadron. Like any experienced Nail, he dodged flak not by dramatic maneuvers, but by slight changes in direction, enough to make the red balls move left or right on the windscreen. If they were moving, they could not be a collision course.

The A-1s assigned to them for the evening checked in.

"Nail, Zorro 33 Flight, two A-1s with nape and four funnies apiece."

"Good evening Zorros. We're on the 105 at 60 off the NKP Tacan. Call when you have us in sight."

"Roger that. We're almost there. Hell, that's not you with the lights on is it?"

"Wanted to make sure you found us. You Zorros are not all that competent at navigation."

Kratz finally spoke over the intercom. "There are about 20 trucks under us. Drop a mark and please turn off the lights. Hold to the west."

Sam rolled the O-2 up on its left wing and looked down. The trucks were easily visible looking down through the trees because they were using headlights due to the lack of a moon. The trucks were moving, barely, because of the craters and mud holes in the road. Road crews were trying to push trucks stuck in mud and bridge the craters in front of the convoy. Sam, like the other Nails, never ceased to marvel at the ingenuity and persistence of the North Vietnamese. He turned off the navigation lights, but not the shielded red tail beacon only visible from above to the fighters. He then dropped two ground flares about five seconds apart when he was directly over them. The parachute flares behind them burned out.

Even with the navigation lights off, the flak continued to stream up from every direction although the tracers were becoming more random without the twinkling lights to guide them. Sam continued to keep his cool, not making any abrupt moves, even if the tracers were not moving but appearing as red balls growing bigger as they got closer. When the trajectory looked too close for comfort, Sam banked slightly a few degrees one way or the other until the red balls appeared to move left or right. Then he slowly rolled wings level and watched them go by. The closer ones made the characteristic sound of sheets ripping as they went by, audible even over the airplane engine noise. His coolness under fire was driving Major Kratz to higher and higher levels of exasperation mixed with fear and nausea. Reacting calmly to anti-aircraft fire was not only Bad Sam's standard flak evasion procedure, as well as the more experienced Nails, but it gave him great satisfaction because it was driving Kratz insane.

"Nail, Zorro 33 and 34 are overhead. We have the marks and your beacon to the west of them."

"Well, shit hot!" Sam radioed back. "Let the party begin. The trucks are moving very slowly southeast. They are just inside the western-most mark. Have at them. Your first nape drop should light them up well enough to give your succeeding drops better visibility. We will be well west at 6,500 feet."

Zorro lead responded. "Roger that. Two, wait for my drop and then mix up the headings. I'll pull off north and orbit at 7,500 to see what we can see."

"Zorro 2, Roger that."

Zorro lead hit just inside the western-most mark and the napalm ran along the ground like a surging river for almost 200 feet. It consumed four trucks instantly. As they burned, at least two exploded, meaning they were carrying ammunition to the war in South Viet Nam.

Maybe it saved a few of the grunts in the South, thought Sam.

Thank God, they're distracted from me, thought Major Kratz. Seconds later a string of 15 or more red tracers, obviously from a 23mm, came up from behind and under the nose of the O-2, climbing a few thousand feet higher before culminating in an orgasm of sparkling white flashes, as the rounds detonated at the end of their predetermined existence. It ruined the few seconds of peace the major was enjoying; he wished he was a praying man, but he wasn't. He didn't know how. The old saying about there being no atheists in foxholes didn't apply to Kratz.

The evening progressed in like fashion for another 20 minutes. The A-1 pilots mixed up their drop headings and chatted between themselves as the Nails witnessed the action from a semi-safe distance from the strike. Most AAA rounds fired in the direction of the O-2 were random shots from the gunners below who were guessing where to shoot except when the A-1s reached the low points in their passes. Then, the North Vietnamese got a brief glimpse of their adversary's aircraft even though they were flying black airplanes. The A-1s would be lit up by the raging orange flames of the jellied gasoline as they dropped. The gunners below would attempt to swivel around and get a shot. It was a cat and mouse game, but it was a game in which either the cat or the mouse might be the victim.

The strike continued for another 20 minutes; as the Zorros made their last drop, Sam counted 23 trucks burning or destroyed, their carcasses black smudges of what they once were.

"Nail, Zorro flight is Winchester, so we're going to head back. See you at the Nail Hole. Drinks are on us." Winchester was slang for out of ordnance.

Bad Sam keyed his mic, "Zorro, you guys are shit hot, and I mean that in all sincerity. Great work, and it'll be a cold day in hell before you buy a drink in the Nail Hole. I'm going to try my best not to step on your fingers at the party."

The Zorros didn't respond. Sam assumed it was because they were probably peeing in their flight suits, both from laughing so hard and from pulling all those Gs for almost half an hour.

Years later, when Sam's eyes were so dim he couldn't pass a driver's test, he would remember this mission and many others like it. And he would wonder, as most Viet Nam veterans would, what the hell it was all about and what he had accomplished to make the world a better place.

19

Heavy Hook

At 0500, Ted Thatcher and Lt. Steve Johns, the carnation-growing navigator, entered the Nail Hole, sweaty after a night mission which ended two hours before sunrise. It was still dark, and the sun wouldn't come up for another hour. Captain Bill Stancil, Nail 23, Thatcher's pilot training classmate, came in the door right behind them, all of them looking for the same thing, boiled eggs for breakfast. Thatcher started the coffee pot, not because he thought coffee would help him sleep better, but because there was nothing else suitable for a breakfast beverage. They all sat down at the bar and started cracking eggs, waiting for the coffee.

"So, how did you do last night?" asked Bill Stancil.

"Eighteen ... half carrying ammunition."

"Damn!" Stancil shook his head and took his first sip of the coffee.

"Have you or your Green Beret friends in Heavy Hook seen an increase in truck counts?" Thatcher wasn't asking to be polite. He knew his pilot training classmate was way ahead of the standard Intel reports because the Green Berets were feeding information hourly. The Nails flying with them, such as Bill Stancil, knew what was happening on the trail hours before the rest of the Nails heard it at their own pre-takeoff briefings.

"Hell yes. To be honest, scheduling airstrikes on everything we find is getting to be problematic. They move this stuff around so fast our Intel is often worthless after half a day. I've been here six months and I can see a big increase in NVA activity. B-52 strikes based on our Intel are getting to be less and less effective. The 12 or more hours it takes to get a B-52 strike in the pipeline means a lot of our stuff is hitting nothing but dirt. The road cuts made by the B-52s are still helpful, but the NVA logistics are getting better every day."

"Are the Heavy Hook guys seeing any increase in the threat to their ground operations?"

Bill Stancil didn't hesitate. "Absolutely. They're having to run more and observe less. There was a time when they could camp out for a week or more. Now they're lucky to get a few days before the shit hits the fan."

"Well, watch your six. I'm going to hit the hay. What time are we having dinner tonight?"

"I land at about 1400, so any time after that is fine."

"Alright. I'll meet you back here about 1600."

Bill Stancil, Nail 23, took off one hour before sunrise; this allowed him to be in place to monitor Trail Watch Team Beethoven as first light appeared. Sgt. Mrozek, the Green Beret 'back seater' in the OV-10 was a veteran of over 20 Trail Watch missions and was paired to fly with Stancil, still a relative newcomer to Heavy Hook. The two had quickly become a well-oiled team, having at least two close calls necessitating more than half a dozen airstrikes in support of emergency exfils. An exfil on the Ho Chi Minh Trail was the extraction of a Trail Watch team and was rarely done neatly and cleanly, according to the pre-arranged schedule, because the teams were operating in a very fluid environment. The NVA patrols were constantly looking for the teams, which they knew were always on the trail somewhere.

Today's mission was to be a standard check in to ensure Beethoven was secure after a night of trail observation. Green Berets had a long and distinguished history of furnishing much of the Intel concerning truck traffic and other activities on the part of the NVA. Their efforts were among the riskiest of all Viet Nam operations. Once inserted on or near the trail by Jolly Green crews, they were on their own. If discovered, they called for an exfil, an emergency rescue, while running like hell to a location safe enough for a Jolly Green pickup. The Nails flying in support of this mission could not employ airstrikes in support of the teams at night. So, the Nails operated mainly from first light to an hour after sunset although they could serve as communication facilitators 24 hours a day in the event of an emergency.

There were many heroic stories told of the Trail Watch Team exploits and some were even funny. One was about an indigenous team member who was a Montagnard, an important part of the team because of their jungle survival abilities. 'Yards', as they were affectionately known, were not Vietnamese: they were a mountain people descended from, but no longer similar, to Chinese. This particular Yard left the team's carefully constructed hiding place in the middle of the night to relieve himself. Right in the middle of doing so, he was tapped on the shoulder by a North Vietnamese soldier who told him it was his turn to take guard duty. Needless to say, the team quickly and quietly exited the area. Today, though, the Heavy Hook team didn't suspect anything out of the ordinary.

Team Beethoven had been left in a secure location perched on a piece of karst that would have required a vertical attack of over 100 feet of very rough rock. There was no significant hostile activity near their location in the last two days and their observations on the truck traffic and other activity was valuable. Several airstrikes based on their Intel were conducted. Secondary explosions occurred, meaning munition shipments were part of the truck traffic. A dozen more trucks carrying rice, and seven trucks towing artillery pieces were all destroyed as well. All of these trucks were camouflaged and parked in a truck park just off the trail. An airborne FAC would never have found them.

Airborne FACs could cover a lot of territory, but the NVA were quite adept at transmitting aircraft positions to each other via radio. What was on a dirt road one minute could easily be covered with camo or hidden under trees in the next. Once a FAC left a given area, information was transmitted to the other North Vietnamese and the trucks in the now-safe area started running again. The ground watch teams were invaluable in observing and reporting trail activity when the noise of airplanes was absent and the NVA activity was done in the open.

As Nail 23 reached an altitude high enough to allow radio reception, Sgt. Mrozek made a call to Beethoven and was immediately informed of a serious problem. The team, despite its seemingly secure location, was discovered. As was standard protocol, they headed for high ground to pre-established pickup points. The team booby trapped whatever supplies they didn't absolutely need with grenades and high-tailed it out of their location. By the time Nail 23 reached the original location, the team was over a mile away on another piece of high ground, spread out like a covey of quail in a circle, weapons pointing outward. In the jungle, locating the team from the air with precision was not easy, so Stancil ordered fighter support and waited without getting too close and giving away their position. His request to Hillsborough was for some A-1s from NKP, but he was able to snag some A-7s from a carrier, diverted to him by Hillsborough, the airborne command post.

The four A-7s, Bobbin Flight, checked in so Stancil dropped down to a few hundred feet, located the team visually, and began directing the attack. The Heavy Hook team suggested some coordinates based on what they were hearing. The NVA used whistles to direct their troops. Based on the noise, Beethoven's team leader called for a drop around 200 meters east of their position. Stancil made a low pass and spotted the exact location of the enemy soldiers. They made the mistake of firing, and the flashes gave them away.

He marked the target with a Willy Pete. He then asked each of the A-7s to drop two of their 12 Mark 82s on the first pass. As usual, they were right on target. He continued the process until the ground team heard no more gunfire. By then, the A-7s were out of ordnance and returned to their ship.

The Jolly Green Giant flight, consisting of two CH-53 helicopters, Jolly Green 1 and 2, and four A-1s, 'Sandy Flight', checked in five minutes out. Bill Stancil gave them the standard briefing on target elevation, the headcount of Green Berets on the ground, and the observed gunfire. The Sandy flight leader, Captain Jim 'Jimbo' Powell, assumed the role of on-site commander and went to work. He dropped down to tree top level and scoured the ground below his A-1, looking for any sign of enemy activity while the other members of his flight observed from above, also looking for any sign of hostile action. Seeing and hearing nothing, he led his flight in a coordinated drop of CBU 29, the cluster bombs that shot stainless steel pellets over a football-field sized area. The Green Berets were also a player in this phase of the exfil since they were the only ones who could hear enemy gunfire. After multiple low level CBU drops and passes all around the area with no sign of hostile activity, they reported no noise. Nail 23 and Sandy 1 both agreed the risk was minimal and Stancil advised Jolly Green 1 the area appeared safe.

Jolly Green 1 began the let down from its secure holding area, lowering cables with Jungle Penetrators to the Beethoven Team. Just as the cables were within reach of the ground watch team, a rocket-propelled grenade (RPG), fired from somewhere on the opposite side of the Ho Chi Minh Trail from the Heavy Hook Team, hit the Jolly Green in the tail rotor, rendering the Jolly Green completely uncontrollable. The fiery, tragic crash of the helicopter took only seconds, and the fireball that ensued left no doubt the crew of Jolly Green 1 were killed instantly.

It would be impossible to describe the sick feeling of both the Trail Watch Team members still on the ground and the aircrew members who witnessed the tragedy. Sandy Lead was on the radio instantly telling Jolly Green 2 to move to even safer territory. There was no one to blame. This was, unfortunately, not uncommon, part of the 'fog of battle'. The fact this wasn't the work of an anti-aircraft gun, but a shoulder-fired RPG, made the situation even more tragic. An anti-aircraft gun was much easier to locate than a camouflaged soldier with a camouflaged tube only five feet long. The enemy soldier was certainly a pro, knowing how to remain hidden and safe during the sweeps from Stancil, the attacks from the A-7s, and the CBU drops from the Sandys.

"Chicago, Sandy 1, where did that come from?"

"It came from the bend in the road east of us. It was an RPG."

"Sandy Lead, Nail 23. I was overhead watching. I know about where it came from."

"Mark it, Nail. Sandys follow me to the south and watch for the Nail's smoke. Let's obliterate that son of a bitch. Use your Mark 82s."

The Sandys pulled off to the east. Bill Stancil rolled in and fired a single Willy Pete. It impacted 300 meters away from the team in a brushy area on the other side of the trail. There was no reaction from the ground, probably because the soldier or soldiers were trying hard to be invisible.

"Hit my smoke," radioed Nail 23.

"Sandy Lead is in hot."

"Two's in."

"Three's in."

"Four's in."

The four A-1s created a huge crater in the landscape. The marked target was obliterated. The area around the white smoke became instantly denuded of vegetation for over 300 meters. It left little doubt that whoever was there was now dead.

"Sandy, Nail 23. That asshole is now in hell."

"Roger that. Sandys let's set up a daisy chain and kill every monkey within 500 meters of the team. Follow my lead. Let's use our Mini guns."

The SUU-11 minigun came with 1,500 rounds of ammunition and A-1 pilots could spray bullets effectively using the rudder pedals to push the nose of the A-1 left and right. As an anti-personnel weapon, it was ideal because the guns spread so many lethal projectiles so quickly and thoroughly. The A-1s spent five more minutes flying in a circle 25 meters from the team to over 300 meters out.

Sandy Lead called for the second pickup attempt and Jolly Green 2 didn't hesitate. He flew aggressively down to the team and the hoist pulled up all team members in record time. As the chopper pulled up and away, the Sandys followed in close formation. In a matter of a few minutes, they were out of gun range and heading for NKP.

In an act few non-combatants could ever imagine, the crews of both the Jolly Greens flew into a hostile area to rescue American soldiers, knowing there was a probability of enemy fire during a maneuver requiring them to hover in one position. They didn't hesitate. If that realization was not enough to demonstrate bravery on the very highest scale, the second Jolly Green crew had watched their fellow squadron mates and personal friends die a horrible death. Did they hesitate? Hell no! It was no wonder the Jolly Green crews were the most highly decorated airmen in Southeast Asia.

Nail 23, Bill Stancil, and his Green Beret observer, Sgt Luke Mrozek, decided to spend a few more minutes over the target area in case the fog of battle resulted in someone else being left behind, either from the crash of Jolly Green 1 or the Heavy Hook team. They decided a single low-altitude, high-speed pass would be the safest way to accomplish this. Stancil rolled in from the trail side of the exfil site and leveled off 100 feet above the ground doing 200 knots.

As they flew abeam the site, the front cockpit of the OV-10 disappeared. There was no explosion. It just disappeared. The top two-thirds of the front cockpit of the OV-10 was Plexiglas. Whatever was fired at the OV-10 didn't even detonate, although it obliterated the front canopy, killing Bill Stancil. Sgt. Mrozek, in the back seat, who was untouched, didn't have time to think. He ejected immediately. His chute deployed perfectly, and he was on the ground in less than a minute. He detached from his chute and headed for high ground. As soon as his chute deployed, the automatic beeper told the departing rescue team yet another rescue was needed. It was the decision of the departing team leader to continue back to NKP with the rescued Beethoven Team. Low fuel and depleted ammunition would put a second rescue with Beethoven team aboard at unnecessary risk. After a grueling evasion up the side of the karst mountain where the Beethoven team was rescued, Sgt. Mrozek was successfully rescued an hour later by yet another Jolly Green team.

NKP was a somber place that afternoon and evening. Ted Thatcher was sitting on the sofa in the Nail Hole, waiting for his pilot training classmate and close friend, when the Squadron Commander, Lt. Col. Melendez, walked in with the news about Captain Bill Stancil. The Nails were stunned, no one more than Ted Thatcher. Their faces said more than they could have with words. Later, they all began sharing memories. Someone chalked in a quatrain from the *Rubáiyát* on the blackboard behind the bar:

And when Thyself with shining Foot shall pass
Among the Guests Star-scatter'd on the Grass,
And in thy joyous Errand reach the Spot
Where I made one-turn down an empty glass!

No one ever confessed to writing it there, but everyone agreed it was a fitting tribute to the NKP sacrifices made that day, especially by their comrade, Captain Bill Stancil, Nail 23.

20

Turkey Shoot

Nail 77, First Lieutenant Tom Stevens, and his navigator, Nail 218, Major Art Kazinski, or 'Major K' to his friends, launched their O-2 at sunset. They were fragged to Sector II, which stretched from the North Vietnamese border at the legendary Mu Gia Pass almost to Ban Karai Pass, ten miles south. Kazinski was an experienced strike control navigator and was paired with the most inexperienced pilot in the squadron for obvious reasons. First lieutenants were by definition inexperienced. Pilot training took a year, and a second lieutenant became a first lieutenant after only 18 months in the Air Force. That meant a first lieutenant couldn't have very much flight time. The 23rd Tactical Air Support Squadron did have three, but one of those was shot down trying to kill a truck being used as a decoy.

There was one advantage of being a first lieutenant in the 23rd TASS: one hell of a resume if he survived. This meant better than average future assignments. Tom Stevens was a volunteer, an indication of his character and a harbinger of some good assignments in the future. His preference, like all Air Force pilots, was to be in fighters, but his class of 25 got only one F-100 and four F-4 backseat slots. He took a KC-135 co-pilot slot and volunteered for fighters after arriving at his first base in Mississippi.

Despite his football-hero background, he was not boisterous or even socially extroverted, preferring to listen to the other Nails telling their war stories or off-color jokes. His experience in combat was typical of most Nails: nervous for the first couple of missions, and then more relaxed, but not complacent.

He and Major K would check in shortly with Moonbeam, the nighttime airborne command post orbiting somewhere. Nails spent hours talking to men they would never meet in person but whom they held in the highest regard. The Moonbeam crew, like the daytime crew of the airborne command post Hillsborough, controlled the flow of fighters to FACs, and responded to FAC requests for ordnance. Radar was useless for providing airplane separation in such a fluid environment. Sectors were mapped out based on prominent landmarks such as rivers or karst ridges to provide visual separation during the day. After a few daytime missions, FACs learned the boundaries of their playground and could operate in relative safety, even in night environments by using their TACAN navigational systems that provided direction and distance from the TACAN beacons, especially the one at NKP.

Because friendly forces, such as Heavy Hook (the Green Berets), might be snooping around on the ground, Moonbeam also provided battlefield control to what could be a disastrous misuse of firepower. B-52 strikes, a daily occurrence, also were factored into the equation. One of the daily Snoopy cartoons in the debriefing room showed an O-2 FAC looking down at a string of ongoing bomb blasts under him that could only be from a B-52 mission, saying, "What the hell, over?," or something a little stronger. Close calls were rare, however, and the Moonbeam and Hillsborough crews did a great job maintaining control in what could be a difficult environment. Keeping the participants in this drama aware of each other's situation was more an art form than a science, but by war's end, a reasonably efficient war-making machine was developed. It just wasn't large enough to match the huge number of trucks spilling into Laos from North Viet Nam.

Kazinski pulled the starlight scope out of its bag and began checking it out.

"Well, Tom, this looks like a good night for hunting. Clear skies, a little cooler than normal, which is always a blessing. Tell me a little about your family. I know you're from Georgia, and I know you played football in college."

"Well, Major K, I grew up on a farm. A few thousand acres. Cotton, soybeans, corn and tobacco. The usual stuff in the South. Went to Georgia Tech, married my high school sweetheart, pretty normal, I guess."

"How'd you get here? First lieutenants are kind of rare at NKP. As a rule, you leave pilot training and get a little experience under your belt before you're sent here."

"Just lucky, I guess." he chuckled.

"Well, let's hope some of that luck rubs off tonight. The sooner we win this war, the sooner we can go home."

Lt. Stevens laughed and then opened communication with the command-and-control system. "Moonbeam, Nail 77. Good evening." His nervousness disappeared as it did for most Nails once the action started. The air over the trail was always much cooler compared to the Laotian surface temperatures, but at night it could actually get chilly. The perspiration that normally accompanied daytime flights was non-existent, and the crews were always grateful.

"Good evening 77. Got some A-1s inbound for you in about five minutes. Zorro 33 and 34. Time to get to work."

"Roger that."

Major Kazinski warmed up his starlight scope and started searching the ground below. Without taking his eye off the scope, Kazinski, in the right seat, held up his left hand and tilted it right. Tom Stevens banked slowly in response, and when his navigator leveled his hand, the pilot leveled the wings. To key the mic would require the navigator to put the bulky starlight scope in his lap, an awkward and time-consuming exercise. In an age of computers and space travel, the Nails were reduced to simple hand signals to direct complex airstrikes on enemy trucks and guns.

Kazinski jerked his thumb downward and the Stevens dropped, or pickled, as the crews liked to say, a mark (a red ground flare) from under the right wing.

Only 23 more to go, Lt. Stevens noted mentally.

After a few seconds, Kazinski put the starlight scope in his lap and keyed his mic, "Perfect. Drop one more and do a 180 to the left. Let's hold west to give the A-1s the advantage of the mountains in case they have to punch."

The lieutenant dropped a second ground flare from under the left wing and initiated a turn to the west. An eastern holding pattern over the mountains of North Viet Nam would have been safer for the Nails since there were no anti-aircraft guns in the mountains, but the A-1s would be given a slight advantage on bailing out since they were closer to the impenetrable jungle on the North Viet Nam side of the trail. The Nails were orbiting higher than the A-1s would be at the low point of their bomb drop and should be able to maneuver away easier from the expected anti-aircraft fire. It normally started after the first bombs exploded and all hell would break loose.

To the uninitiated, it may sound like madness to deliberately fly into a sky filled with streaks of red death shooting up from the ground night after night, but it was either accept the reality or truly go mad. It was common to be the target of multiple guns firing from several different directions at the same time. That created some very exciting moments for the aircrews which required quick but correct action. Lt. Stevens acted appropriately on his first mission, confirming the direction of the red balls screaming toward him soon after the muzzle flashes alerted him to start looking. He had not pulled hard enough to hurt the O-2 and he chose the right direction to break.

The assigned A-1s checked in. "Nail 77, this is Zorro 33 and 34, CBU 29, napalm, and Funny Bombs. Lots of time."

Maj. K responded, "Zorro, we've already prepared a little present for you. A dozen or so presents under the palm trees. All between the marks. We'll be holding west. Hit the southern part of the string first. Come in from either the north or south but break west. That will put you over the mountains. Call in hot. Do you have the marks and our beacon?"

"Roger that Nail. FAC and marks in sight."

The young Nail pilot headed east and started to orbit. He was nervous but not as nervous as on his first mission. He had a few trucks under his belt. Tonight, the roads were dry, and the trucks were out in the open but not moving, not an uncommon situation. A mechanical breakdown of the lead truck or craters in the road caused by daylight airstrikes could be the reason. Road cuts, the unglamorous missions disliked by daytime FAC's, could often be productive. The young pilot, nervous at takeoff, was soon immersed in the mission and hoping for a yet another war story to tell his grandchildren one day when his hair was gray. Lt. Stevens started a shallow right turn away from the target in response to Maj. Kazinski's hand motion designed to give the A-1s more room to maneuver. The ground flares reached a brilliant red, similar to, but much larger than those truckers used on highways when they broke down in his native Georgia. The first A-1s drop of CBU 29 created the usual oval pattern: dozens of sparkles of light 100 meters long and 50 meters wide. But, they were centered slightly west of the trucks. Kazinski gave a correction to the wingman who had more luck, starting two of the trucks on fire with his first drop. Red streaks from 37mm guns had started in earnest as the first bombs exploded. Snaking up into the dark night, the red balls vainly sought the soft aluminum skin of the O-2 or the armor-plated underbelly of the A-1s making the drop. The A-1s began mixing up the attack directions, making the gunners unsure where in a 360-degree arc the planes would be coming from or going to next. The seven-round string of the 37mm anti-aircraft shells reached over 15,000 feet before the shells self-destructed in brilliant sparkles of light.

Kazinski triggered his intercom. "OK, Tom, quick lesson, just to refresh your memory. Those strings of seven tracers you see are 37mm shells. If the first one misses you, the following shells will probably miss too. The airbursts you see above us are the shells self-destructing, so they don't come back down and hit the assholes on the ground. A 37mm shell looks just like a bullet from a high-powered rifle, but the entire round, the casing and the warhead, is about 28 inches long. The warhead itself looks like any typical hunting bullet, but it's about ten inches long and filled with gunpowder. A fuse blows it up if it doesn't hit anything after so many seconds. One shell can take off the wing of this airplane.

"Thirty-sevens are the most common AAA you will experience out here. You've never seen this on your daytime checkout missions because the tracers don't show up during daylight. This is why you were taught in your daytime missions to look up from time to time. If you saw seven small black clouds, a 37mm had been hosing you down. Twenty of so airbursts and it's a 23mm. The guns are old, and they tend to spray the shells which make them more deadly than a 37mm. If all you see is one big black airburst, it's a radar-guided 57mm or 100mm. If one of those hits you, it won't take the wing off of the airplane, it will take the airplane off of the wing."

Lt. Stevens turned his head to the major and grinned at the joke, his face illuminated by the soft green light from the instrument panel. The obvious competence and calm demeanor of his much older companion instilled a sense of confidence in the young pilot. The jitters he experienced at the first sight of red balls screaming up toward his aircraft abated, but they hadn't—and never would—totally disappear. Like most Nails, once he engaged in an actual airstrike, his emotions became much more atavistic, and his performance became second nature, breaking right or left as the situation warranted. It was a transformation those who had never been in combat could not comprehend.

Major K interrupted his flak lesson to give the A-1s additional guidance. Their first drop hit the front truck in the column, which was headed south.

"Way to go Zorro 33. Zorro flight extend in a line north, fire at anything you see, and don't quit. We're well west holding at 6,500 feet." Kazinski motioned with his hand to the right and Stevens started a slow right turn.

Zorro flight leader responded, "Roger that Nail. Two, you heard the Nail. I'll follow you this time."

"Roger that. Zorro 34 is in hot from the south."

For the next ten minutes, the A-1s took turns dropping napalm, the flaming orange splashes of jellied gasoline setting off truck explosions, one after the other, punctuating the night's blackness. The fires gave off enough light to see the remaining trucks and the FACs did not need to intervene to give corrections; the A-1s talked to each other about the next drop each would make. The Nails held a ringside seat to a show few people ever saw, and they relished the moment. As the trucks started burning, they lit up the surrounding area. Trees, illuminated only from the sides, took on an eerie look; the shadows were four times longer than the trees were tall.

The A-1s methodically worked their way through the trucks trapped behind the convoy lead, always mixing up the attack headings to confuse the gunners. Through it all, the anti-aircraft fire never diminished. At least a dozen guns were within range of the A-1s and the O-2. Major Kazinski reminded his young pilot not to get caught up fixating on the A-1s, but to keep his head on a swivel.

Though holding off to the side in a rough figure eight pattern, they still could be hosed down from behind at any moment, even if the targets were the A-1s.

The Zorros worked over the trucks for the next 20 minutes, destroying the entire convoy with spectacular results. Fires and explosions punctuated the black night, and the gunfire even slacked off a little, probably due to ammunition depletion. Most of the gunfire was in response to bomb drops, and although the O-2 was orbiting a quarter mile to the west, a generous portion of the red balls also came in their direction. While they observed the airstrike, Major K schooled his young protégé on the proper way of avoiding flak.

"Remember, the basic technique is to not do anything if the red ball appears to be moving, even a little, because it's obvious the anti-aircraft round is not on a collision course. If it appears stationary, the rounds are on a collision course and a slight turn in either direction is all that's necessary to escape harm. Unless, of course, the round detonates near the aircraft. In that case, put your head between your legs and . . . well, you know the rest."

"I get it!" The young Nail was smiling.

Zorro lead came up on the radio. "Nail, we've got a great map of the guns, and since all of the trucks are on fire, what say we drop some funnies on the guns?"

"I say Hallelujah! This will sure please the daytime FACs headed this way tomorrow. We're way west, so use all the airspace you need."

"Roger that. Three-four, take the east side of the road. I'll take the west."

The Zorros made two passes each and destroyed four of the guns and noted secondary ammunition explosions as well, meaning they were hitting stockpiles of even more shells. The magnesium of the Funny Bombs continued boiling over in brilliant white clouds for five minutes or more, ensuring that what was left below would be nothing but a molten mass of metal. It would remain there forever, unrecognizable as a gun, and unusable for anything except as a paperweight for the gods of destruction. The aircrews were careful not to stare directly at the hellish scene to preserve their night vision.

Zorro Lead interrupted the Nail conversation. "Nail, that's all we've got. Thanks for serving up that soft ball."

"You're welcome Zorros. Drop in at the Nail Hole and we'll buy you a beer."

"See you there," radioed Zorro Lead.

Major K triggered the intercom, "Let's go home. There won't be any more trucks coming by here tonight. And we don't have any fighters to use anyway."

"Shit hot!" Tom Stevens responded, wheeling around to the west and heading home.

Major K packed up the starlight scope and the lieutenant now had a resumé. He would not be buying any drinks at the Nail Hole that night.

The Zorros spent over an hour killing guns and destroying trucks carrying ammunition and supplies bound for South Viet Nam. It took the Nails three hours to locate the trucks and direct the strike. Unfortunately, as they were destroying one convoy, dozens more were rolling uninhibited down the trail with ammunition to kill more Americans in South Viet Nam, assured of a safe trip, at least until they entered Sector III, the next sector to the south. After the war, intelligence officials would find, despite all the destruction wrought by the U.S. forces on the trail, the North Vietnamese could have suffered substantially more damage with no appreciable impact on their ultimate victory. The only possible path to victory would have been to block the trail on the ground. He was beginning to realize that his automotive manufacturing experience didn't work very well in a jungle war. Sadly, he didn't

189

act on that right away, and thousands more Americans would die before the truth was revealed.

As the Nails enjoyed the quiet flight home in the cool night air coming in from the open window on the right side, they looked down the trail to the south, toward Viet Nam. It was a busy night. Thirty miles south, over South Viet Nam, parachute flares were swinging and swaying through the inky blackness by the dozens, looking like a collection of surreal flowers. On a black night, both the flares and the tracers from the enemy guns were clearly visible. It was quite a show: red tracers from the anti-aircraft guns screaming upward, parachute flares dropping toward the earth, and bomb explosions punctuating the dark canvas below.

Major Kazinski finished his cigarette and motioned with his hand to the south. "Those flares you see are being dropped by Candlesticks. Those are the black C-123s you see parked on the tarmac back at our base. They light up the sky with dozens of flares when their navigators find trucks through their starlight scopes. Their scopes are much bigger than mine and they look out through doors in the airplanes while standing up. The A-1s follow along behind and above and are directed to the targets by the Candlestick navigators. Candlesticks can't operate up here where we are because the flak is too thick. They were pretty effective before we quit bombing the North and the guns doubled. You can see the tracers from the guns down there and it's obvious the guns are fewer and smaller."

"What's their altitude?" asked Lt. Stevens.

"A minimum of 10,000 feet, usually. The air is a little thin there but a 23mm anti-aircraft gun can't reach that high and a 37mm would have to be shooting straight up to hit anything. I don't see any Spectres tonight. They're C-130s with 40mm recoilless cannons which can directly attack the trucks from the side doors. They have a computer which flies the plane in a perfect 360-degree orbit. When they're operating, you'll see red tracers from the bad guys going up and red tracers from the gunships going down. It's never boring up here."

After landing, Major K and his young pilot/protégé checked their weapons and parachutes and headed for debriefing. The debriefer, Staff Sergeant Todd Brady, listened to the report given by the O-2 crew and was obviously impressed by their exploits. They left debriefing and caught the TUOC Trolley back to the Nail Hole. They debarked from the TUOC Trolley in front of the Nail Hole where the party was in high gear. The other Nails and a few A-1 pilots crowded around them to hear the latest war story. Major Kazinski stepped back and let his young lieutenant bask in the spotlight. Tom Stevens, although young, had enjoyed a fulfilling life. He was the son of a wealthy father, who owned a large farm, and a doting mother who, like most mothers of Viet Nam soldiers, was worried sick on a daily basis. Stevens somehow managed to escape the arrogance others might have assumed under similar circumstances. But up to this point, his success as a college athlete and the husband of the head cheerleader from his alma mater could not begin to touch the elation and attention he was receiving in the Nail Hole.

The evening passed quickly, with more missions reporting in, all successful. The Nail Hole would once again be a rollicking, testosterone-laden party of warriors, each with his tale to tell. Lt. Stevens had finally arrived with his own tale to tell, a member of the Band of Brothers, all wearing sweat-stained flight suits or camouflaged fatigues. Hands were seen in the air, weaving and rolling, describing aerial maneuvers an outsider would have thought strange if not weird. Members of the Lafayette Escadrille from WWI would have been right at home.

Lt. Stevens continued to swap the details of his mission with the arriving Nails. Major Kazinski drifted up to the bar to speak with the new Squadron Commander, Lieutenant Colonel Melendez.

After a brief handshake, he ordered another Johnny Walker Black Label and the Squadron Commander nodded in the direction of the young pilot.

"Sounds like you did well this evening. You're doing a great job with him, Major K. I don't suppose it would surprise you to know I got a call from his congressman."

"Not really. I'm wondering why a guy with so much money would want to be here anyway. But I will have to tell you, he's a very quick learner and I think he's gonna be one of the best pilots we have. He anticipates. Tonight, for example, after we dropped the ground flares, he turned 90 degrees to the trucks and got out of the way of the fighters before I even opened my mouth. I think he's ready to fly with any, but the very youngest, pilots." The Squadron Commander took another drink and thought about it for a few seconds.

"I completely trust your judgment, but I don't see any rush. I spend a lot of time trying to match the abilities of the crew members and, quite frankly, I don't think pairing him with another navigator would lead to any increase in efficiency."

"Well, it's fine with me. Maybe he's my good luck charm."

"Major K, did you ever think maybe you were his good luck charm?"

"Me thinks it's time for another drink, don't you?"

"Roger that, you old turkey."

"Let's take the sofa in the corner. I'd like to talk to you about something."

As the two senior officers sat down in the corner, the Squadron Commander took a long swig from his drink, and asked, "What do you think about this war, Art?"

Kazinski smiled and didn't answer immediately. He took another drink and finally spoke. "Probably the same thing you do. There's no way in hell we're going to win anything. The only questions are,

'What the hell are we doing here, how do we get out, and how many more lives do we lose doing it?'"

Colonel Melendez nodded and after a long pause responded, "It appears there is a plan."

Major Kazinski swiveled around on the sofa they were sitting on, paused briefly, and then spoke, somewhat dramatically, "You have my attention."

The commander continued, "I'll be briefing the squadron at our next monthly meeting, but in a nutshell, there is a plan to block the Ho Chi Minh Trail using Vietnamese infantry from South Viet Nam. In December, there will be an initial test of enemy resistance. A battalion of Laotian mercenaries will be moving west from the Laotian/Vietnamese border into eastern Laos at Tchepone, one of the major trail entry points into South Viet Nam. If the test is successful and enemy resistance can be measured and found within appropriate levels, then in January, five South Vietnamese tank battalions supported by infantry will move up from South Viet Nam. The plan is to physically block the Ho Chi Minh Trail on the ground at Tchepone more effectively than we've been doing with air alone. If we can stop the trucks headed to South Viet Nam, their supply chain will be cut, South Viet Nam will be able to manage their own defense, and we can disengage much more quickly. The operation is called *Lam Son 719*. The 'seven-one' comes because it will be launched in 1971, this coming January, and the 'nine' from Route 9, the main road into South Viet Nam."

"Sounds like bullshit to me. South Vietnamese troops will cut and run, and mercenaries may work in the short run, but they'll never hold the trail long enough for us to disengage."

The Squadron Commander smiled. "Major K, there you go again, reading my mind. I would have used a little less colorful language, but it would have conveyed the same thing. Now I need some advice. I've been asked to provide a liaison with the CIA who is directing the Laotian part of the operation. They want someone who has worked with the Laotians and who is smart enough to provide a plausible, and hopefully workable, plan for our support. The Geneva Conventions, as you know, won't allow uniformed Americans so we can't use American troops or Air Force officers in uniform. This is why we have Raven FACs in Laos. They'll be working with us in any event, but a Nail needs to represent us at the planning session in Laos. He'll be briefing us on a daily basis and will be the lead Nail flying directly in support of the five test battalions. Give me a name."

"That's easy. Ted Thatcher. He flew here three years ago, when the Trail wasn't as hot. He flew O-1s, knows the trail better than anyone, and he speaks French, which can come in handy with the Lao and the Vietnamese."

"I remember his personnel records. He's got quite a record. Been hit twice, as I recall."

"Yep. Got it from a ZPU near Ban Laboy Ford. He was one of the first FACs shot down and rescued here. Their call sign back then was Cricket. He told me Walt Disney designed their squadron patch using Jiminy Cricket floating down in a parachute, the same patch we wear today."

"What's he doing back here? And why is he flying an O-2? He could have any airplane over here."

"First, he wanted to continue as a FAC, not a strike pilot. He says the FACs are battlefield commanders, every other pilot is just following a FAC's orders. As for the O-2, he says the OV-10 is not the best choice for a FAC platform. Way too noisy and way too large. His perfect FAC airplane would have stealth engines and a very small footprint, as it were. He thinks the O-2 is a good compromise: not as noisy as the OV-10 but its twin engines give it more survivability than the old O-1 Birddog."

"Maybe OV-10 pilots are braver." The Squadron Commander was smiling, being an OV-10 pilot.

"Every pilot over here is brave. Putting O-2s without ejection seats over the most heavily gunned region in this stupid war is just short of criminal. I wonder where we get such brave young men to fly them. And by the way, I think we navigators are as brave if not more so than the pilots. We have to crawl into airplanes we don't even control. There used to be a certain lieutenant in our squadron I would just as soon ... never mind."

The Squadron Commander chuckled. "I know who you mean, and my predecessor transferred him home. Maybe he won't shoot himself down there. And I wonder where we get such brave over-the-hill men like you. But, back to the plan to end the war, *Lam Son 719*. I agree Thatcher needs to coordinate air cover for the Nails. He has more experience than any of the other pilots with the Laotians. I'll speak to him tomorrow. Now what say we join the poker table over there?"

Major K chuckled. "Boy, oh boy. You've had a few too many methinks. You're the world's worst poker player."

21

La Rue Sans Joie: The Street Without Joy

Bad Sam and Ted Thatcher met late one afternoon after bumping into each other in debriefing. They agreed to have dinner together at the Officers' Club since they hadn't eaten there in a while and because the popcorn and boiled egg diet at the Nail Hole was getting a trifle stale. They arrived as the Thai sun was setting, embracing the coconut palms around the Teak-sided structure with a halo of gold. Super Thai exchanged the traditional Thai greeting with Ted as they entered, bowing with hands together in prayer fashion while ignoring Bad Sam. Sam, as usual, acted disgruntled, but it was just an act. She led them to a table away from the crowd. The cool air conditioning rapidly dried out their perspiration-laden flight suits.

As the pilots finished placing a drink order with the waitress, Lt. Col. Travers, the 23rd TASS Executive Officer walked in followed by the Squadron Commander, Lt. Col. Melendez. They were wearing wrinkled khakis and obviously hadn't been flying but probably wished they had. Spotting Thatcher and Bad Sam, they ambled over, shook hands, and asked if they could join them. It was a request Thatcher and Bad Sam enthusiastically agreed to.

The new arrivals added to the drink order and then sat down. The colonel's dark hair streaked with wisps of gray complemented a five o'clock shadow and gave him a look of maturity and distinction. His avuncular demeanor would instill confidence and respect in any subordinate, and Thatcher was instantly at ease. Lt. Col. Travers was taller than his commander, but thinner and grayer and displayed a more serious look on his face. He didn't smile often, although he was pleasant enough. Sam was at ease with both officers but Sam was always at ease. He would have been at ease with Jack the Ripper as long as he held a drink in his hand. After a few seconds to get comfortable, Col. Melendez paused a moment, looked at Ted, and began the conversation.

"I've been over your file Ted. You were here 24 months ago as a lieutenant. What in the hell prompted you to volunteer a second time?"

"Bernard Fall, colonel."

"Bernard Fall?"

Thatcher paused, took a sip of his scotch, and began. "Bernard Fall was a teenage Jewish resistance fighter in France in WWII. He and his friends, mostly orphans, aided our American troops as scouts and spies. His own mother was sent to a concentration camp where she disappeared. I'm sure we can all guess how. He never found out what happened to his father. Fall and his friends served the Allies with distinction in some very dangerous guerilla operations, reporting on the location and strength of German forces and carrying Allied messages to and from other guerilla forces.

"After the war, he came to the U.S. and got a PhD from Howard University in Washington, D.C. He did his dissertation on the French disaster in 1954 at Dien Bien Phu. That became a book entitled, *Hell in a Very Small Place*. He returned to Southeast Asia many times to do research for his other books and often embedded with French forces and, later, the Americans. He accurately predicted failure for both his French brothers, and later for America. Three years ago, February 21, 1967, he died literally right at the DMZ on Route 1 while on patrol with U.S. Marines from their base in Dong Ha, seven miles south in South Viet Nam. My brother served there as a Marine and was wounded and air-evaced out three months after Fall was killed. My brother was only there a month, if that gives you any idea of the situation three years then.

"Of course, we've all flown right over that spot because Tchepone and Route 9 are only a few miles north, and we occasionally fly down there so we can tell our kids that we, too, were in Viet Nam since no one will know where Laos is. Dong Ha and Khe Sahn were both abandoned because they were indefensible. Route 1 is the coastal highway, the one the French dubbed, '*La Rue Sans Joie*', or 'The Street Without Joy'. That's also the name of Fall's most famous book.

"But, back to the history lesson. Robert McNamara hated Fall because Fall taught there was no justification for our being in Viet Nam and our tactics were completely ineffective in any event. Interestingly, the American military drew heavily on his observations. He actually lectured at the Army Command and Staff College."

"I'm sorry about your brother. Is he OK?" Lt. Col Melendez was, if nothing else, a man whose concern over issues such as this was genuine and appreciated by his entire squadron. Popular commanders were often thought of as too soft, but Col. Melendez combined an all-too-rare ability to merge toughness and compassion in the proper proportions.

"He's alive but doesn't have complete use of his right arm. That doesn't stop him though. He's a Marine. He could still take me anytime he wanted to. I once heard a Congressman telling the Marine Corps Commandant Marines were too extreme. The Commandant thanked him."

The other officers laughed. "Sorry to hear about your brother but I'm glad he's alive."

"Thank you Sir."

The waitress intervened to take to their orders. They all ordered lobster, and a bottle of wine. Then the dialogue continued.

"How did Fall die?" asked Colonel Melendez.

"The Marines he was with paused to take a break before heading back to Dong Ha. He, his photographer, and some of the Marines were just walking around looking for souvenirs. Fall and his photographer went down a small embankment. Fall stepped on a Bouncing Betty, one of those mines that jumps up a foot or so after it's stepped on before it explodes. Nine Marines and his photographer died with him.

"Among other accomplishments before his death, Fall interviewed Ho Chi Minh at his home in North Viet Nam. Fall wrote that neither the French nor the Americans had a clue as to what the dynamics were in Southeast Asia. Both governments hated him because he documented their failures and produced statistics disagreeing with their rosy predictions of victory. He was not anti-war. He was anti-stupidity."

"But what are the dynamics Fall was speaking about?" asked Lt. Col Travers. "Let's start with the French. Why did they lose and what can we do to avoid their mistakes? Don't we have the benefit of their hindsight? As I recall, Dien Bien Phu, the second French Waterloo, so to speak, was a stupid exercise in trying to fight a set-piece battle in a guerrilla war. We aren't doing what the French did, are we? The last thing we need is another Dien Bien Phu. Our tactics are far more fluid—we have fixed bases, such as Danang, but our airpower alone is light years ahead of the French." The colonel's arguments seemed logical.

A waiter appeared with the drinks and the officers all paused a few moments to overcome the heat and dust of Northern Thailand.

"Before we get to Fall, let's talk about how we got here. You may not believe this, because not many news sources have ever published it for general consumption, but the reason we are involved in this war today is directly correlated with our entry into WWII. We were supporting Britain and the European Allies with programs such as Lend Lease long before our entry, but there was no desire whatsoever to get directly involved on the ground, especially in Asia. In fact, there was a substantial bias toward non-involvement. We lost 40,000 Americans in the First World War and were never in any imminent danger then. We were not in any perceived danger in 1944, either. Although a high percentage of Americans were of European origin, we were oceans away from any of the action. Why watch more American boys get killed for a second war not of our making? So, Americans were watching WWII with a certain sense of caution.

"Our greatest defenses were two giant bodies of water between us and the Germans and Japanese, which seemed to counsel, 'Don't risk more American lives just to save the Europeans again.' Pearl Harbor, of course changed all that. Admiral Yamamoto feared he had awakened a sleeping giant, and he was right. He would live to regret it and die because of it. By 1944, the Japanese had captured all of the colonies in South East Asia including what was called Indochina: Laos, Cambodia, and Viet Nam. They installed a puppet French government called the Vichy Regime to manage the territory since they didn't have the manpower to both govern and continue their expansion.

"There were several groups in Indochina, including the communists, who established operations in the early forties to fight the Japanese. Most of the Vietnamese opposition was based over the border, in China. Our allies, the Nationalist Chinese led by Chiang Kai-shek, created and funded a Vietnamese resistance movement called the Dong Minh Hoi, later called the Viet Minh; this included both communists and non-communists. They were hoping for Intel on their common enemy, the Japanese, and when it didn't materialize, they released Ho Chi Minh from jail. Ho returned to Viet Nam after 30 or so years in exile to lead an underground movement to liberate his homeland from the Japanese. Western intelligence agencies assisted Ho, primarily the American Office of Strategic Services. The Free French also used him to undermine the Vichy French-Japanese collaboration. Ho was employed by the O.S.S. (Office of Strategic Services, forerunner of the CIA) in our clandestine operations against the Japanese. He also rescued American pilots shot down and brought them back to safety.

"We weren't in the war with the Japanese because there were two big oceans protecting us, but were obviously sympathetic to the French and other European allies. At the request of the French, we put embargoes on exports of steel and oil to Japan. In retribution, Japan bombed Pearl Harbor, both to punish us for the embargo and hoping to defang us to allow them to solidify control over the entire Pacific."

"Are you saying Pearl Harbor was payback for our support of the French in Indo-China against the Japanese?" The colonel was obviously puzzled. This was not a topic widely discussed in most history lectures he ever attended. Of course, as he admitted later, he was an engineering major.

Thatcher took a sip of his drink and answered, "Yep. The die was cast. We would have been involved sooner or later, but the oil embargo triggered the resultant Pearl Harbor attack and resulted in two dramatic changes: first, it accelerated our involvement by leading to a huge outpouring of nationalism which would never have materialized without the direct provocation to our nation. Think about it for a minute. Can you imagine a huge influx of young American men volunteering for service to help the French and British? Volunteering to put their lives on the line to save the French, again? It's doubtful a draft would have been successful without a direct attack on us. So, our support of the French, while not entirely altruistic, indirectly led to the attack on Pearl Harbor and a sea change in our outlook on the war. The draft boards were overwhelmed. American boys were being drafted right out of high school, although some volunteered without waiting for a notice. The change in American attitudes was not only dramatic, but also in some sense it's why we're here today."

Dinner was served and the history lesson was suspended. Then Thatcher continued.

"In a nutshell, the French were here before the war to exploit the natural resources. To be honest, they weren't inclined to come back after the drubbing they took in WWII, but Eisenhower encouraged and supported them to return. Eisenhower was concerned both as General and President that a domino effect such as we witnessed in Europe and Korea would be replicated in Southeast Asia. Remember, the communists took half of Germany, and all of Czechoslovakia, Hungary, and Poland. Eisenhower was the author, if you will, of the policy of containment. In Southeast Asia, he feared the Chinese Communists taking everything as far as India, including Laos, Thailand, Viet Nam, Cambodia, and Indonesia. Ironically, he was worrying about the wrong communists. The Russians were far more aggressive in the final analysis. That's why our F-105 pilots are flying against them in North Viet Nam raids, not the Chinese."

"In any event, the French came back to re-exploit their colonies, if I may use that expression, especially Viet Nam, with our encouragement using tanks and mechanized vehicles and by building an impregnable fort, the now infamous Dien Bien Phu. They suffered a humiliating defeat there in 1954 despite our effort to assist them with aerial re-supply and bombardment."

"Eisenhower, incidentally, originally wanted to use Laos as the stopper in this western policy of communist containment, not Viet Nam. How Viet Nam became ended up as the line in the sand is a long story, but we'll pick that up another time."

Coffee and desert were served. Then the history lesson was concluded, beginning with Col. Melendez. "But we're not French, and we're not using mechanized convoys in this current war. We're using Green Berets and Smart Bombs, infrared photography, and seismic and acoustic sensors transmitting real-time information on truck traffic."

"Without being insubordinate, colonel, is there really that much difference in the French approach and our efforts to stop human porters walking under triple canopy jungle on the trail using F-4s and B-52s? We all know how much of their operation is hidden underground and under triple canopy jungle. We all know about the Tonkin Gulf Incident in which we probably faked at least one of the two attacks on the U.S.S. *Maddox* and how that led to Congressional Authority to support the Southeast Asia Treaty Organization. That opened the door to insert American ground forces over here in August of 1964. What we should have done was to recognize Ho Chi Minh as more of a nationalist than a communist and supported him with some anti-Chinese strings attached. America, and only America, could have intervened in 1954. It was a great opportunity. China will never be a friend of America as long as the communists are in charge.

"There was a perfect model in President Tito in Yugoslavia. He was a communist, but like Ho Chi Minh, he was considered one of the most effective resistance leaders in WWII Europe. Some have suggested he was too authoritarian, but most Yugoslavs liked him, and he was considered one of the leaders in the non-aligned movement along with Nehru in India, Nasser in Egypt and Sukarno in Indonesia. Expecting an American style democracy in a third world nation with practically zero educational attainment was, if I may opine, not rational."

"Well," answered the colonel, "our Bomb Damage Assessments say we're doing a pretty good job of containment. As a matter of fact, you're doing a pretty good job. Didn't you kill 12 trucks night before last?"

"I just did what my navigator, Steve Kelso, told me to do, colonel. The A-1s that dropped the napalm destroyed the trucks. I always find trucks with Steve, but the real question is, while we were attacking them, how many more were driving with impunity a half a mile away, knowing they were completely safe since we were preoccupied? My assessment is that we are spending enormous sums of money to destroy what I am sure is a very small percentage of the total capacity. We might be better off just offering to buy the trucks from them."

The two senior officers laughed. Coffee was brought, and there was only a temporary lull in the conversation. The Squadron Commander resumed the questioning. Sam was starting to doze.

"Let's change the conversation to something more strategic." The commander was showing true concern, not simply a casual interest. "Based on your first tour and this one, what does your personal experience tell you about the future? Is there no hope at all?"

"No Sir. As my mother used to say, 'If you want to make God laugh, tell him your plans'. Our efforts here are hopeless. The outcome of this was determined before we ever got involved."

"Based on what? Tea leaves? A Ouija Board?" Colonel Travers asked. Travers was perhaps a little belligerent, not at all as sincerely interested as the Squadron Commander.

"No sir, rice." Thatcher was not insubordinate but calm, showing no sign of irritation.

"Rice?" asked Colonel Melendez.

"Yes sir. Bernard Fall answered your question with an old Viet Nam proverb: 'A grain of rice is worth a drop of blood.'"

"Does that mean something as simple as food is a part of the North Vietnamese motivation?" Travers replaced his former belligerence with more than a little curiosity.

"Actually, yes, sir. Its significance is that our concept of democracy, which means so much to us, is not even in their top ten. Democracy doesn't work very well when starvation is an ever-present threat and people couldn't read a constitution if there was one. According to Bernard Fall, the Asian economy is highly sensitive to food, especially rice. The population growth is outstripping the food supply in many Asian regions, including North Viet Nam. A bad crop there can mean starvation for thousands. South Viet Nam is a rice-surplus region. They can actually triple the crop there, although they don't bother, and rice is a major factor in the war. The North would love to squeeze every grain they could out of the South to feed their people. And let me insert one more little-known fact: North Vietnamese and South Vietnamese aren't monolithic: they are more like Yankees and Rebels here in the United States. Their dialects are noticeably different, much like our Northern and Southern dialects. South Viet Nam is much warmer. It rarely dips below 68°F in Saigon, even at night. In the North, average temperatures can average 60°F from January to March. During these months, you'll see people in the North wearing thick winter jackets; the mornings are especially cold, even dipping into single digits. Farther North, in the mountains, it snows. Coffee there is less prevalent; most Northerners would prefer a cup of tea and cafes are rare. Northerners prefer noodles to rice, although rice is still the staple crop in most of Southeast Asia. While you'll certainly find exceptions to this rule, Southerners tend to be quick to smile, whereas Northerners are seen as more aloof. I'm not suggesting the presence of foreigners, 'round eyes', as we're called, doesn't offer a tremendous incentive to launch an invasion of the South. No one wants a foreign country dictating its policies. Let's not forget our own Revolution. And we were fighting people who looked like us and spoke the same language. But in a nation where starvation is an ever-present threat, a grain of rice is, literally, worth a drop of blood. We view communism as evil, which certainly makes sense in a western nation where liberty is cherished, but we don't understand that simple survival, and especially food, trumps everything else in Southeast Asia. On a personal level, it's obvious. What hasn't been so obvious to the planners in Washington is the North can't give up trying to unite the two halves of Viet Nam since they mate perfectly, the North being the industrial sector, and the South being the food supply. And it's not just Viet Nam. The same situation exists in many regions of the Orient, as Professor Fall pointed out."

"So, is that the major lesson of Viet Nam?" asked Lt. Col. Travers.

"Probably the most misunderstood. Imagine our Midwestern breadbasket states being forcibly carved out of the U.S. and given to another country, such as Canada. How would we react?"

"I get your point." The colonel, finishing his coffee, motioned for another. "One last cup, Ted? Sam?"

His question woke Sam up; he was hoping for something a little stronger than coffee, but he decided to put on a good front.

"Thank you, sir." They both spoke at once. While waiting for the coffee, Thatcher made one concluding remark.

"One last factor here is the corruption that exists in an artificially contrived government. For example, on his many visits here, Professor Fall kept reading reports in Saigon newspapers about the South Vietnamese government claiming loyalty from a suspiciously high percentage of the towns and villages, around 80-percent of them. This is important because the culture here is that the rule of the Emperor stops at the Bamboo Gate, meaning the state doesn't control the towns or villages even though their loyalty to the government is obviously important. Kind of like our concept of States' Rights. By reading the same newspaper every morning in Saigon, Fall plotted the reports of the assassinations of the regional governors and village chiefs. He found the actual territory controlled by Saigon was about 20-percent, not the

80-percent claimed by the Vietnamese government. The U.S. hadn't even questioned the reports of the South Vietnamese government and the Western press parroted the remarks of the Saigon officials. What we have here is an artificially created government with little loyalty from the population. The money we gave them, and still do, for public works and other government services is largely pocketed by corrupt officials. We've already lost the war. If the U.S. Armed Forces were not here, pandemonium would be instant and not very pretty."

Lt. Col. Melendez was silent for a while, pondering the implications. "I guess what Fall was saying is that a western nation, even one with no economic aspirations, cannot possibly appreciate the dynamics of the economic and social structure of a third world nation."

"You get an 'A' from Professor Fall, colonel. Frankly, the North Vietnamese soldiers we face are well fed, some for the first time in their lives, and they have a sense of importance they would never have growing rice. And the southerners, like our American southerners, have a culture that despises a central government. And all they want to do is live at peace, behind their Bamboo Gate, with no interference from anyone. The government we created in South Viet Nam has very little loyalty."

Thatcher paused and finished his coffee. He didn't speak right away, but collected his thoughts and then replied.

"Ho helped us get rid of the Japs, and he'll have no problem getting rid of us. Now all we have to do is figure out what we're doing here."

Lt. Colonel Travers responded somewhat emphatically, "I know why I'm here! Getting ahead in the military means logging some serious duty. There may never be a WWIII, but if there is, we need men with experience in combat. I'm not so naïve as to believe we're making the world safe for democracy, but the atrocities of the North

Vietnamese against civilians and our own POWs allows me to sleep at night after a successful airstrike."

Thatcher nodded. "I understand what you're saying colonel, and I don't disagree. But I'm also here for the same reason Professor Fall was. I'm hoping the pressure we're applying may result in a negotiated settlement to prevent a bloodbath when we realize we can't win. But, I'm not optimistic."

Sam, who had dozed through much of the conversation, chimed in, slurred in actually. "Hell, this is the only war we've got. What are we going to do without it?"

The other three officers laughed. Sam was a character, one who endeared most men to him. The ones who didn't like him were, as a rule, arrogant and superficial. The great dinner made the evening a pleasant diversion from the flak-filled skies the four officers would encounter in the days to follow.

Col Melendez lit a cigar and looked directly at his dinner companions. "Ted and Sam, I have enjoyed this. Thanks for the company and the conversation. I have no quarrel with your prediction of failure, Ted. We've done nothing but backpedal for years, and from what I've personally seen, we can't blow up enough trucks to win this war. If we destroy one, two more take its place. So, how exactly, and when, do you think the end will come?"

Thatcher finished his drink, paused briefly, then concluded: "based on what I've seen since my last tour two years ago, colonel, we won't have to wait long. I can't see any decrease in truck traffic despite the substantial increase in bombing, and the anti-aircraft fire is much greater now than two years ago. My guess is there are plans in the works in Washington to try one last desperate attempt to close the trail long enough to get us out. How, I don't know, but the trail is the key. Stop the supplies and the NVA and Viet Cong will be weakened. The war will still be lost because of the rice problem, but it might take years more.

Thatcher paused for a few seconds.

"While I'm at it, colonel, I would like to encourage your continued support of our Laotian allies. The war in the Plain de Jarres is not going well nor is our effort right across the River. Laos is practically submerged in the news because of the attention Viet Nam is getting. Most Americans back home couldn't find Laos on a map. The Laotians aren't hopeful. Maybe we can discuss that over dinner the next time we meet."

"I would look forward to it, Ted. Let's do this again."

The officers finished their drinks and exited from the cool air conditioning of the Club to the oppressive humidity and hot air of a Thailand summer. As they put on their flight caps, an OV-10 roared by overhead, outbound for the trail. The war was back on.

22

Tanks for the Memory

Nail 77, Lt. Tom Stevens and his navigator, Maj. Art Kazinski, launched at 2200 hours, paired again by the Squadron Ops officer to put the most inexperienced pilot with the most experienced navigator. On three previous missions, they performed well, amassing a total of over 50 trucks, thanks to good weather and the professional job done by the NKP-based A-1s. In the past week, no one on the night missions was hit, let alone shot down by AAA. The daytime FACs were not so lucky. One O-2 returned, miraculously, missing half of the rear propeller. Capt. Ron McClannahan, the pilot, was marking a 23mm gun for an attack by F-4s and got hit as he pulled off after firing a Willy Pete. That night in the Nail Hole a cluster of Nails, anxious to hear his story, asked what it felt like.

"It felt like the plane was going to shake apart."

Someone asked if he shut down the rear engine.

"Hell no! As long as that puppy was turning, I was going to get all the push I could out of it."

The laughter was immediate and predictable. Staying alive meant getting as far away as possible from an active gun. Saving an aircraft engine was so far down the list it didn't register.

Lt. Stevens, the Georgia football star, heard the story and made a mental note to remember aircraft were expendable, his life was not.

He and the major logged the last three missions in Sector II, near Mu Gia Pass. This night, he and Major K were fragged to Sector III, which covered the territory near Ban Karai Pass. It was south of Sector II meaning the trucks were able to stay safely in North Viet Nam longer before crossing into Laos on the trail. As they climbed east, Art Kazinski briefed him on the difference in the sectors.

"Tonight, the North Vietnamese trucks you see will have logged another ten or so miles in safety because their trucks were able to travel farther in North Viet Nam jungle before turning west into Laos. It's taken them a while, but they never stop hacking roads through the jungle. The farther they can get in North Viet Nam before they enter Laos, the safer they are since we don't bomb the North anymore. We're not authorized to strike them until they cross the border. They've become so brazen, they sometimes line them up in broad daylight, waiting for bad weather or darkness to move them. How's that for a screwed-up war?"

"I guess I have to ask: Do FACs ever cheat on those restrictions?" Tom Stevens was exhibiting the same reaction all new FACs did: Were we here to win or not?

"It's been known to happen. Sometimes the border is difficult to pinpoint." Major K was grinning, his face softly illuminated by the instrument panel lights.

"I'll have to remember that," laughed the young pilot, adding a little more elevator trim and his own grin to the dialogue. The two officers made a strange pair. In addition to a 15-year age gap, Stevens was a southerner, Kazinski was from the north. Stevens was a football star, Kazinski was a sedate, intellectual who loved reading history books, particularly books about WWII. Stevens was six-foot-two; Kazinski was five-foot-eight; Stevens was a newly-wed; Kazinski a grandfather.

Major K took the starlight scope out of the bag and started scoping the ground below. The sun's last glow was replaced by tracers, visible as far as 30 miles farther down the trail. Parachute flares by the dozens were already swinging lazily in darkening sky in South Viet Nam, meaning the black C-123 flare ships, called Candlesticks, were hard at work trying to find targets for their A-1s. Tom Stevens saw other large red tracers to the south, also many miles away, but they were not coming from the ground up toward an airplane, they were coming from an airplane toward the ground.

"Those are the C-130 gunships you told me about on our last mission." Lt. Stevens pointed to the south.

"Roger that. They can be extremely effective, but they can't operate in most places we do because they can't jink when it gets hot. That's why they fly a little above 10,000 feet. Since they're 4,000 feet higher than we are, the AAA is at its peak unless it's firing straight up. Remember, what they can do, which is unique in aerial combat, is fly in a computer-driven parabolic arc allowing them to fire their recoilless cannons continuously as they fly in a 360-degree circle."

Tom Stevens broke hard left as a string of 37mm shells came up suddenly, low and from the left. They went under the O-2 and lit up the sky above them high and to the right as the shells airburst in a sparkling crescendo. The display was beautiful, but the fact that the shells were intended to kill them tended to dampen any pleasure the observation might have provided otherwise. After recovering from the break, both crewmembers rechecked the tightness of their seat belts and shoulder harnesses and adjusted their mental and psychological state to ensure maximum concentration and emotional control. It was time to get serious.

"Good move on that break Tom! What the hell is going on? The main part of the trail is still a mile or so ahead. Let me see if this can find something." The starlight scope was on, but Kazinski was waiting for the functional part of the trail to start his hunt. As a rule, the guns were silent until the attacks began. The gunners didn't want to advertise themselves as targets in the absence of any other targets. It was like hanging a sign on themselves saying, "shoot me." But on this particular night, they made a mistake, and it would cost them dearly. They opened up on the O-2 before any provocative action on the part of the Nails. Major K immediately started scanning below.

It wasn't long until the reason for their aggressive behavior became clear: there were a dozen tanks on a side road leading to the main portion of the trail. They came into view a few minutes after the warning shot from the gunners below and were getting ready to turn south.

"Damn!" Major Kazinski's shock was understandable. This was the first sighting of tanks on the trail and it probably meant a further escalation of the North Vietnamese attacks in South Vietnam.

"Call Moonbeam and get something here fast. Tell them we've got tanks."

"Moonbeam, Nail 77, we've got tango alpha november kilos in sight. Need something right away."

As Tom Stevens finished his request, he banked quickly once again, dodging two more strings of 37mm shells, this time from separate guns.

It took a few seconds for the Moonbeam controllers to figure out 'tank' was spelled phonetically to disguise, or at least obscure, the message from anyone listening in. Lt. Stevens encoded the message on his own; it wasn't necessary since radio transmissions were scrambled. Nevertheless, it showed he was being extra cautious, and Maj. Kazinski smiled to himself. Moonbeam controllers reacted quickly and redirected two A-1s from NKP that were outbound to Sector II to the north. In less than two minutes, they checked in with Nail 77.

"Nail 77, Zorro 21 and 22 five out from your position. Eight napalms apiece, four Funny Bombs and pistols. We have your overhead beacon."

Lt. Stevens keyed his mic, "Zorro flight, what we have down here has tracks if you get my meaning. We'll drop two marks and suggest you mix up the roll-ins more than usual. We've already taken 37mm fire and haven't even dropped anything yet. Let me know when you see our beacon and the marks. We'll be well to the west to give you room. Let's use the nape first to light up the area. We're dropping the marks now."

Major K was smiling to himself. His young pilot was only on his third mission, but he was learning fast. He figured out, on his own, that napalm would provide illumination for the succeeding drops of the Funny Bombs. They could easily melt the tanks, barrels and all. Major K, his head buried in the hood of the starlight scope, used hand signals to direct Lt. Stevens over the drop zone. Then he gave the thumbs down drop sign twice, a few seconds apart. As the last ground flare dropped, he put the starlight scope in his lap.

"Okay, let's head west and watch the show." The ground flares took a few minutes to ignite before they became visible.

Lt. Stevens started a steep turn to get as far away from the target and the A-1s as quickly as possible. Within three or four minutes, the red ground flares reached a brilliant glow visible from miles away. Major K motioned for a 180-degree turn to the left to place him on the side where the show would begin so he could give corrections to the A-1s. As the black O-2 was halfway through the turn, he pushed the starlight scope out of the window again. "Shit hot!" he shouted over the intercom. Then, over the radio, "Zorro the marks are perfect, one on each end of the column. Send everything between them to hell. We'll be south of the target at 7,000."

"Roger that," responded Zorro lead. "Zorro 21 is in hot. Two, delay until you see what the nape lights up." Zorro 22 acknowledged, and the show began.

Within seconds, a sight very few people would ever witness appeared on the inky black canvas below. Napalm, basically jellied gasoline, doesn't erupt instantly, like a bomb; it splashes in a line of bright orange flame, lighting up the ground around it as if it were day. It runs along the ground like a flaming avalanche burning anything it touches and sucking the air out of anything close to it. At the end of the 300-foot stream of hell, everything under it is on fire. The flames die slowly, over several minutes, but that was all the time Zorro 22 needed to assess the damage. The tank column came to a complete halt, but only the first four were burning. If there were any crew members alive in the rest, they were undoubtedly trying to reverse course to get out of their death traps.

Zorro lead radioed his wingman to come from the rear, both to ensure the remaining tanks didn't reverse course and to confuse the gunners who were probably still looking in the direction Zorro lead came from. Zorro 22 had a cake walk. The light from the remaining napalm was still adequate to see precisely where to drop and he didn't miss. The rear of the tank column was now ablaze and ammunition from the tanks started to erupt in a furious series of explosions. With each new explosion, the tanks jumped a few feet off the ground and disintegrated a little more.

During the entire episode, North Vietnamese gunners in the area were furiously shooting randomly into the sky. Red tracers were screaming up from the ground in all directions since the gunners had no idea where the black A-1s were. The Nails enjoyed a front row seat. They could see Zorro 22 at the bottom of his pass even though the A-1 was painted black; that was how bright the flames were. The FACs, even from their higher vantage point, were still forced to dodge both 37mm and 23mm tracers; some of the AAA rounds fired at the Zorros were fired in their direction. Other gunners, not sure of where to shoot, were firing wildly, not at all uncommon in night conflicts.

The attack continued for another 20 minutes, with both Zorros exhausting everything except their Funny Bombs. After they paused the attack, Kazinski entertained Lt. Stevens and the Zorros with a little humor. "Guys, you're not going to believe this, but they're down there kicking dirt on the burning tanks."

"Kicking dirt? You've got to be kidding," radioed Zorro lead.

"No, I'm not. They are trying to put the fire out." Apparently, the crews abandoned ship, as it were, hid somewhere in the vicinity, and then reemerged when they thought the attack was over. "Okay, guys. You destroyed the tanks on each end of the column, let's use the Funny Bombs on the rest. You're cleared in hot. Start from the front of the column and work backward." Major K motioned with his hand to Lt. Stevens to turn north to give the A-1s plenty of room to maneuver. Stevens started the turn.

"Zorro 21, roger that. In hot from the east. I'll be breaking south Nail."

"Zorro 21, roger. We're well north at 7,000."

Funny Bombs, the phosphorus bombs with thermite initiators that start with a flash, and slowly grow into a boiling white hot magnesium cloud from hell, were tailor made for tanks. The FACs observed only using peripheral vision to avoid night blindness. The Zorros spent ten minutes dropping on the tanks that were either undamaged or damaged but not burning. Major Kazinski called for the last pass on the second tank, which was stopped but still not burning, and Zorro 21 called in hot.

The 'fog of battle', a common term in military affairs, afflicts military operations everywhere and has throughout history. It results from the confusion and uncertainty surrounding battle whether land, sea, or air. On this evening, it manifested itself once again as Zorro 21 dropped the second Funny Bomb. Seconds later, a clip of seven shells from a 37mm anti-aircraft gun streamed up from behind the O-2 and ripped off four feet of the right wing. The two Nails were trapped in an airplane with no ejection seat. The panic was indescribable. The cramped cockpit left no room to maneuver and the O-2 was instantly uncontrollable. It disintegrated on the ground in less than a minute. It was downed by a random shot fired wildly by a gunner with no idea what he was shooting at in the black, Laotian night.

On the ground, the 37mm gun crew commanded by North Vietnamese Sergeant Ca, the gunner whose name meant 'brave warrior', shouted with joy at the vengeance his three-gun anti-aircraft battery wreaked on the American spotter plane. He knew it was a lucky shot, but to him it was a tribute to his father who died recently. He was now the oldest member of the family, a family that fought first the Japanese, then the French, and now the Americans. This was his second 'kill' and would earn him another promotion.

Major Art Kazinski and Lt. Tom Stevens had been trapped in a completely uncontrollable airplane, one with no ejection seats and with faint hope of opening the door and bailing out given the cramped cockpit. After the war, records would show only one successful bailout from an O-2. A total of 178 would be shot down. OV-10 losses were 73; and the OV-10 had an ejection seat. The next day's photo-recon pictures showed the O-2 lying on its belly, four feet of wing missing. Apparently, it went into a flat spin and crash landed on its belly. Bailing out of an O-2 was difficult under normal circumstances, particularly for the pilot. If the navigator in the right seat was incapacitated, bail out would have been impossible under any circumstance. There would be only one documented bailout.

No one would ever know why, but two opened parachutes were lying in a pile on the ground next to the remains of the fuselage the next day as the RF-4 reconnaissance aircraft photographed the scene. There was no indication the parachutes had been used; they were too neatly piled up. Apparently, they were removed unopened from the bodies, popped open, and piled neatly to discourage any search and rescue attempt. Sergeant Ca and his gun crew weren't being kind; they just didn't want any interference with their normal activities. His father would have been proud. This was his third American aircraft destroyed.

The Nail Hole was predictably somber that evening. The Viking atmosphere was subdued. Conversations were in hushed tones, not the boisterous banter which normally prevailed. The Nails had suffered the loss of two heroes, men who fought bravely with no thought of fame or fortune. Men who served their country when it called. Men whose names would be etched in stone on a wall with over 58,862 other names. Family members and veterans would visit the wall over the years and remember their comrades. Many would say a prayer. Some would shed a tear. Nearly all would silently vow to oppose any commitment of American lives in the future without a clear and compelling justification for putting American lives in harm's way. And, one day, people would stop coming.

23

The Beginning of the End

Captain Ted Thatcher landed after a day mission over Sector III, a mission marked by two airstrikes on suspected truck parks in triple canopy jungle. Not uncommonly, there was no discernible BDA. He had flown over the crash site of Major Art Kazinski and Lt. Tom Stevens on the way to his target. Not surprisingly, there was nothing left. The North Vietnamese moved the wreckage and dumped the bodies in the jungle to prevent any attempt at recovering them. As he climbed out of the cockpit, hair rumpled from the helmet and camouflaged fatigues wet dark with sweat, he was met by the squadron orderly, Airman Blake, driving a Jeep. "Sir, the Squadron Commander wants to see you as soon as it is convenient."

"I'm not in any trouble, am I Airman Blake?" Thatcher was smiling.

"I don't think so, sir. I think it's about a meeting he wants you to attend."

"Must be important. Want to give me a ride?"

"Yes sir. How was your mission today?"

"Typical. Tree parks, airstrike on targets I couldn't see, and no discernible damage. I may put myself in for a medal of some sort. There must be a medal for frustration. Take me by the armory and let me get rid of this stuff."

Thatcher loaded his parachute, AR-15, .38 caliber revolver, survival vest, and helmet into the back seat and climbed in the front seat next to the squadron clerk. They stopped at the armory on the way to headquarters and Thatcher dropped off his gear. A few minutes later, the Jeep pulled up to the Headquarters of the 23rd Tactical Air Support Squadron.

"Well, that was better than walking in this insufferable heat. Thanks for picking me up."

"Not at all, sir. Have a good day."

Thatcher entered the headquarters building and knocked on the door post of the Squadron Commander's office. Col. Melendez looked up and motioned him in.

"Hi Ted. Did you win the war today? Can we go home now?" He was smiling. Thatcher saluted,

"Not quite, sir. Just created some more firewood for the locals."

Col. Melendez returned the salute and motioned the captain to a chair.

"Ted, I called you here to see if you would be interested in a very delicate assignment. It involves working with the CIA, the Laotians, and the South Vietnamese military. You've already demonstrated a great rapport with our Laotian military. The X-Rays you fly with have a very high regard for you. I've already talked with Major Khampat and he picked you above the other Nails he flies with on the Cricket West missions. You're the only Nail we have who speaks French, another plus for this mission."

"First of all, colonel, I don't speak French fluently. I learned what little I know on my first tour over here and I can get by. But if that's a criteria for ending the war, we've lost. I will gladly accept your invitation based on the fact Major Khampat has recommended me. I assume the assignment is about a change in strategy. When we talked in the Officers' Club a few months ago, I more or less predicted as much based on both the French experience and the obvious observation we are already pulling out. The abandonment of Khe Sanh and Dong Ha, our two northern most bases, was a signal to everyone watching this fiasco we couldn't plug the supply line from the North. From what I see in the little news we get here; the U.S. is about to explode."

"Ted, your guess is probably right on the money. What I've been told—and my paygrade doesn't allow me access to much else—is that the South Vietnamese are going to invade Laos with infantry and tanks and block the trail from the ground. And, we are going to beef up Dong Ha and Khe Sanh in support. You will know more than me in a few days because you are to represent our squadron in the planning session at the Raven compound in Pakse, Laos. The Raven commander there will fly over and pick you up at 1300 hours tomorrow. You know the drill. Civilian clothes, no ID."

"Do I have any authority to commit us in any way or am I just an observer?"

"I've been told we are to give them anything they want." Ted Thatcher didn't respond immediately, and the Squadron Commander finally broke the silence. "What are you thinking?"

"I'm wondering what the hell is going on. An invasion of Laos by the South Vietnamese is just short of insane. Has anyone heard of Dien Bien Phu?"

"Dien Bien Phu was a fortress. This is a mobile maneuver. Maybe there's an ace in the hole we don't know about." Col. Melendez lit a cigar and tilted back in his chair.

"Yes sir. And we may be it. We can't win the war because we can't plug the supply lines from the air, despite ten years of constant bombardment. American ground troops aren't allowed in Laos by the Geneva Convention. We need to pull out of Viet Nam with minimum loss of face, so we arrange for the South Vietnamese and Laotians to launch a major ground offensive into Laos, probably with tanks. We direct air strikes around the clock based on the fire they're getting. They're the cheese in the trap, so to speak. They will cut and run, of course, and it will be a total disaster. So, we use it as an excuse to pull out, but at a faster rate than we have been. Since American troops won't be involved directly, it won't an American defeat."

He paused and neither officer spoke for a few minutes, pondering the situation. Finally, Thatcher spoke again. "Maybe it will give us a chance to negotiate something short of a complete disaster, politically and militarily."

Col. Melendez pondered his subordinate's theory for a few moments and then broke the pause. "If you're right, and I think you probably are, our squadron is going to revert to a lot of low level, close air support situations at the expense of bombing the trucks on the trail. We don't have a lot of experience there, except for Nails working with the Green Berets and you Cricket West FACs supporting the CIA stuff. How do you see this unfolding?"

"Until I attend the meeting, I won't know but here's a guess: We are going to be asked to provide around the clock air cover and the number of anti-aircraft guns will grow like mushrooms. American air power will be used to give as much cover as possible, but there is no way we can stop the massacre. The Nails without experience in close air support of ground troops can be used on the guns, and they'll be very busy. But there was already one friendly fire incident with a Cricket West operation. You know the lieutenant I'm talking about. He killed a half dozen of our Laotian allies."

"I remember." The colonel shook his head with an exasperated look on his face.

"The NVA artillery capability is very credible. And I can't believe they won't be bringing SAMs with them. Another problem, the territory around the DMZ, as you know from experience colonel, is basically flat, 50% covered with trees and somewhat featureless. The lack of defined physical landmarks means a lot of confusion over exactly what coordinates are in play. This doesn't smell good to me."

He paused for a few moments; the colonel picked up a smoldering cigar from his desk ashtray and took a drag, blowing the smoke toward the ceiling. Then Thatcher continued.

"Colonel, you know what happened at Dien Bien Phu in 1954 better than anyone. The French picked a site for a set-piece battle, thinking they had the advantage. They thought their trenches, barricades, and breastworks made them safe from artillery. In fact, they were in a hole. General Giap did something the French never dreamed he could do, hauled artillery up jungle-covered mountains and rained down pure hell. Our bases at Dong Ha and Khe Sanh just south of the DMZ were abandoned for the same reason: they were hammered from a distance at night. There were very few frontal assaults. My youngest brother was a Marine at Dong Ha and is now medically retired with a mangled right arm. My brother told me he never got the chance to shoot at an enemy soldier; the NVA just sat back a few hundred meters and hammered away with artillery and missiles 24 hours a day."

Thatcher paused, frowned, and then continued, "By the time the NVA finishes with artillery and rocket attacks at night, they won't have to mount any suicide charges. Their artillery can fire up to 22 miles. The South Vietnamese, still alive, will run like hell. I wish someone would read Bernard Fall."

The Squadron Commander shook his head in a sign of agreement and dismay and then paused. "Well, do whatever you can do to make all that clear in your meeting."

"Yes sir."

After another long pause during which neither officer spoke, Thatcher stood up and the two men shook hands without any further discussion. The faces of both men were expressionless. Ted Thatcher saluted and left.

The next morning was uncharacteristically cool. Captain Thatcher, Nail 79, was seated on the NKP ramp near Base Ops, wearing blue jeans and a green golf shirt, waiting for a pickup by Raven 1, the commander of the Raven Detachment near Pakse, Laos. The early flights of daytime Nails were cranking up and taxiing out for take-off as the last of the night flights were landing. Right on time, at 0700, Raven 1 touched down and taxied over to the Nail portion of the flight line. Ted Thatcher waved to the O-1; the aircraft headed directly to him, shutting down the engine, and coasting to a stop a few feet from Thatcher and his overnight bag. The pilot, also wearing blue jeans, completed his ensemble with a Hawaiian shirt, and a cowboy hat. He stepped briskly from the Bird Dog and met Ted Thatcher halfway to the plane. He was slim, sported a smile on his face, and held out his hand. Thatcher shook it before picking up his bag,

"Hi. Brandon Sugg. Raven 1. I hope you're Nail 79."

"So do I." Thatcher was smiling. "I'm Ted Thatcher. Do you need to make a pit stop?"

"Negative, but thanks for the offer. I'm ready if you are."

"Let's go. I'm ready to hear the strategy for our upcoming victory."

Raven 1 laughed. "I see why you were selected for this mission. What's your outlook on this war?"

"I don't have an outlook. I just practice what I learned hunting doves in North Carolina: 'shoot at everything that flies and take credit for everything that falls.'"

Brandon laughed again and motioned to the open door of the O-1.

They climbed into the small O-1 Bird Dog, Major Sugg in the front seat and Thatcher in the back. Before Thatcher fully strapped in, the O-1 was taxiing toward the runway, but they didn't make it. Raven 1 gunned the engine on the O-1 and was airborne in about 400 feet, using only the taxi way. Ravens prided themselves on being a little out of the ordinary and made every effort to demonstrate how unconventional they were. Within two minutes, they leveled off at 400 feet and Major Sugg checked in on the intercom.

"I was given the highest recommendation for you by your Squadron Commander. Apparently, you've had some previous experience here. My only question is, why in the hell did you come back?"

"Before I answer, you have to tell me why you volunteered to become a Raven. Have you lost your mind?"

"That's simple enough. Where else can you fly without someone looking over your shoulder every minute and asking why you did what you did?"

"*Verstehen*. I guess you knew Paul Bartram."

"Of course. He was a Raven through and through. I feel for his wife and family. How did you know him?"

"He was my introduction to the Air Force Academy, my element leader the moment I walked onto the campus. He trained me to walk, talk, march, sleep, and everything else."

"Well. I'll be damned. I didn't know he went to the Academy. I thought he got right off a tractor and into a cockpit."

"Not hardly. He was definitely a farm boy, but he was also in the top 25-percent of his class. And he was tough as nails, pardon the expression."

"I'll pardon it. We Ravens don't think the Nails are tough at all."

"Look," laughed Thatcher, "I fly with our Laotian X-Ray friends, just like you, but when I get back, my next mission may very well be flying an O-2 over Mu Gia Pass. Want to join me?"

"Hell, no! That's Air Force stupidity. Why would they ever put an airplane without an ejection seat into that environment?"

"It didn't start that way. Initially, the anti-aircraft fire was lower caliber stuff. As it grew from heavy machine guns to real anti-aircraft artillery, the O-2s didn't show any more or fewer casualties than the newer OV-10s. Know why?"

"I would guess they are smaller and not as noisy."

"Bingo. When I volunteered for a second tour, I specified O-2s. Quite frankly, you Ravens would be a lot safer in O-2s."

"We would be, except we have to make a lot of short field takeoffs. Sometimes we land in rice paddies, dry ones of course."

"Of course. What's your guess on this meeting? From the Nail perspective, we're losing, which I predicted two years ago. We can't even begin to slow the truck traffic. Every time we launch an airstrike at night, the rest of the trail looks like an interstate highway. They even turn their lights on once we start an airstrike knowing we can't strike in two places at the same time. By the time we put in one airstrike, there's no telling how many other trucks have moved several more miles."

Brandon Sugg chimed in, "I agree we're losing. There's been no letup in Pathet Lao activity in the western half. It's definitely increasing. More villages are losing their rice to the bad guys. It means there are more bad guys. We're seeing gunfire from areas that were friendly a year ago. Maybe that's what this meeting is about."

"Maybe."

* * *

The secret meeting to win the war in Laos and Viet Nam began at 1400 hours on December 1, 1970. It was held in a briefing room at a Raven compound in southern Laos. There were no uniforms of any kind, and no full names were used, only call signs. It was not because the meeting was super-secret, which it was, but because those attending would be using their call signs in the upcoming campaign. This way they could put a face with the call sign during the upcoming battle. An American in civilian clothes began the meeting. He was apparently the CIA officer in charge.

"Gentlemen, thank you for attending. Let's see who's represented here."

Raven 1 started, "I'm Raven 1 and I represent the Raven FACs at this location, four of whom are with us here. We have a half dozen pilots and eight Laotian fighter pilots flying AT-6s."

Ted Thatcher went next, "I'm Nail 79 and I represent the Nails. We have four Nail/X-Ray teams at NKP and we can supplement them with as many solo Nails as necessary. Our squadron has 28 pilots and ten navigators who can operate day or night in both O-2s and OV-10s. I have been instructed to commit to this operation whatever is needed."

The CIA leader, who introduced himself as Bob, began the briefing by describing an anticipated major infantry invasion of Laos by South Vietnamese forces, spearheaded by five tank battalions. Entitled *Lam Son 719*, it would begin in early 1971 to block Route 9, the main road into South Viet Nam for the trucks on the Ho Chi Minh Trail. The designation "719" represented the year the South Vietnamese attack would commence, 1971, and the Route into South Viet Nam it would concentrate on blocking, Route 9 through Tchepone. The town of Tchepone, the bombed-out Laotian village just north of the Laotian/South Vietnamese border, was the intended focal point. Well known to the Nails, the convergence of the roads there would be captured and held for an indeterminate period using 12,000 Vietnamese infantry supported by their own tanks and U.S. air power. A push by U.S. troops into Laos had been seriously considered but rejected by the Nixon administration since it would be a violation of the Cooper Church Amendment prohibiting U.S. troops in Laos.

To provide intelligence on potential enemy reaction, there would be an initial probing test launched not from South Viet Nam, which might telegraph the punch, but from the Laotian side of the Mekong River across from Ubon, Thailand. This test would use one battalion of mercenaries from Laos commanded by a CIA officer and would measure the resistance from the Pathet Lao and North Vietnamese. It would occur in December 1970, one month in advance of the major invasion. The information gathered would be used in planning the major invasion.

For the major invasion itself, Dong Ha and Khe Sanh, the abandoned U.S. Marine bases just south of the DMZ, would be reactivated to provide artillery support. Army helicopter gunships and all available U.S. air power would be used to accompany the infantry/tank offensive, but no U.S. ground troops would be used. All of the ground operations, including the initial test by Laotian mercenaries in December, would depend heavily on U.S. airpower from the Thai airbases at NKP and Ubon, as well as the closest U.S. bases in South Viet Nam, such as Danang.

The briefing officer concluded, "Our major goal is to plug the Ho Chi Minh Trail from South Viet Nam by using South Vietnamese infantry, tanks, and U.S. airpower, including B-52 strikes. By stopping the flow of men and materials from Laos into South Viet Nam, it will allow the U.S. to ...." The briefing officer didn't finish the sentence because he didn't have to. Everyone in the room understood the U.S. was politically unable to continue prosecution of the war.

When asked if there were any questions, Ted Thatcher asked if anyone was familiar with the French defeat at Dien Bien Phu. The CIA officer responded quickly, "Of course. The NVA used artillery hauled up the mountains and rained down hell on the French who expected a set piece battle. They expected a frontal assault which they could defeat with artillery and airpower. The difference here is there are no mountains close enough to give the North Vietnamese that advantage."

"That's true." continued Thatcher, "but the enemy doesn't commit in broad daylight. Their tactics have always been rocket, mortar, and artillery fire, especially at night. They have artillery that can reach 20 miles. They don't have to be on a mountain. The South Vietnamese infantry will have nothing but foxholes. We can't use air attacks safely at night, even with flareships. The use of tanks is also questionable, at least in my mind. We're not dealing with the farmland of Europe; we're dealing with the jungle of Southeast Asia. Even where there are roads, they'll be mined heavily. What do you call a column of tanks with the lead tank blown up and blocking the rest of the tanks behind it? It's called a shooting gallery, and the French learned it the hard way."

The room was quiet, and the briefing officer paused before speaking. When he did, it was with very measured language.

"I hear you loud and clear. All I'm authorized to say is the U.S. effort here is winding down and this is the opportunity for the South Vietnamese and Laotians to assume the lead role in protecting their countries. You are all in this room to provide air cover, you know the territory, you know the enemy, and you will have unlimited access to whatever you need." There was a long pause while the reality of the situation sunk in.

"I understand." Thatcher was the one speaking but the rest of the room nodded in agreement. There was no need to expand the discussion any further at this point.

That night, Ted Thatcher, the CIA officers involved, and the Raven FACs assembled at a local restaurant in the nearby town. The Crown Prince of Laos, resplendent in his dress uniform, the Princess, his very attractive wife, the Laotian X-Rays headed by Major Khampat, and the Laotian T-28 fighter pilots joined the Americans at a long banquet table. To Thatcher's acute embarrassment, some of the American CIA radio operators brought prostitutes into the room as dates as well. The meal was served, along with wine and mixed drinks consumed by the Americans only. After dinner, the Crown Prince delivered a very moving speech directed to the Laotian fighter pilots present. Although the Americans could not understand him, the emotional content was clearly discernible. The Prince obviously conveyed the utmost seriousness of the upcoming offensive, and the Laotians present displayed very somber faces both during and after the speech. The Prince finished his remarks, and the diners rose in respect as the Prince and his wife departed. He probably suspected 1,000 years of the monarchy were coming to end. And he was right. He would ultimately escape across the Mekong River into Thailand, but much of the rest of the Royal Family, including the King, would be sent to camps where they lived until they died.

After dinner, the American pilots moved upstairs to a bar that featured a Laotian rock band trying hard to mimic American music. A number of Laotian 'ladies' and Americans who were not in the meeting were already dancing.

Thatcher assumed the Americans were the aircraft mechanics and radio operators who supported the Raven FACs in their missions in the Cricket West missions in the Laotian territory bordering Thailand. Raven 1 and two other Ravens Thatcher knew only by call signs from previous aerial encounters, ordered beer, and spent a few minutes trading backgrounds with each other before launching into a discussion on the upcoming operation.

Raven 1 started with a direct question to Thatcher. "Nail 79, you were a little rough on the briefers in there. We agree with you 100 percent, but you know as well as we do it's over. We'll do our duty, as you Nails will, but the end is not going to be pretty."

Thatcher paused a moment before answering. "Every American soldier, sailor, and airman in Southeast Asia knows it's over. This operation, in my opinion, is designed to allow the administration in Washington to say we tried, and that it's not our fault the South Vietnamese couldn't step up to the plate."

Then he spoke in a lower tone of voice to avoid anyone hearing other than the FACs at the table. "As far as this initial test from Thailand into Laos to block the trail, our CIA test battalion coming in from Laos on Route 9 will be sitting ducks; they won't even have a tree to hide behind. Route 9 is basically a dirt road through abandoned rice paddies. Our air power is impressive, especially the

B-52s. But the NVA will strike unexpectedly and retreat quickly. And all of this will be at night, when we're sleeping. The battalion won't last a week.

"The South Vietnamese invasion scheduled in January will be a different story, but with the same ending. There is nothing to hide behind, and all the tanks in the world won't change this because this is not the open farmland of Europe, this is the jungle of Southeast Asia. This is an historic moment, and we are right here at the starting gate. Maybe I should say we're at the finish line. But the most painful part to me is that our Laotian friends, the ones we have all been flying with for our entire tours, are going to endure hell, and we all know it. The Viet Nam fiasco has been an inexcusable exercise in American ignorance. Ho Chi Minh was probably the logical choice to be the leader of his country. But the Laotian communists are not patriots, and they do not have the support of the people. They're Chinese puppets. They are thugs and we all know it."

No one argued, and the rest of the night was somber. The FACs turned in early. The following morning, the Ravens and Nail 79 bid goodbye and good luck. Raven 1 ferried Thatcher home to NKP. They shook hands and Thatcher watched as Raven 1, true to form, simply turned around and took off from the taxiway, ignoring all the flight line rules.

"Ravens," Thatcher laughed to himself as he picked up his bag and headed for base ops.

24

Lam Son 719

Thatcher went straight to the Commanding Officer upon landing to report on the visit to the Raven Base. Col Melendez closed the door after Thatcher saluted and then settled back in his reclining office chair with its squeaky wheels. If a face could convey curiosity, his would win the Academy Award, and he wasted no time on niceties. "Have a seat Ted and give me the bad news."

"Well, Sir, it isn't good news, I am sorry to say. But I'm not surprised. I know the end had to come sometime, but I don't have a good feeling about what I heard in Laos. I was told that the South Vietnamese are going to invade Laos and block the Ho Chi Minh Trail with five tank battalions supported by South Vietnamese infantry. This is supposed to give the United States an opening to begin accelerated withdrawal of the troops in South Viet Nam. The Operation is code named *Lam Son 719*. The number is a conjunction of the year it will be launched, 1971, and the defined operational territory, Route 9, the main road used by the NVA into South Viet Nam. 'Lam Son' was a famous Vietnamese victory over the Chinese in 1418, so it's meant to inspire courage. The plan is a two-pronged invasion aimed at capturing Tchepone.

"As you well know sir, Tchepone is nothing but a bombed-out village at a conjunction of dirt roads one mile north of the DMZ used by trucks headed to South Viet Nam and Cambodia. You and I have created a few of the bomb craters there because there are always trucks passing through there at night, and it's a good place to hunt. The anti-aircraft fire there is as bad as anywhere on the trail. 'Capturing Tchepone' is probably a poor choice of words since there is no village left to capture, but the basic idea is stopping the trucks traffic until the rainy season starts in May, and win the war. I'm being facetious, of course, but the unspoken strategy is to do something all our bombing for the last decade has been unable to do stop the guns, ammunition, and supplies from getting into South Viet Nam. As we all know, the Viet Nam War could not continue without the supply pipeline. At its most basic level, this is a supply war. Strategically, the operation makes sense. An army moves on its stomach; stop the trucks and the VC in South Viet Nam can't continue. Tactically, it will be a blood bath for us and them. We'll lose planes, including FACs, and choppers supporting the South Vietnamese troops."

Col. Melendez, obviously concerned, asked, "Whose idea is this? Who's running the show?"

Thatcher paused for a moment to collect his thoughts. "Hard to say. Obviously, the CIA is involved since they're running the show in Laos. That's who briefed me on my visit to Laos. This is the first time in our history that the CIA has fielded its own army and air force. But I suspect this is straight from Washington designed to get us out. Plugging the Ho Chi Minh Trail is the key. From the news reports we've been seeing here second-hand; veterans back home are leading a lot of the demonstrations. Infantry and tanks could do something we haven't been able to do with air power in the last decade. Theoretically, if they could block the trail, the North Vietnamese supply chain into South Viet Nam would be blocked, at least temporarily. That could allow our withdrawal from South Viet Nam at a faster pace. Weather, which precludes us from operating, would no longer be a factor. Realistically, though, they'll be sitting ducks. NVA rockets and mortars will be relentless. It'll be Dien Bien Phu all over again. Expect the worst. The French at Dien Bien Phu used underground bunkers and extensive trenches to facilitate troop movement. These poor guys will have nothing but a foxhole if they're lucky.

"There will be a test, a battalion of South Vietnamese infantry will march from western Laos to Tchepone led by the CIA. It will begin next week. The objective is to see if they can reach Tchepone and how long they can stay there. They'll measure the level of resistance. No one expects a battalion to hold it for very long. We'll have joint responsibility with the Ravens for air cover for the troops. So, although the official start of the operation isn't until early in January, our squadron will be engaged ahead of it in supporting this probing operation. The code name of the American contact for the test is Red Man. We shared a few drinks at a bar during my visit to the Raven compound last night. He must be out of his mind.

"The actual invasion in January will be with five battalions of tank-supported South Vietnamese infantry. It will be modified as necessary based on this test. Our responsibility is to offer all the air cover we can muster in both the test phase next week and the actual invasion which will follow in January. Nails will be the primary FACs, but Coveys from Danang will also be used in the actual invasion. Obviously, we can't do anything at night, so the troops on the ground will be subject to most of their attacks at night."

The Commander frowned, aware of the dangers facing his squadron in the weeks ahead. Supporting infantry and tanks was one thing in South Viet Nam where the quantity and size of the AAA was much smaller than in Laos. The rule of flying 5,000 feet above the ground in Laos was mandated because of the obvious risk/ reward ratio. In the case of *Lam Son 719*, the support of infantry and tanks meant accepting the risk of flying far lower altitudes.

The anti-aircraft threat from large AAA that could reach well over 10,000 feet would be supplemented by lower caliber machine guns. That meant double the risk to the pilots. He didn't speak for a while, obviously mulling things over. How many Nails would be lost? What would happen to the truck traffic on the trail if so many resources were shifted south to the DMZ? If the operation failed, what next? If the U.S. pulled out, how would it affect his squadron? The thought of losing even one of his crewmembers in a lost cause was disturbing to the commander. Thatcher didn't interfere, and patiently waited for his commander to speak. Finally, he did.

"Obviously, Ted, you need to brief the squadron. I'll schedule a meeting day after tomorrow. Don't hold back I want you to speak clearly and forcefully. I assume you and the other Cricket West FACs will be in a front row seat for this operation."

"Yes Sir, but it will take all of the 23rd if I don't miss my guess."

There was a long pause. Finally the Squadron Commander spoke. "This operation doesn't stand a chance in hell, does it?"

The commander was normally not this blunt, and Nail 79 didn't mince words either. "Not a chance, colonel. The moment the lights go, the NVA will move in. They'll use fixed artillery, and they also have much more advanced Soviet rockets. Between those weapons and the mortars, which will be moved frequently, the attacks will come incessantly and mostly at night. Mines will hamper the South Vietnamese tanks along with the terrain. When it's over, the North Vietnamese are going to realize there isn't anything stopping them from continuing on … and by that, I mean to Saigon."

"I guess you're right. If we've thrown everything we have at them, and they've demolished the five tank battalions, why would they pack up and go home? If all of I Corps is sitting there for the taking, why turn around and leave?"

Another long pause. Then it hit both of them at once. The war was over! The American effort was already unwinding, papered over with 'Vietnamization', Washington's term for turning the war over to the South Vietnamese. When, not if, this *Lam Son 719* attempt at closing the supply lines of the North Vietnamese collapsed, why would the North Vietnamese just stop and turn around? The war really was over; only the headlines were waiting to be written!

That night in the Nail Hole, Elvis Presley was singing, appropriately, *There Goes My Everything*. Thatcher entered after taking a short nap and found the party in full swing. Roger Brown brought him a beer and asked him what he'd been up to.

"Just finished briefing the Squadron Commander on the upcoming plan to win the war."

Brown laughed. "You're going home soon, if memory serves. Coming back for a third tour?" He was being intentionally sarcastic.

"No, I was thinking of writing a book."

"Well, nothing ruins a good war story like an eyewitness."

Thatcher laughed. "Ain't that the truth?"

25

The Big Test

On December 5, 1970, the sun rose on a cloudless sky as two men in camouflage fatigues strapped into parachutes on the Pierced Steel Planking (PSP) that covered the flight line at Nakhon Phanom Royal Thai Air Force base. Ted Thatcher and his Xray for the mission, Lt. Tonsonnai, squeezed into the cockpit from the open door on the left side and strapped in. Thatcher started rear engine first followed by the front engine and started taxiing while receiving clearance from NKP Ground Control. They took off on a pre-planned mission to provide air cover for the first infantry incursion onto the Ho Chi Minh Trail. It never would be reported to the press and would never be mentioned in any articles after the war. It was intended solely to assess the reaction of the North Vietnamese to infantry activity in and around Tchepone. And it would provide an omen of things to come.

Thatcher and Lt. Tonsonnai arrived at daybreak over the base of a mountain on the western side of the valley/flood plain that was the flat land hosting the Ho Chi Minh Trail and its various tributaries. They found a long string of infantry already descending from the safety of the gorgeous green mountains to the dusty brown plains of Laos. The mountains they were leaving were decorated with gun-metal gray karst formations erupting vertically from the lush green jungle and topped with sunshine like frosting on a cake. It was a beautiful day. The camouflage-clad soldiers below Thatcher's O-2 were Vietnamese except for Red Man, the American commander who was the contact. No one was wearing uniform insignia of any kind. The guerilla fighters were marching east on Route 9, the dirt road that was the primary target for blockage of the truck traffic. They were 20 miles east of Tchepone, their intended target. And they were, to put it mildly, guineas pigs.

The rice paddies on either side of the dirt road were abandoned years before because of the war. This dry, brown landscape was interspersed with water-filled bomb craters, many dating back a decade or more. Azure blue water filled the craters that looked so out of place, a beautiful collection of topaz jewelry on a piece of rough burlap.

Red Man called on the VHF radio. "Nail 79, Red Man. Is that you?"

Thatcher looked down and saw 1,500 troops waving their rifles in the air, obviously happy to see air cover. "Sure is. How're things Red Man?"

"I've been expecting you and you sure look good. So far, so good down here. How do things look ahead?"

"Don't know yet. Just got here. Let me take a look."

"Roger that. The troops would sure appreciate a little air show."

"Well, I always wanted to fly with the Thunderbirds. Hold on to your hat."

Thatcher dove down to tree top level and zoomed over the column of troops, using his excess air speed to pull up and over into an aileron roll. While inverted, he fired a few rockets for effect in the direction the column was headed. The response was immediate.

"Shit hot, Nail!" Red Man keyed his mic to allow Thatcher to hear the cheers of the troops below.

"Glad to oblige. I've got three hours of fuel. I'll be ahead of you checking things out. If you hear any anti-aircraft fire, let me know. I can't hear it in the airplane."

"Roger that."

Tonsonnai tapped the mic on his helmet and Thatcher informed Red Man his X-Ray wanted to talk to the Laotian troop commander. The conversation was in Lao, and Tonsonnai spoke for several minutes before signing off.

"How are things?" Thatcher asked Tonsonnai over the intercom.

"Good. Everyone is what you call gung ho."

"Well, I just hope this is a short-term thing. I can't imagine them lasting for more than a few days. The bad guys will keep pouring more and more men in here until they outnumber Red Man and his people, and it won't be a pretty sight."

Thatcher pulled up from treetop level to 1,000 feet above the ground. This was 4,000 feet lower than the standard operating altitude over the Ho Chi Minh Trail and subjected the O-2 not just to the standard large caliber anti-aircraft fire, but to small arms fire as well. To compensate for the increased risk, he jinked aggressively, banking 45 degrees in random directions while he and Tonsonnai kept their heads on a swivel.

Surprisingly, after three hours of searching for signs of enemy activity, there was not a single shot fired. It was nothing short of a miracle because this was one of the hottest areas on the trail. Thatcher knew from experience there were dozens of anti-aircraft guns easily in range. He was amazed that he couldn't find even one. The NVA camouflage techniques were truly incredible. There were, of course, no signs whatsoever of any current agricultural activity. He was surprised by the obvious age of many of the bomb craters. There were small trees growing in some of them, giving a clue as to the age of this war.

Thatcher, although far from relaxed, was enjoying the experience. A year of flying a mile high above the landscape never gave the same impression as flying right on top of it. From the ground, Red Man would have heard anti-aircraft guns several miles away but continued to report nothing. The North Vietnamese were masters of camouflage. Thatcher knew they were there somewhere but were choosing not to engage for some reason. Perhaps they wanted to lure the CIA battalion deeper into the trap. He knew from experience a lot of NVA operations were underground, so hiding was not that difficult. At the end of his fuel capacity, two hours over target, he flew over Red Man one more time.

"Red Man, I flew all the way to Tchepone and never saw the first sign of the bad guys and never got shot at, least as far as I know. I've put a lot of airstrikes in here at night and I know they use this road a lot. But there isn't a lot of cover so I suspect your daytime activities will go uncontested. This evening, you'll be getting a lot more attention, so dig deep and stay small. I'll be back in two days, but other Nails will be overhead at all times."

"Roger that Nail. Thanks for everything. I enjoyed the beers the other night."

After landing, Thatcher reported and gave the debriefer, Lt. Sanford, his report.

"I stayed with the column for several miles and observed no ground fire. I flew ahead of them over a fairly wide area 100 feet to 1,000 feet where I know there is a substantial amount of AAA based on my previous trail missions. I was surprised at the lack of ground fire. I suspect they were aware of our ground forces and were baiting the trap, waiting to get our guys into a vulnerable position before giving their positions away. Just a guess. Captain Mark Tinga was shot down once in this area, so I know the AAA is there."

Lt. Sanford interjected, "do you suppose the NVA isn't prepared for an infantry attack since they are primarily engaged in anti-aircraft activity? They can't even lower their barrels past 20 or 30 degrees. Maybe they don't have infantry in that area."

"Possibly, but it still doesn't explain why they didn't hose me down. I almost made myself sick with the extra jinking I did. My X-Ray, Lt. Tonsonnai, started to look green around the gills, so I pulled up occasionally to a higher altitude and smoothed it out a bit. He made it through, barely."

"Thanks captain. Let's hope this all goes as well as it did today. You flyin' tomorrow?"

"No, thank God. Capt. Sam Dixon and Capt. Jim Tyler will be covering for the next few days. I'm going back to Bangkok to complete my short R and R."

"Have a good time, captain. See you when you get back."

26

The Best Laid Plans ...

Thatcher stepped off the C-130 from Bangkok after a two-day pass and was met by the squadron orderly who saluted. "Sir, the C.O. wants to see you right away. I have a car."

"Airman Blake, we're going to have to stop meeting like this. People will be starting to talk."

"Sorry, Sir. Orders."

Thatcher walked down the hall at the headquarters building to the C.O.'s office and knocked on the open door. The commander was on the phone, his back to the door in a swivel chair. As he turned around, he motioned with his hand to Thatcher to come in. After hanging up he spoke in a very serious voice.

"Ted, the test for Operation *Lam Son 719* was a complete disaster. Your CIA friend retreated back to a mountain top where he has been parked for the last 24 hours. He's surrounded by at least a battalion of NVA and getting hammered by mortars every night.

"To make matters worse, one of our junior pilots, Lt. Pridgen, was directed to their location to provide air cover. He screwed up the strike. Put the smoke too close to the troops. The F-4s killed a few dozen of our own guys. The ground commander has been asking for you personally and I don't know how much longer he can hold out."

"Sir, I can go now if there's a plane ready." Thatcher was still wearing his camouflage fatigues from the return flight from Bangkok. Military personnel often sacked out on a pile of parachutes on the cargo planes which were transporting them around Southeast Asia.

"There is."

"I'm on the way."

"Thanks, Ted. By the way, how was the French Onion Soup at Nick's Number One?"

"Superb, as usual," Thatcher answered as he headed out the door. "When are you scheduled for leave?"

"I was waiting for you to get back. This CIA thing is going to get worse, isn't it?"

"Yes sir, it is. Do I have an X-Ray?"

"Lt. Boun Tang has been waiting for you to get back. I took the liberty of sending him to the briefing room."

"Thank you, sir." Thatcher saluted and departed.

Thatcher met Lt. Boun Tang in the briefing room. The lieutenant, like all of the X-rays, was short with pearly white teeth and black hair. Unlike the others, he didn't smile much, but was always friendly. After a very short briefing and receiving the launch code for the day, the two walked to the flight line and started the preflight. Minutes later, they lifted off and headed east.

Thatcher contacted the airborne command post. "Hillsborough, Nail 79 outbound to Sector III."

"Roger that Nail 79. Let us know what you need. We'll have some F-4s available in about 20 minutes."

"That's great. Any CBU?"

"Affirmative. CBU 29."

"Fantastic. I should be on station in 20 minutes."

"Roger that."

Thatcher reverted to intercom and continued his climb to 5,200 feet.

"Boun Tang, have you been on any of the support missions since I left?"

"No. Maj. Khampat and Lt. Tonsonnai have been flying. They say Red Man got attacked with mortars first night at Tchepone. Started back next morning. Made it to mountain. Had air cover most of way but that night very bad. Lose many men. Next morning airplane trying to kill bad guys hit Red Man's position by mistake, kill many men."

Most Nails didn't work with troops, but all were trained back in America to provide close air support. This friendly fire incident directed by a Nail was disgusting. Lt. Boun Tang pronounced a word Thatcher could not mimic, but it sounded angry. Thatcher turned his attention to the radio, having gained enough altitude to permit reception.

"Red Man, this is Nail 79, over."

"Nail 79, this is Red Man. Thank God. When can you get here?"

"Twenty minutes out."

Red Man apparently had apparently made it to Tchepone, the former town, but was driven back almost to the starting point the following day and was perched not far from where he started on a meadow near the top of one of the ubiquitous karst formations embracing the trail on both sides. He recited some coordinates which Thatcher found easily after reaching the area. He increased his altitude to avoid drawing attention to the friendlies on the ground, but it was unnecessary. The Pathet Lao or North Vietnamese already knew where Red Man was.

Red Man spoke again in a very strained voice. "We've been hammered all night long by mortars. I've lost half my men." He didn't say how many were killed by friendly fire the previous day directed by the young Nail, and Thatcher didn't ask. Red Man's radio operator was killed, and the main radio was shot off the operator's back. Red Man was using a handheld radio. Thatcher's anger at the

Nail who misdirected the airstrike was mixed with overwhelming sorrow at the devastation he saw below him.

Red Man and his troops came into sight, perched at the high side of a meadow at the top of a karst peak surrounded by jungle. On the eastern side of the wide grassy meadow, the side next to the trail, the rocky terrain dropped off very steeply and provided a fairly good defense against a ground attack from the trail itself. The western side was a gently sloping downhill meadow, about 600 yards in length, gradually changing into jungle. It was the only path home to western Laos and safety. On left and right sides of the scoop-shaped meadow, were walls of vertical karst formations, not suitable for moving troops, enemy or friendly. The geography meant the ground troops were safe from attack both from the trail and from the sides. Unfortunately, the only way home was downhill, directly into the enemy mortar position in the trees, which was more than likely supported by infantry in sizeable numbers.

The CIA-supported troops on the trail side of the meadow were in a dug-in infantry position, a large circle of foxholes easily visible from the air. Black spots of earth dotted the circle, and it was obvious the enemy forces had worked hard on them the night before with mortars. Bodies were scattered around the site; a few dozen were in clear view with more probably in the trees.

"What do you need, Red Man?" Thatcher's mood had changed from anger to an overwhelming sense of compassion as he contemplated the possible actions that might save the remnant below him.

Red Man answered, his voice raspy and tinged with a sense of helplessness. "There's at least one 82mm mortar down the slope to the west of us in the trees, maybe more. I don't know how far down. They move up close after dark and hammer us. They're killing us. Most of my survivors are wounded. We won't make it through another night with them blocking us. We need to go over or through them to get back home."

Thatcher had been flying over the area downhill from the troops and 500 feet above the ground, but he couldn't see through the canopy of trees at the lower end. Like most jungle in Southeast Asia, it was 'triple canopy', which meant vegetation with multiple layers even sunlight couldn't penetrate.

"Consider them gone Red Man. God Bless." Thatcher startled himself. He had never invoked the name of the Lord in combat before, but the visible evidence of the hell that was the current home of Red Man overwhelmed him. Much of his war was impersonal: trucks on the trail, guns in the trees, storage depots. This was a different scenario. This was personal. Thatcher had met Red Man personally at the meeting in Laos, shook his hand, shared a few beers, told a few war stories. Thatcher was emotional, but he knew he needed to remain in control. So, he suppressed his emotions and did what he had to do.

"Hillsborough, Nail 79. Troops in Contact! I need that CBU 29 and fast."

"Roger, Nail 79. Your F-4s are a few minutes away."

As a command-and-control system, Hillsborough and Moonbeam were well designed and operated efficiently, as Thatcher once again discovered. Thatcher never knew the people behind the radios, but they had earned his respect. In his year of combat, they never failed him. In his later years, he would regret not having met any of them.

While Thatcher waited, he spoke with Red Man again, if for no other reason than to bolster his spirits. "Red Man, it should be raining in a few minutes." Since it was a clear day, Thatcher's meaning was obvious.

"Thanks, Nail. I've sent several patrols down there to locate the mortar position, but they've all been wiped out. We lost our mortars two days ago. All we have are rifles and a few .50 cals."

"Well, when we're finished, you should be able to walk home on the bodies. I need you to tell me when you hear noise indicating a hit on the mortar rounds."

"Roger that, Nail."

As he finished, the Phantoms checked in.

"Nail 79, this is Denver 44 flight, flight of two F-4s with CBU 29. We have you in sight, O-2 circling left over the karst peak. We'll be orbiting above you until you're ready."

"Roger, Denver. The scorched earth right under me is home to a bunch of good guys who have been hammered all night. That is sacred ground. Do not come anywhere close to it. Below them and to the west is a U-shaped valley covered in jungle. Do you have it?"

"Affirmative, Nail."

"Okay, I'm going to locate the bad guys in that jungle and put in two smokes. Your job is to kill everything between the marks."

"Roger."

Thatcher told Lt. Boun Tang to keep his eyes open and dove for the trees on the V-shaped slope below Red Man. He made the first pass perpendicular to the valley a few hundred meters down the slope and 100 feet above the trees. The triple canopy jungle was as effective a screen as could be imagined, and he saw and heard nothing.

Thatcher used the excess airspeed from his first dive to climb up the opposite side of the V-shaped funnel. At the top of his climb, in a near stall, he wheeled the O-2 around, pivoting on one wing. Then, he swooped down in the opposite direction a few hundred feet farther down the slope from the first pass. Again, nothing.

On the third pass he was rewarded with what he was been looking for—a series of bursts that sounded like popcorn popping. Machine gun fire! Where there were machine guns, there must be mortars. He firewalled the throttles, pulled the aircraft quickly wings level, clawed for altitude, and armed his rockets as he climbed. At the top of his climb, with airspeed near a stall, he kicked left rudder, dropped the nose and reversed course. As he rolled wings level and nose down, he fired two rockets, 100 meters apart, at the pollution below him and then headed back toward the troops flying at tree-top level, staying as low as possible to give the jets room to maneuver. His rockets produced two distinct white plumes puffing up from the trees.

"Okay, Denver. Between the marks."

"Roger that Nail. One's in."

Denver 44 Alpha, the lead F-4, rolled upside down and then rolled out 45 degrees nose low. Seconds later, Denver 44 Bravo followed suit. Thatcher never tired of watching the superb airmanship of American pilots from his vantage point as a strike commander. He had been in love with a dancer once and he often imagined himself as a kind of choreographer. This was a great ballet, although a deadly one. The finale of the 1812 Overture was thundering in the back of his mind as he conducted the F-4 Phantom Philharmonic. Within seconds, the F-4s, one after the other, rolled out wings level 500 feet above the ground and saturated the entire jungle between the parallel ridges with their deadly calling cards in the first of a series of passes. They pulled up hard and left and circled around for the next pass. The hundreds of sparkles each CBU bomblet created as it exploded looked like a field of stars in the dark green jungle below.

CBU didn't cause as much noise as conventional bombs; they sounded more like firecrackers. Thatcher knew from being shot at just a few moments before that the CBU must have hit something, but he was looking for more noise, lots of noise, but Red Man heard nothing but the pops of the CBU.

"OK, Denver. Good work. Right on target. I know you got some troops, but I want the mortars. Let's move down the slope a little." He fired two more rockets, one after the other 300 meters farther down the slope. Again, the F-4s were right on target, and once again, Red Man reported nothing but the CBU pops.

On the third pass, still lower down the slope, Red Man began screaming over the radio. "You got him Nail! Their mortar rounds are cooking off like popcorn!" Thatcher found what he was looking for, and as if to confirm, every time Red Man pressed his mic button, Thatcher could hear the troops below shouting, ecstatic after a night of hell. The bad guys, Pathet Lao, or maybe even NVA, apparently anticipated a reaction and had moved well away from the friendlies on the ground. That's why it took three passes to find them.

"Denver flight, you got the mortars and the ammunition. Our troops below are shouting and waving to us. Drop your remaining load a little farther down to give them a clear path home. Then make a low pass over the troops and give them a farewell air show."

"Roger that Nail."

The F-4s dropped the remaining CBU with no more appreciable secondary explosions and departed after a tree-top, vertical, after-burning climb.

Shit Hot, Ted thought. In the midst of all this crap, there is some glimmer of justice, some hope that maybe the bad guys don't always win.

"How about that, Boun Tang?"

Lt. Boun Tang didn't answer. Thatcher looked over at the right-hand seat for the first time since the battle was joined. Lt. Boun Tang, his eyes wide open and filled with fear, were looking at a bullet hole in the window just inches behind Thatcher's head. The bullet, probably a .51 caliber, apparently came in through the rear right hand window of the O-2 leaving a very neat hole three quarters of an inch in diameter and exiting through the top of the cockpit over Thatcher's head.

The two comrades looked at each other, neither speaking. Thatcher would live with the picture—and many more like it, for the rest of his life: pictures of people, men—and women—enveloped in orange swirls of napalm; squadron mates blown out of cockpits; trucks with people inside being vaporized by Mark 82s; human beings on the ground being punctured by stainless steel ball bearings from cluster bombs. If the North Vietnamese were like the Nazis in WWII, sympathy would have been out of the question; but these weren't Nazis, they were Vietnamese trying to reunite their country. Their enemy was a different race of people from a nation halfway around the world who had arbitrarily cut their nation half and invented a government to their liking. On the ground, the few surviving North Vietnamese, all wounded, were picking up their dead, including their unit commander, Sergeant Ca, who, from his 14th birthday, had spent his entire life at war. He had been promoted from an anti-aircraft battery commander to an artillery company with over 100 men. He was a father to a son he had never seen, and a husband to a wife who would join the throngs of North Vietnamese widows who had almost forgotten what their husbands looked like. American would suffer 58,862 deaths in the war; the North Vietnamese would experience over 1,000,000 but no one could really count the cost of the Viet Nam war.

27

Farewell

The Air Force has a long-standing tradition called a Dining In, a rite of passage at which significant events are celebrated, awards are distributed to worthy recipients, and much alcohol is consumed in the assumption that anyone getting inebriated with another airman must, by definition, be solidifying the bands of the brotherhood for which they had pledged their lives and sacred honor. The 23rd TASS upheld this tradition once a month, not only to bid farewell to those leaving, but to welcome their replacements. Col Melendez called the December Dining In to order on December 29th, 1970, at 1800 hours at the NKP Officers' Club. This Dining In was both a celebration and a memorial. The event was a celebration of life, first and foremost, but also a memorial to those who did not survive to celebrate.

As the northern-most FACs in the Viet Nam War, the graduating Nails faced death many times, flying an average of 200 missions over the course of the year they served. From their very first mission, they faced a continuous escalation of gunfire from the largest caliber of anti-aircraft guns in the most heavily bombed country in the history of the world. They were also witnessing what appeared to be the beginning to the end of the war.

Dramatic events in the past year? One could write a book. Nails watched as a North Vietnamese MiG shot down a Jolly Green helicopter on a rescue mission in their own playground. They heard briefings every day on the escalation in Viet Cong victories in South Viet Nam. They watched the news as Americans, including Viet Nam veterans, were escalating their criticism of the war. So, they were leaving their brothers behind with mixed emotions. At one end of the emotional scale was a sense of relief that they still were alive; at the other end was a sense of profound sorrow at the death of many of their friends, both Nails and others with whom they fought their battles. Perhaps, somewhere in between, was the nagging thought that those to whom they were bidding farewell might not have the opportunity to do the same when their tour ended. Pilots were still dying all over Southeast Asia as were Marines and Army troops on the ground. No one wanted to be the last man to die in a war that, to paraphrase Shakespeare, was a 'tale told by an idiot, full of sound and fury, and signifying nothing'.

Each of the departing Nails at The Dining In spoke in turn and there was no censorship of any kind. At the end of the ceremony, they were each presented with the coveted Brass Balls Award. This cherished award, a red, white, and blue ribbon consisted of two small brass balls and would hang next to their other medals when they returned home. And they would have a lot of medals.

The first after dinner speaker and the presenter of the awards was the Squadron Commander, Col. Melendez. His avuncular manner and demonstration of courage in flying as many missions as his schedule allowed had endeared him to the Nails.

"Gentlemen, we are gathered here tonight to celebrate our victories but to also remember with sadness those who are not here to celebrate with us, those who perished in the service of their country. We have all witnessed the acceleration of enemy activity, the continued drawdown of our military presence in South Viet Nam, and the turmoil in our nation back home. Many of these protests are being led by Viet Nam veterans, as you all know, and the civil unrest is becoming more and more pronounced. I have no crystal ball, but I suspect we will see a conclusion of this military activity in the foreseeable future. In fact, there is a dramatic operation intended to start our withdrawal in the near future, one code named *Lam Son 719* awaiting those of us who remain. It will start with a South Vietnamese tank invasion across the DMZ at Tchepone in January."

"Ted Thatcher, who is leaving us tonight, represented us in the planning session in Laos. You will be briefed on the operation soon. Ted was also involved in providing air cover for a CIA-led infantry probe from a safe area down Route 9 to Tchepone. It was a disaster. The NVA just waited for nightfall and wiped out half the force. Ted and I think this may signal the end of the war, but only time will tell.

To those departing our band of brothers tonight, my thanks for your devotion to duty and your courage in carrying out your mission assignments with aggressiveness and skill. You have served your country well. This event is an opportunity for your remaining comrades to honor you as they will be honored by their replacements. There is no doubt the engagement here by our nation will be debated for years after it ends, but I say to each of you honored here tonight, you have done your duty. I salute you. Return to your families and your new assignments and never doubt your actions were honorable. It's a tradition for each departing Nail to say whatever he wants, with no censorship, so let's begin."

The Commander then introduced each of the departing Nails in turn with a few remarks about their more notable achievements. There were six departing Nails, each of whom made remarks, some humorous, some profane. Each then had the Brass Balls Award pinned to his black party suit, the one with the red Laotian Flag patch on the left pocket and the American flag patch sewn on the right. According to tradition, each was honor-bound to chug down a mug of beer. If the honoree was unable to get the entire mug down, tradition also required him to empty it ceremoniously on his own head. The first five Nails made comments, mostly humorous, some profane, but all received warm rounds of applause. Some got the mug all the way down, others didn't even try.

Thatcher, sitting at the head table with the Squadron Commander and the other departing Nails, stood last and approached the podium. He paused, took a deep breath, and began. "Gentlemen, I am reminded of a line from Macbeth, 'it was a tale told by an idiot, full of sound and fury, and signifying nothing.'"

The laughter, hoots, and whistles that erupted showed the assembled Nails the message was understood clearly.

"I am also here to announce tonight that the War is over!"

More laughter erupted, followed by cheers and whistles. After it died down, Thatcher continued. "I'm not kidding you drunk bastards, so listen up. There is going to be an attempt to end this nightmare, and it ain't gonna be pretty. As you know, we've been fighting two wars in Laos, making it the most devastated country since the end of WWII. One war was the Truck War which was really a part of the Viet Nam War. The Viet Nam war will be over soon. We all know that; the U. S. Government knows that; the North Vietnamese know that. It was conceived by successive American leaders to prevent the unification of Viet Nam. I won't go into the history, but suffice to say we didn't have a clue how to create a viable government in a third world nation whose people can't read or write and whose economy is not based on producing cars or any other manufactured product. Their economy rises and falls on the success or failure of the rice crop. North Viet Nam can't grow rice, at least reliably; South Viet Nam can triple crop. So why did we divide it? And if you were Ho Chi Minh, what would you have done? The need for rice alone would have justified North Viet Nam's war efforts. But we also know we shouldn't be in Viet Nam for political reasons. Whoever was responsible for dividing the country and creating a government in the South out of thin air was a few beers short of a six pack. That's why we use the 'F' word to describe the Truck War and sing a few disgusting songs when we've had too much to drink in the Nail Hole. Come to think of it, most of the songs we sing in the Nail Hole are disgusting. I'm surprised those songs and the jokes we share every night haven't peeled the paint off the Nail Hole walls.

"But back to my Master's Thesis: What you and I were supposed to do here was simple: stop the trucks, win the war, starve the invaders. We all know how that's working out. It's not because we aren't killing trucks, but when we blow up one, two more take its place. And while we mourn the loss of over 50,000 of our countrymen, South Viet Nam has suffered three times that at last count. Civilian casualties We've done our job, but that won't win the war, if the definition of winning is stopping the convoys full of troops, supplies, and ammunition headed to South Viet Nam. We all know triple canopy jungle is impossible to penetrate on any meaningful scale from the air and our efforts, spectacular as they may be and as brave as you are, will never be enough."

Someone from the crowd shouted, "Tell it Ted! Tell it!" and was met by howls of alcohol-induced laughter.

Thatcher paused, smiled, took another swig, and then continued. Dignity and drunk Nails, after all, were mutually exclusive.

"OK, I will tell it: News flash. The powers that be have decided to win the Truck War by invading Laos from South Viet Nam using South Vietnamese infantry and tanks supported by American air power. The goal is to block the trail from the ground in Laos, physically stopping the trucks, and plugging the supply pipeline. That would allow faster American troop drawdowns in South Viet Nam. The name of the operation is *Lam Son 719*. *Lam Son* is an ancient battle won by the Vietnamese. The '71' comes from the planned launch year, 1971, just next month, and the '9' comes from Route 9, the major road through Tchepone, or what's left of Tchepone. *Lam Son 719* has disaster written all over it. Unfortunately, you will be heavily involved in the coming weeks. So be careful."

The formerly boisterous audience became more attentive. Thatcher paused for another drink and then continued, obviously serious. "Last week I provided air cover for a battalion-sized test of the concept. A CIA operative I only knew as Red Man led an indigenous force down Route 9 toward Tchepone from the mountains just west of the trail. I was able to do something I was never able to do before, except in the rainy season. I dropped down to a few hundred feet above the ground ahead of the infantry column. It was the only mission I ever flew where I wasn't hosed down. Of course, I was jinking like a hummingbird on steroids and my X-Ray, Lt. Boun Tang, got a little green around the gills. I suspected the lack of gunfire was a trap to get the battalion coming up behind me farther into the trap.

"It was. Two days later, when I flew my next mission, half the battalion was dead, and the other half was back on the mountains just west of the trail where they originally started. They got Tchepone but only held it for a few minutes. The men were being hammered by mortars as I arrived and wouldn't have made it much longer. It was obvious there was a substantial North Vietnamese force parked there. I was able to snag some F-4 pilots with CBU who saved those who were left. The survivors made it back to the Mekong, but the test was a complete failure if the definition of success was being able to penetrate and hold a position on the trail. Now, believe it or not, despite the obvious failure of the test, the South Vietnamese invasion into Laos is going ahead as planned anyway, so you guys be careful. If there is any good news, the failure of this idiotic scheme may end the war because it's going to show how little control we have over anything." Then Thatcher, after a pause, got more serious.

"Looking back over the past year is painful. I don't know why … some would call it fate, I suppose … but I showed up in this fairly small squadron and found a lot of friends from my previous days in the Air Force. Statistically, it really doesn't make sense. Bill Stancil, who we lost a few months ago on a highly dangerous Heavy Hook mission, was a classmate of mine at Moody Air Force Base in pilot training. I knew his wife when she was just his fiancée. I feel so sorry for her. Can you imagine not even having your husband's body to bury?

"The senior cadet who met me as I got off the bus my first day at the Air Force Academy, the element leader who trained me, Capt. Paul Bartram, was killed by Pathet Lao troops a few weeks after I got here. He was a Raven and I was on the radio with him when he was shot. I hadn't met him here in country, but I recognized his voice over the radio as I was trying to vector the Jolly Greens to his position. They didn't get there in time.

"Nail 33, Tex Robertson, whom most of you senior Nails knew, was two years ahead of me at the Zoo, but we were both in the same squadron. He was shot down near the ford at Ban Laboy directing some Navy A-4s. He scrambled up a slope and hid in a clump of bamboo. A North Vietnamese officer climbed up the hill within a few feet and was staring right at him when some Navy A-4s roared in overhead. When the NVA officer heard the noise of the jets, he just turned and walked away, blowing a whistle and taking his troops with him without firing a shot. If nothing else, it shows their respect for CBU. Tex is home now, thank God, but he'll be staring at that face for a long time. A long, long time. I suspect we'll all be staring at things from this war as well.

"Nail 52, Mark Tinga, was a Zoo classmate of mine, and a fierce competitor on the Rugby Field. He knocked the crap out of me more times than I can remember. He was, as you all know, a full-blooded Indian. Mark watched as a MiG shot down a Jolly Green at Mu Gia during an attempted rescue of two F-4 pilots he was directing who got shot down by a 23mm. He was sent back to the States after getting shot down for the second time himself only a week later.

"Another Air Force Academy classmate of mine here at NKP, Al Carpenter, was the pilot of the Jolly Green shot down a month ago on a simple training mission to the airfield at Ubon, Thailand, 30 miles south of here. Unbelievably, his Jolly Green was right over the Mekong River in Thailand. He was not even over the trail! Al and I lived on the same hall at the Zoo. His room was about 30 feet away from mine. Let me repeat: he was shot down over the Mekong River just ten miles south of here! He wasn't even in Laos!" Thatcher paused again composing himself. Then he continued.

"Our loss of Art Kazinski, our most senior navigator, and his pilot, Tom Stevens, a New Bean, were especially painful. I didn't know Tom well, but I flew more night missions with Art than any other navigator here. We've lost many others here at NKP as well, airmen I didn't know personally: A-1 drivers, EC-47 crews, the C-123 crews flying the Agent Orange missions over the trail that give us so much better visibility, and the Green Berets that provide so much of our Intel.

"I'm trying to make the point that I'm not a disinterested observer. I have an emotional investment here just as you do. I conclude after my year here that despite the courage and sacrifice of all the aircrews, we can't possibly win either of these so-called secret wars.

"To conclude, my conscience tells me the Viet Nam War was an inexcusable exercise in political arrogance and will soon be over. My instinct also tells me the gentle people of Laos will be left with a very uncertain political future in a country scarred by the most intense bombing campaign since Germany in WWII. I hope our nation won't walk away from the damage we did here and the destruction we leave behind. God Bless you. Do your duty, but don't be a hero.

I would finish with this classic Nail salute: 'You Nails is 'shit hot!" It has been my honor to serve with you."

The Nails stood and applauded. Thatcher took the ceremonial beer mug and tried to chug it down; he got halfway and poured the rest over his head, a mandatory punishment for Nails who were not chuggers.

Col Melendez stood and presented Thatcher with the Brass Balls Award, pinning it on Thatcher's black party suit and shaking his hand as he did with the previous honorees. After the rest of the speeches and ceremonial presentations, the meeting adjourned to the bar. Ted Thatcher approached Col Melendez and shook his hand.

"Colonel, I want to thank you for your support of the Laotian activities. I don't know what will happen to our Laotian friends, but I trust we will do the right thing."

"I will do my best, Ted. Thank you for your efforts here and best of luck in whatever future endeavors you undertake. I haven't forgotten our discussion on *Lam Son 719*. I agree with you that it will probably be the end of the war. Maybe someone will write a book one day on how all this nonsense got started."

"Maybe they will, colonel, maybe they will."

Thatcher joined the rest of the squadron who adjourned to the bar where the party continued until late in the evening. As was customary, the Nails started the monthly party with the Nail song:

> *Run, run, Cricket run,*
> *Ho Chi's coming with a loaded gun.*
> *He's mighty angry, you've caught his eye,*
> *He's throwing flak up in the sky.*
> *Run, run, Cricket run,*
> *One thing is no lie,*
> *If you wanna get back to your wife in the States,*
> *You better damn well fly high.*

You've been blowing up all of his guns,
And killing all of his trucks.
You keep doing things like those,
And Ho Chi, he's fed up!
So, run, run Cricket run!
As fast as you know how.
If you wanna be a Cricket any more,
You better be a chicken now!

Author's Note

Other than the Civil War, few events in American history have brought so much acrimony as the Viet Nam War, a long, costly, politically divisive exercise initiated in ignorance, pursued in arrogance, and terminated in shame. Television images of the hordes of frantic South Vietnamese clamoring to grab the skids of U.S. helicopters evacuating the U.S. Embassy in Saigon at the end of the war have become iconic. Interspersed with those images were those of Viet Nam veterans marching on the United States Capital. Never before in America have anti-war protesters been led, in large measure, by those who were veterans of their war.

The Viet Nam War was a blunder; most Americans, including most veterans, would agree. The War actually started soon after WWII ended. Here's how we got there: After the defeat of the Japanese in 1945, President Eisenhower encouraged France to re-colonize Viet Nam. Eisenhower, painfully aware of the communist successes in Europe, coined the phrase "Domino Effect" to describe the expansion of communism there and thought the same thing could occur in Southeast Asia. So, the French marched back in to re-colonize Viet Nam with American encouragement. Looking through the lens of history, the fear of monolithic communism overshadowed Allied thinking in 1945, thanks to Stalin and the Soviet Union, so the decision was not totally imprudent.

Ho Chi Minh thought differently however. He had been the leader of a guerrilla force helping the American O.S.S (Office of Strategic Services and forerunner of the CIA) against the Japanese in WWII. He rescued American pilots shot down by the Japanese, was fluent in English, French and all the Vietnamese dialects, and was the logical leader of post-war Viet Nam. No other Vietnamese had a fraction of his public stature. He was, unquestionably, a nationalist first and a communist second. The Communist Party of China, formed in 1921, fell under Mao Zedong's control in 1927. Mao led a revolution, defeating American ally Chiang Kai-shek and took control of mainland China in 1947. So, Eisenhower's caution about communism was not completely unwarranted, but history showed Ho was much more a nationalist than a communist.

When the French returned after the War, Ho immediately became an adversary. The subsequent and infamous defeat of the 'impregnable' French fortress at Dien Bien Phu on May 7, 1954, by Ho has become legendary among military historians. (Does the image of a nation achieving its independence in a war against a powerful nation from another continent sound familiar?)

After the French defeat at Dien Bien Phu, the 1954 Geneva Accords divided Viet Nam into northern and southern halves at an arbitrary line, called the Demilitarized Zone, or DMZ. This division was based on nothing but expediency to permit efficient administration of the two halves of Viet Nam pending the scheduled 1956 nationwide elections. Ho Chi Minh would have won the election overwhelmingly, but the U.S. never permitted the election to be held. President Eisenhower, still alarmed over the Balkanization of Europe, formed a totally separate government in the southern half. Even though the situations in Southeast Asia and Europe were not identical, Eisenhower's fear was far from imaginary. China was already telegraphing its Communist intentions outside its own border. So, the 'temporary' DMZ became permanent and Ho proceeded to continue the war for independence he had been fighting since WWII. America made another decision which would come to haunt it: it selected a Roman Catholic, Ngo Dinh Diem, to rule a country that was only 9% Catholic, and where Buddhism, Taoism, and Confucianism were the predominant religions. Twenty-one years and 58,620 dead Americans later, the War was finally over.

In this book, I demonstrate the Viet Nam War, 'The War That Should Never Have Been Fought'. Ho Chi Minh was a communist, but there was nothing else to be in a country that was illiterate and poor and whose only concern was the success or failure of the next rice crop. The end result of America's failure to reunite Viet Nam was tragic. Civilian casualties on both sides have been estimated at between one and two million, but an accurate number would be impossible to ascertain. Over 250,000 South Vietnamese soldiers were killed in South Viet Nam and another 65,000 in North Viet Nam. North Viet Nam and Viet Cong military casualties have been estimated at over one million.

One more mitigating factor was ignored by American planners: Rice. North Vietnam was lucky to get one good rice crop a year; South Viet Nam could triple crop but usually didn't bother. If the insult of denying Ho Chi Minh control of the country he devoted his life to were not enough, rice alone would have been a compelling economic reason to declare war. An old Vietnamese axiom is illustrative: 'A grain of rice is worth a drop of blood' and it literally came true in the Viet Nam War.

One final comment: The *Pentagon Papers* proved material misrepresentation in the *Maddox* incident by the U.S. government to justify a war in Vietnam. The Gulf of Tonkin incident, also known as the USS *Maddox* incident, was an international confrontation that led to the United States engaging more directly in the Vietnam War. The *Maddox* was a U.S. destroyer involved one real and one falsely claimed confrontation between U.S. ships and those of North Vietnam.

So much for background. Now, to the main focus of this book: the Viet Nam War was not lost in Viet Nam. It was lost in eastern Laos on what became known as the Ho Chi Minh Trail. Over *80-percent* of the bombs dropped in the Viet Nam War were dropped in Laos, not in Viet Nam. Why? *Because Viet Nam at the DMZ consisted of flat, open, rice paddies. There was no way to march an army south let alone supply it with the necessary guns and supplies necessary to fight a war.* To reunite his country, Ho Chi Minh needed food, ammunition, and other supplies and the only way to transport them to his forces in South Viet Nam was through the triple canopy jungle of Laos by trucks. An army travels on its stomach, if we can believe Napoleon. Ho Chi Minh certainly did. His routes through the jungle became the infamous 'Ho Chi Minh Trail'. The United States Government realized very early in the conflict that choking off this Laotian pipeline was the key to winning, if indeed the war could be won at all. America devoted billions of dollars and invented new technologies specifically aimed at stopping trucks being used to transport war-making material. The transportation battle became known as '*The War Against Trucks*' and is one of the two main stories in this book.

The number of bombs, cluster bombs, and napalm canisters dropped in Laos on North Vietnamese truck and storage facilities over a decade long war surpassed any other war ever fought. Because of this decade-long bombardment, Laos has earned the unenviable title of 'Most Bombed Country on Earth'. To be clear, that would include any war, fought anywhere, at any time. How it happened is answered in this book, and the answer is not especially comforting

264

to those who take pride in being an American, as I do. I refer to the 'Truck War' as *The War That Should Never Have Been Fought*. Why? If Viet Nam had been united in 1956 in accordance with the 1954 Geneva Conventions, Laos would not have been needed as a transportation corridor. It would not have suffered such horrible bombardment and America would have not suffered a decade of dissension at home, the loss of 58,620 American lives, and a monetary cost which may never be fully measured.

Ironically, and sadly, few Americans know that the U.S. was simultaneously involved in a *second* war at the same time in northern and western Laos. This war was fought by the United States and its allies to preserve the popular and benevolent 1000-year-old Laotian monarchy from Chinese-sponsored Laotian communists. These were not the equivalent of the Vietnamese patriots trying to oust a foreign country from their land. They were solely interested in personal power and monetary gain and allied with communist China. I term this conflict *The War That Should Never Have Been Lost*. The 'People War', as it has been called by other accounts, was lost soon after the Viet Nam War was concluded, but few Americans know when or how it happened.

This book focuses on American military involvement in Laos in both the 'Truck War' and 'People War' in the critical year of 1970, a sharp turning point in both wars, and it shows how those wars overlapped. American efforts in Laos were all but hidden from the American public by the smokescreen of the war occurring in Viet Nam. Unlike Viet Nam, with reporters 'embedded' with U.S. forces often broadcasting live, there were no reporters or TV cameras covering operations from the front lines in Laos. There *were* no front lines in Laos. The entire country was a war zone except the very western part bordering the Mekong River across from Thailand. After the war, it was discovered only a few POW's from Laos had been transported to North Viet Nam, but very few.

Nearly 600 Americans lost in Laos disappeared. Not one American held in Laos was ever released. Pilots shot down in North Viet Nam had publicity value so, ironically, many survived.

The 'People War' to preserve the Monarchy of Laos, was prosecuted by the United States through a CIA-sponsored indigenous army composed of several indigenous tribes in the north, and Laotian military in the South. Notably, this was the CIA's first attempt at active military involvement. The army was supplemented by military contingent of FACs using the call sign 'Raven'. Flying out of safe bases in western and far northern Laos, the Ravens flew out of uniform in unmarked O-1 Birddogs, directing air strikes of Laotian fighter pilots flying T-28s against Chinese-supported Pathet Lao (communist) troops. Ravens were supplemented, in turn, by three of the Thailand-based Nail FACs (out of 25) who were assigned to both the Truck War and the People War in southern Laos. I was one of those FACs flying in both wars.

FACs, were, in essence, battlefield commanders. They located targets (North Vietnamese trucks and hidden supply centers), requested appropriate fighter-bomber aircraft, and directed their bomb drops by firing white phosphorus rockets (or dropping red ground flares at night) to mark the targets and attain maximum destruction. Nail observation aircraft were O-2s and OV-10s from which they directed untold thousands of airstrikes using both Air Force and Navy/Marine attack planes in both secret wars. Ravens flew exclusively in the people war in O-1s.

Our activities in these two wars were not without peril. The usual minimum altitude for Nail aircraft in the Truck War was 5,000 feet 'AGL' (above ground level). We never flew a mission, day or night, good weather or bad, where we weren't a target of North Vietnamese anti-aircraft fire. In bad weather, North Vietnamese gunners simply fired at engine noise in an attempt to dissuade us from even looking for targets.

This story begins on Christmas day 1969, and ends in January of 1971, the year the U.S. decided to extricate itself from the Viet Nam War by plugging the North Vietnamese supply lines with a desperate invasion of Laos. The invasion, code named *Lam Son 719*, consisted of five battalions of South Vietnamese tanks and infantry supplemented by Nail FACs from Thailand and Covey FACs from South Viet Nam. Since Laos had been declared neutral according to the proposed Geneva agreements at the end of WWII (which the United States never signed, incidentally), the U.S. chose not to openly violate the agreements using uniformed American troops. There were American Special Forces teams on the ground, but they were out of uniform, as were the Raven FACs. (When I visited the safe areas of Laos bordering the Mekong River with my Laotian X-Rays for briefing sessions, I always wore civilian clothes.) *Lam Son 719*, finally launched in February of 1971, failed miserably; the collapse of the invading South Vietnamese force broke down the imaginary wall between Laos and South Viet Nam. Victorious North Vietnamese troops poured through it on the way to Saigon which they finally overwhelmed on April 30, 1975, totally subduing the South Vietnamese and Americans on the way.

I chose to write this book as historical fiction with some explanation required. The background and political histories of the Viet Nam War as well as both the Truck and People Wars in Laos are as accurate as I can relate them. The aerial combat missions depicted herein actually occurred; they were not fabricated, but details such as radio transmissions and ground conversations between me, my fellow FACs, and other aircraft/parties involved were depicted based on my recollection and conversations with my squadron mates. I 'filled in the blanks' using standard terminology and radio protocol. I also changed the names of everyone, including my own. I did this for several reasons. I did not wish to add to the pain of families of my squadron mates who did not return from the war. Secondly, I wanted to bring alive the emotional calculus present in these 'Secret Wars' to allow others the experience of what these wars were all about. What were participants saying and feeling? How did it feel to see red tracers screaming up from anti-aircraft gunners on the ground intent on killing them as they were directing napalm strikes on trucks or truck parks and the people driving and maintaining them? Why do flashes of light today still remind Nail veterans (and other Viet Nam aircrew members) of the flashes from anti-aircraft gun barrels spitting out their strings of deadly projectiles? How did they feel about fighting a war they knew they couldn't win? What must the North Vietnamese gunners have thought when they saw our aircraft coming or saw a sudden splash of light from a parachute flare popping open at night over their position? I couldn't achieve those objectives using third person descriptions. So, I endeavored to put the reader 'in the cockpit', as it were.

Finally, the book confirms, once again, the Viet Nam war was, in large measure, made far worse by Robert McNamara who hid the problems from the American public as long as he could. Immense amounts of American dollars, weapons, and lives continued to be invested into an unwinnable conflict marked by stupidity, outright lies to the American people, and ultimately rebellion by millions of Americans, including tens of thousands of veterans.

Ho Chi Minh, a U.S. ally against the Japanese in WWII, posed no threat to the U.S., Thailand, or India although Cambodia did fall to a different and brutal breed of communists late in the war. Tragically, the benevolent and revered Laotian Monarchy was overthrown in 1975, the King was executed, and a coalition government of Chinese-backed Laotian Communists was fashioned after the Monarchy fell. In northern Laos, Communists massacred hundreds of thousands of indigenous Hmong and other tribes at the end of the War, people who remained loyal to the United States but who were abandoned in one of the saddest and least known

268

histories in the Southeast Asian drama. Today, in a bizarre twist of fate, Viet Nam is our number two trading partner while Viet Nam veteran decals adorn the windows and baseball hats of Viet Nam veterans all over America. Laos has become somewhat of a tourist designation due to its cultural attractions including palaces and shrines. As a lasting monument to the Laotian Wars, the pathways for tourists at the Shrine sites are carefully delineated using markers to prevent inadvertent contact with unexploded American cluster bomblets still lurking in the ground.

* * *

An Unexpected Footnote

I must acknowledge the contributions of the late Dr. Bernard Fall, the indisputable expert and former French resistance fighter who worked for the Americans while a teenager in France as a spy and guerilla fighter in WWII. Fall was the quintessential interpreter of the Viet Nam experience, first for the French and later as an American resident of Washington, D.C. In his books, beginning with *The Street Without Joy*, an expose of the French debacle in Viet Nam, Fall vividly described the causes of the French failure, which presaged the American failures and the inevitable disaster at the end. His final book, *Last Reflections on a War*, was actually finished by his wife Dorothy after his death at the DMZ.

I had the honor of not only studying him at the Air Force Academy, but later conversing with his wife under extraordinary circumstances. One day at my wife's gift shop in New Bern, NC, an elderly Cherry Point Marine Viet Nam veteran came in with his wife. Don't ask me how I know a Viet Nam veteran, I just do. Don't ask me how I know a Marine, either. They still have Marine haircuts, for one thing. I struck up a conversation, and it was obvious he was impacted by his experience. We went outside to sit on a bench and talk. He was at Khe Sanh and Dong Ha, two of the most dangerous bases in Viet Nam, which both were abandoned because of their proximity to the DMZ and North Viet Nam. My brother was wounded at Dong Ha and med-evaced home, so I was always alert for opportunities to speak with vets from those bases. Knowing Fall's works, I asked him if he knew the French name for Route 1, the coastal highway. He didn't hesitate. "Of course: 'The Street Without Joy.'"

"How did you know that?" I asked, somewhat surprised. Bernard Fall was not required reading for grunts, the term used for enlisted Army and Marine soldiers.

"I was with Bernard Fall when he died at the DMZ. I put his body on the armored personnel carrier which also took the bodies of nine dead Marines, his interpreter, and his photographer back to Dong Ha."

He paused for quite a few moments. Tears came to his eyes. "I have his ID bracelet."

I wish there was a word stronger than 'stunned' to describe my reaction, but if there is I can't think of it. Fall was an icon among students of Southeast Asia, and his death was a tragedy not just personally for his family but for the United States as well. The Army invited him to lecture at their Command and Staff College. Presidents Johnson and Nixon and Secretary McNamara hated him for undermining their war. But few grunts knew who he was.

Incredulous, I asked my new friend what happened. He told me he had no idea at the time who Fall was or why he was there. He said Bernard and his photographer walked down a small slope during a break right at the DMZ. The photographer and Fall were smoking and were obviously scoping out the area around them. One of them stepped on a Bouncing Betty, a mine that springs up from the ground when stepped on before exploding. They were killed instantly along with several Marines. But that's not all. My friend was given the job of cleaning up the site, collecting the bodies, body parts, weapons, and equipment, and loading them on a tank. In the process, he picked up canteens, eyeglasses, and helmets as well as a stainless steel chain-link I.D. bracelet with no apparent value. It was old and scratched. He put it in his pocket and forgot about it. It was in a box of mementoes at his home. Fall's credentials on his clothing identified him, and both his name and the written numbers on the ID bracelet issued to him by the O.S.S. in France had no significance to a Marine Corps private in Viet Nam. The bracelet was forgotten for years. He could sense my excitement and asked if I would take the bracelet. He told me he didn't know until many years later who Fall was and was reluctant to come forward. I had no doubt my friend was concerned someone might interpret his actions as less than honorable, and I know they were not.

I knew quite a lot about Mrs. Fall because Bernard wrote about her. However, I didn't know if she was still alive. Calling Washington, D.C. information, I asked for Dorothy Fall. To my surprise, she answered immediately. I explained, as delicately as possible, who I was, how I came by the bracelet, and asked if she would like it back. She was, as I feared, taken aback. After a very, very long moment of silence, which was completely understandable, she asked how I got it. I explained. She couldn't talk and we hung up.

After a few days, she called back and asked me to return the bracelet, which I did promptly. Not long after that, she graciously sent me the book she wrote on Bernard: *Bernard Fall: Memories of a Soldier-Scholar*. It was, as I would have expected, a truly fascinating book. She is as much a gifted writer as was her very talented husband. God truly made a match in heaven for those two. I thoroughly enjoyed talking with her and was amazed she never moved in all those years. As strange as it may sound, I think it gave me closure. I tried writing this book for 40 years. And now I've finally finished. I submit it in the hope we never again waste lives, American and otherwise, on military actions that do not pose an existential threat to our national security or that of our allies.

As a sad footnote, just as I finished writing this book in New Bern, NC, 60 miles east of my last duty station at Seymour Johnson AFB in Goldsboro, NC, the remains of an RF-4C navigator killed in Laos in 1968 were returned there and buried with full military honors. The remains of Col. Edgar "Felton" Davis were discovered by a Laotian villager who remembered his father burying the American. As of this writing, 1,589 Americans are still listed by the DoD as missing and unaccounted for from the Vietnam War. Here are the numbers of missing listed where they were last seen: Vietnam: 1,246 (North Viet Nam: 452, South Viet Nam 794); Laos: 288; Cambodia: 48; People's Republic of China territorial waters: 7.)

I also think it more than appropriate to encourage the United States Government to exert more effort to assist the Laotians in the removal of the millions of tons of unexploded ordnance which inflict their country and kill and maim their children even to this day.

Tom Thompson

This is a picture of the rugged mountains of North Viet Nam I took on one of my missions while flying over the Ho Chi Minh Trail. It's apparent why the flat plains of Laos were the only feasible transportation routes to South Viet Nam. The small white spots are not defects: they are reflections of the sunlight on water, some from small streams, and some from rain-filled bomb craters.

Glossary

A-1	Skyraider
AAA	Anti-Aircraft Artillery
AR-15	U.S. Army Assault rifle with a folding stock used by O-2 pilots
B-52	Major U.S. strategic bomber
Ban Karai	Southernmost pass from North Viet Nam into Laos close to Tchepone
Ban Laboy	Northernmost ford adjacent to the famous Mu Gia Pass
BDA	Bomb Damage Assessment
Bingo fuel	Close to empty, necessitating a return to base
BOQ	Bachelor Officers' Quarters
C-123	WWII Glider converted to twin engine cargo plane; sprayed Agent Orange
Candlestick	C-123 with two additional jet engines used for flare ship
CBU 29	Anti-personnel Cluster Bomblets which explode on contact
Chokes	Location on trail where several roads converged
Chute	Short for parachute

C.O.	Commanding Officer
Cricket	Original call sign for the early FACs operating in Laos
Cricket West	Western and northern Laos; west and north of the Ho Chi Minh Trail
DMZ	Demilitarized Zone; dividing line between North and South Viet Nam
Double Click	Hitting mic button twice to acknowledge intercom
EC-47	WWII cargo plane outfitted with electronic listening devices
F-4	Two man, twin engine fighter/bomber nicknamed the Phantom
FAC	Forward Air Controller; pilot who finds targets and directs airstrikes
Flak	Slang for anti-aircraft fire (AAA)
Fragged	Scheduled target, one selected by intel planners
Funny	Magnesium bombs with thermite initiators used to melt gun barrels/tanks, etc.
Gooney Bird	Nickname for C-47
Grunt	Nickname for infantryman
Gunship	Any cargo aircraft outfitted with side firing weapons
Heavy Hook	Code name for Green Beret units operating on the trail
Hillsborough	Daytime airborne command post
Hobo	Call sign of First Special Operations Squadron A-1s at NKP
Hot or In hot	Preparing to attack, munitions armed
Igloo White	Program name for electronic and acoustic sensors

Jolly Green	CH-53 Rescue Helicopter
Karst	Volcanic Rock Formations common in tropical locations
KC-135	Boeing 707 outfitted for aerial refueling of other aircraft
M-1	WWII infantry rifle
MACV	Military Assistance Command, Viet Nam;
Mark 82	500-pound bombs
MiG 21	Soviet Jet Fighter
Minigun	7.62mm machine gun
Mu Gia	Second pass from North Viet Nam into Laos
Napalm	Jellied petroleum product which spreads like a river of fire
NCO	Non-commissioned officer
Negritos	Very small (about four feet tall) Filipino natives
New Bean	New Nail FAC reporting for duty
NKP	Nakhon Phanom, Thailand
O.S.S.	Office of Special Services and forerunner of the CIA
O-1 Cessna Birddog	Korean War era FAC aircraft used in Viet Nam
O-2 Cessna 337	Twin engine A/C with in-line (front and back) engines
OV-10	Twin engine turbo prop specially designed for FAC work in Viet Nam
Party Suit	Black flight suit adorned with Nail Call sign, the Jiminy Cricket logo patch
Pathet Lao	Laotian communists attempting to end 1000-year-old benevolent monarchy
Paveway	Laser guided bomb

PJ	Crew member responsible for operating rescue hoist on helicopter
POL (Pipeline)	Gasoline pipelines, usually hidden in ditches or under foliage
Preflight	Walk around inspection of airplane before takeoff
PTSD	Post-Traumatic Stress Disorder: emotional impairment due to stress, trauma
R&R	Rest and relaxation
Raven	FAC stationed in Laos as a CIA officer
RF-4	Photo Reconnaissance aircraft
RPG	Rocket-propelled grenade, a shoulder-fired hand grenade
RTB	Return to Base
SAC	Strategic Air Command; specializing in bomber and aerial refueling aircraft
Salvo	Continuous stream of firepower (rockets, machine guns)
SAM	Surface to Air Missile
Sandy	Call sign of A-1 aircraft on search and rescue missions
SAR	Search and Rescue
S. E. A.	Southeast Asia: Viet Nam, Laos, and Cambodia
Sector (I, II, III)	The three geographic sectors of the Ho Chi Minh Trail in Laos
Sensors	Acoustic or seismic sensors disguised as shrubs
Skyraider	Nickname for A-1 Aircraft
SOG	Studies and Observations Group: Green Berets out of uniform on trail

Spectre	C-130 cargo plane outfitted with side firing guns and night vision capability
Squawk	Transponder (radar signal emitter) code
Staff Weenie	Caustic term used for a staff officer in headquarters units
Starlight Scope	Night vision scope; gave a somewhat eerie green and white picture
T-28	A 1950s Air Force and Navy Trainer outfitted for limited combat in Viet Nam
TACAN	Tactical Air Navigation Beacon; gave distance and direction to known location
Taoism	Middle Eastern religion
TASS	Tactical Air Support Squadron: unit of forward air controllers
Tchepone	Bombed-out city at a critical junction on trail in Laos, just north of South Viet Nam
The Hump	Himalayan Mountain Range between China, Burma, and India
Thud	Nickname for F-105, major fighter-bomber; used over North Viet Nam and trail
Tracers	Red streaks following anti-aircraft rounds; allowed gunners to see the path of fire
Transponder	Radio beacon readable by ground control radar
TUOC	Tactical Unit Operations Center: building with all aircraft/mission control
TUOC Trolley	Step van used to transport crew members to and from TUOC
UHF	Ultra-High Frequency Radio: static-free radio used for most air/ground contact
Viet Minh	Communist Army in Viet Nam

Willy Pete	White phosphorus rocket; primary daytime target marker
Winchester	Slang for out of ammo
X-Ray	Code name for Laotian officers flying with Nails on Cricket West Missions
Zoo	Nickname for the Air Force Academy; used primarily by graduates
Zorro	Call sign of the 22nd Special Operation Squadron flying A-1 Skyraiders
ZPU	Older antiaircraft gun used against French; still operational in Viet Nam War

About the author

Tom Thompson is a 1966 graduate of the U.S. Air Force Academy. His father, 2nd Lt. Loren Raymond Thompson, was killed on flying a mission over China 34 days after Tom was born. His step father was a Coast Guard pilot and Tom spent his childhood living in such disparate locations as San Juan, Puerto Rico, Kodiak, Alaska, and, Newfoundland, Canada. Both his half-brothers served in Viet Nam, the youngest wounded after 34 days and sent home. In 1970, Tom flew 194 missions as a Forward Air Control pilot in Laos as a member of the 23rd Tactical Air Support Squadron. He was awarded two Distinguished Flying Crosses and 13 Air Medals. After returning to the States, Tom resigned his commission, earned an MBA from East Carolina University, and pursued a career in economic development. He and his wife Wanda Kay reside in the first colonial capital of North Carolina: New Bern.